COIGN OF VANTAGE

BOOKS BY JOHN M^CALEER

Ballads and Songs Loyal to
Hanoverian Succession • *1962*

Theodore Dreiser: A Biography • *1968*

Artist and Citizen Thoreau • *1971*

Notes on Life: The Philosophical Writings of
Theodore Dreiser (with Marguerite Tjader) • *1974*

The Matter of the Red Man
in American Literature • *1976*

Rex Stout: A Biography • *1977*

Justice Ends at Home: The Early
Crime Fiction of Rex Stout • *1977*

Rex Stout: An Annotated Primary and
Secondary Bibliography (with Judson Sapp,
Arriean Schemer and Guy Townsend) • *1980*

Unit Pride (with Billy Dickson) • *1981*

Royal Decree: Conversations
with Rex Stout • *1983*

Ralph Waldo Emerson:
Days of Encounter • *1984*

Queen's Counsel: Conversations
with Ruth Stout • *1986*

JOHN McALEER

COIGN OF VANTAGE.

OR
THE BOSTON ATHENÆUM
MURDERS

A FOUL PLAY PRESS BOOK

The Countryman Press
Woodstock, Vermont

FIRST EDITION
Copyright © 1988 by John J. McAleer

Library of Congress Cataloging-in-Publication Data
McAleer, John J.
Coign of vantage, or, The Boston Athenaeum murders.

"A Foul Play Press book."
I. Title.   II. Title: Coign of vantage.   III. Title:
Boston Athenaeum murders.
PS3563.A2447C6   1987   813'.54   87-8825
ISBN 0-88150-093-3

Jacket illustration and book design by James Brisson,
Williamsville, Vermont
Photocomposition by the F. W. Roberts Company
Belfast, Maine

Printed in the United States of America

A Foul Play Press Book

The Countryman Press
Woodstock, Vermont

To my three angels
Mary Alycia, Saragh,
and Seána

COIGN OF VANTAGE

FROM THE ATHENÆUM ITSELF, from a little high-perched coign of vantage there, a little outside reading-place which fairly overhangs the back of the Granary graveyard, the most striking of all views of the inclosure may be had, for from this point one looks down through the treetops on curving lines of little dull-colored headstones, standing . . . under the gloomy trees, like gloomy spirits of New England consciences forever looking out, with drooping shoulders, through the great iron fence, upon the passing of their descendants and successors.

ROBERT SHACKLETON
THE BOOK OF BOSTON

MEN OF THIS SURCHARGE OF arterial blood . . . cannot satisfy all their wants at the Thursday Lecture or the Boston Athenaeum. They pine for . . . hair-breadth adventures, huge risks, and the joy of eventful living.

RALPH WALDO EMERSON
"Power"

PROLOGUE

A gust of wind coming in from the sea blew hard against the glass paneled doors of the cabana suite and rattled the spiny bayonets of the yucca. Overhead a bolt of cloud scudded across the sky loosening spangles of sunlight which fell like shreds of foil on the aquamarine tiles skirting the pool. On his knees the tall man in maroon swim trunks leaned over the pool's rim to disengage from the filter mesh a small, anxious toad. Though exhausted, it still was alert and blinking. Cuddling it now in his palm its liberator walked to the edge of the tiled apron and set it down upon the grass.

Silsbee Enright, who, from the comfort of his webbed chaise, had watched the rescue operation with mild absorption, nodded when his companion flung himself into a second chaise beside him. "Your Mr. Toad seems none the worse for his adventure," he said. "They're durable creatures—discounting enchantment, of course. Probably survived even the last Ice Age."

"I wouldn't be surprised," said the emancipator. "Somewhere lately a party of citizens opened a cornerstone sealed up fifty years ago. Inside they found a toad, still alive and responsive."

"Don't know as I believe that," said Enright.

"Don't know enough about toads to disbelieve it," his companion answered. "Yet, who's to say? Maybe that's the direction cryogenics will move in. If only the toads will tell us how it's done."

"A futile science, cryonics," Enright said, getting up and stretching his lean, well-muscled body. Belying his forty-seven years, no slack flesh drooped beneath biceps or buttocks. Clearly he kept fit and never had to think about having himself put in a state of suspended animation while science schemed to rout some degenerative disease gnawing away at his vitals. "Who'd want you back after you'd been in the deep freeze a dozen years?" he went on. "It'd be revolting to have you up and around again."

"That's one problem we can leave to the future," his companion said. "We're never going to have to face it. Unless, that is, you've been looking into the possibilities already?" He pointed a gaunt finger at the low, oblong freezer visible through the cabana's glass door—an avoca-do-hued sarcophagus. "What assurance have I that Emily isn't inside that chest right now?"

Emily was Mrs. Enright and Silsbee earlier had informed his visitor that she was in Greece, gone there with a party from Harvard to assess the Stoa Poikile dig.

"The need to preserve Emily that way never will arise," Enright said gallantly. "She's done a good job preserving herself with aerobics, moisturizers, and Geri-Fax vitamins with mineral supplements. Tell you though, as for taking care of ourselves, there's been some excellent beer in that chest. If memory serves there's a couple left. Shall we have one?"

"What better way," his guest said, "for us to wind down in the waning hours of a late September day?"

"I suppose it seems strange, my being here on the Cape in the shank of the season," Enright observed, as they moved indoors. "But, with Emily away, it seemed a good time to get off alone. Get some reading done. Store up a little energy for winter. In Dover, I'm too vulnerable. Constant demands on my time. Quite otherwise at Louis Bay. With October just around the corner no one expects me to be here. I say, why not? Haven't winterized the pool yet and this past week's been pure Indian summer."

"And I had to put in an appearance and spoil your solitude."

"You're no bother. I know you like your privacy as much as I like mine and—dare I say it?—I know you won't overstay your welcome."

"I won't overstay this beer, in fact," the visitor said, taking the bottle of pilsner and setting it beside him on the cabana's portable bar. "Wait," he said then, as Enright began to lower the freezer lid. "Your freezer's empty now."

"Keep your cool," Enright said. He gave a quick grin at the unexpected aptness of his idiom. "I mean to pull the plug."

"Never doubted it," said the man in maroon, "but leave the lid up too. Otherwise you'll get that nasty, smelly, green mold inside."

"That's so!" Enright said. "Glad you reminded me. Saved my neck. If I let that happen, Emily would never let me hear the end of it."

Raising the lid a second time, Enright leaned across the chest to reach the plug, rising on his toes to do so. Instantly, his companion seized him by the ankles, lifting him up and toppling him off balance. As his body sprawled into the chest, the beer he'd held in his left hand smashed to the cement floor shattering in foamy consternation.

Like someone stuffing stale loaves of French bread into a small dumpster, the visitor shoved down Enright's lean, thrashing arms and legs in quick determined thrusts and, with a resolute push, forced shut the lid of the freezer, listening with satisfaction as the lock snapped into place. It had all been done with such dispatch that Enright hadn't even had the presence of mind to cry out. He was crying out now, though, pleading to be released. At least, this was the visitor's surmise. It was a good freezer, snug and well insulated, and, on utterance, Enright's exhortations blurred to indistinctness.

The visitor's later recollection was that the muffled cries and the desperate poundings, flailings, kicks, blows, and thumps coming from inside the chest, and made, no doubt, with fists, feet, knees, elbows, and, he supposed, head as well once true desperation had taken hold, did not subside altogether till the better part of an hour had past. Meantime, the ideal September day moved majestically to its close. The calls of the gulls that gathered on the sea wall, which shut off the fiercest approaches of the ocean, rang through the air with a haunting loveliness that made him newly appreciative of the rare peace that descends on Cape Cod in the off-season. Such bliss!

He drank his pilsner slowly, relishing its tangy vigor, and munched on some macadamia nuts which Enright, with the magnanimity of a Maecenas (if one could believe

4

the TV ads), had produced on his arrival. How typical, he thought, for Silsbee to provide some little extra token of welcome.

Even with the sun sinking, the air temperature still was warm. A final dip in the pool was quite in order. He swam about leisurely, practicing his breaststroke and keeping an eye out for toads which he might rescue. What a miserable world modern man has created, he reflected, when a toad can't hop on its way without running the risk of drowning.

On emerging from the pool, the visitor entered the cabana, slipped the tank suit Enright had loaned him down over his lean hips, showered, toweled himself off thoroughly, and got back into his own clothes. While in the shower a happy thought had struck him. On his arrival, Enright had shared with him an exciting find. Setting in some iris rhizomes that morning he had come upon a long buried arrowhead, dating back surely to the days when the Wampanoags roamed the Cape. Whimsically, Enright had placed his find on his wife's dresser together with a three by five card on which he had written: "For Emily—A treasure not found at Stoa Poikile!" The visitor fetched both now—card and arrowhead. As he walked back to the cabana, he scaled the arrowhead over the sea wall. Then, donning Enright's gardening gloves, so as not to leave prints, he scotch-taped the card to the top of the freezer chest. Finally, before leaving, he double-checked to make certain the freezer was plugged in. It would never do if the agitation which had made the freezer judder about over the past hour had loosened the plug. He was glad to see it was still snugly in place. At least Emily, when she opened the freezer on her return, would not have to confront all that nasty green mold.

When he started up his car he noticed that the sound of the surf pounding on the beach was quite loud, rumbling so as almost to make the sound of the car itself inaudible. A flood tide! Nearly full in! How nice, he thought—the moon must be in its fourth quarter. The sandy Cape roads always looked at their best brimming with moonlight.

1

*T*he rush hour traffic climbing Beacon Hill moved at a sluggish crawl. And there we were, caught smack-dab in the middle of it, Boston Common to our right and, to our left, a solid phalanx of noble nineteenth-century houses, their occasional rheumy purple window-panes leering at us like lewd old men who relished our impotence. Of all the stalemated specks of humanity I had in view, only Ladonna Stanton, sitting beside me in the front seat of the Sun Runner, her hands folded primly on the muted brown tartan skirt that hugged her knees, seemed undismayed.

"To me," I said, "this is penitential. To you it's a day in the country. How do you manage it?"

"I'm sorry, Austin!" she said. "It's just that I'm so glad the Alma-Tadema exhibition's over and the Athenaeum's shipping the whole lot back to New York. Rose Treat's sea-weed collages were so much nicer—and Elizabeth Cameron's botanical watercolors!"

The traffic began to surge forward. We rolled past things that had Alma-Tadema's epic creations beat a mile—St. Gauden's Robert Gould Shaw bas relief, and Bulfinch's

State House, its golden dome pasted against the October sky. I craned my neck to admire it, then peered up ahead and reported, "A stuck truck at the corner of Beacon and Bowdoin. That's what the delay was about. It's under way again and everything looks rosy."

"Probably the truck that's going to cart Alma-Tadema away."

"I hope they're not going to drag those paintings out into plain view on 'the sunny street that holds the sifted few'."

"They're crated now," Ladonna said.

"To protect them from mad slashers or vitriol throwers?"

"Well, naturally."

"Which are you?"

"I use whatever comes to hand. For my last desecration it was a geologist's hammer."

"What unleashed your wrath?"

"A smart aleck boyfriend who asked too many questions." As she spoke Ladonna's hand sought the back of my head, flattening a cowlick (which, at her touch, immediately sprang erect) and finishing with a love pat. No geologist's hammer in sight. I relaxed.

"The people who sponsor the Athenaeum exhibitions," she said, "are that same sifted few you're going to be consorting with an hour from now at the Cart-tail Club."

"You sound envious," I said.

We had finally come abreast of the Athenaeum, Ladonna's destination, and I pulled in close to the curb to let her out. The street in front of the Athenaeum was no place, at any hour but especially this hour, to trade verbal barbs. Knowing this, Ladonna, instead of calling me to account, merely leaned over and kissed me on the cheek.

"They come and go from the Athenaeum all the time," she said, "those 'sifted few.' You could really live in terror of them if you let their manner get to you—so advantaged. Underneath, though, they're really nice."

"Just so long as they're nice to me," I said.

"If they don't treat you right," she said, "tell them I'll spike their asti spumante with cyanide at the next Ives Gammell exhibit."

Sensibly she opened the car door and got out, not expecting me to sprint around, playing the gentleman, and get run over doing it.

"Gotcha, sweeting," I said.

"Sweeting! An antique apple. Should I be flattered?"

"Sure. It's tasty and it's hard to get."

She smiled. "I guess that will do till you think of something better."

"I am thinking of something better."

"You still have an hour to do something about that tie," she said, calling me to order.

"What's wrong with it?"

"It's too small and it droops."

A passing Beacon Hill matron glared at Ladonna.

"Let's not get physical," I said briskly to encourage the inferences the lady had gleaned. "My other girl friends aren't complaining." The eavesdropper moved on, Brahmin shoulders shaking in contempt.

With fine calculation Ladonna swung the car door inward, getting it shut, as only a thoroughbred can, on first try. Her heels clicked with authority on the paving. Without looking back she crossed the sidewalk and, passing between the parted bronze doors and the brass studded, padded red leather doors beyond, entered the world's finest private gentlemen's library, the Boston Athenaeum. She makes it, I thought as I began to inch out again into the traffic flow, still nicer by her presence. Her presence had made my world nicer, too. The scent of Guerlain lingered in the car, mingling with agreeable memories.

"Nice spot for an ambush," I said to the lanky attendant who, ten minutes later, hailed me at the foot of the cement ramp that leads into the parking garage—that grim cavern which the imp of progress has slipped under Boston Common.

Jack Cool, young and not long out of County Fermanagh, greeted me with a smile as broad and beaming as a currach full of moonlight. An oval patch covered his right eye. It seemed not to diminish the watchful twinkle in his left.

"Mr. Austin Layman, sir," he asked, "what would a lad like myself know about ambushes?"

Jack, I'd heard, had arrived in the States not long after two of Ian Paisley's more vehement followers had been gunned down along the road to Omagh. No need to allude to that directly. "It would," I suggested instead, "be a way of keeping your hand in."

With one index finger Jack Cool launched, from a knit brow, just above the oval patch, a salute with a descending trajectory. An unmistakable dismissal.

"That," he said, "is all gone by."

"On the Common above us," I told him, "to uphold what they believed was a good cause, Bostonians once hanged witches and pirates."

"And your occasional comely Quaker lass."

"That, too. You've done your reading, Jack."

"A promised land, flowing with milk and . . . mayhem, was it?"

"Age brings wisdom, Jack. To borrow your own phrase, 'that's all gone by'."

"And the milk with it. I've yet to see a cow at pasture on the Common overhead."

"Herded off, long since, to dairy farms, and mechanical milkers."

"Efficiency was ever a Protestant virtue."

I punched the knob on the ticket machine and took the slip that emerged—an insolent pink tongue poking out at me. I didn't wonder.

"Hold that thought, Jack," I said, "and Dame Boston will clasp you to her bosom."

My foot slid off the brake. The car rolled forward into the garage.

"What?" Jack called out as the distance between us widened. "Those withered paps? Sure I'd perish for want of nourishment!"

I wended my way through the Common's ultimate cow tunnel, one that far surpassed the little honeycomb of passages that once ran under Park and Beacon to accommodate the comings and goings of Boston cows—a place where now Mustangs, Impalas, and Tauruses, brushing one another's fenders, do the only grazing done still on Common ground. Dodging two of them, I brought my non-bestial, non-contentious MG Sun Runner to rest in a dismal corner where even Jack Cool, for all his command of wit and phrase, could not dispute that it, at last, truly had outrun the sun.

From the parking garage I climbed the stairs into the

neon glitter of the October twilight. Overhead, a jet from Logan lifted into a fustian sky, trailing pennants of pollution on its nighttime haul. A sudden gust of wind sent the leaves rustling along the footpaths of the Public Garden across Charles Street. I watched as they rose in flickering eddies, then twisted and fell.

My fingers played along the front flap of my Burberry, securing buttons. I didn't want my onyx and gold studs to stir the greed of the space shots who lounged around the peanut roaster at the edge of the mall where nightly they gathered to disparage the human race and dispense to one another the solace of human companionship. Someone might get the idea that I could be coached to part with those trinkets and with whatever else I had that looked negotiable, right down to the platinum pin (if they but knew I had it) in my left femur, a keepsake of my last days in Viet Nam's An Hoa Basin.

I flipped the vendor two bits and took one of the bags from the corner of his pushcart.

"You gonna feed the squirrels or somethin'?" he wanted to know.

"More like something," I said.

"Get with it, Lennie," said one of the spacies, brandishing a makeshift Cockney accent. "Cahn't you see the bloke's pickin' up the hor d'oeuvres for a bust at the Ritz?" He jerked his thumb in the direction of the Ritz Carlton, poking up through the trees beyond the Public Garden, the place where Winston Churchill stayed when he came to Boston, and the big celebrity movie stars.

"What gave me away?" I asked, stepping up to him and looking him in the eye.

"The cute bow tie," he said, his accent waning even as

he edged away from me. Meeting me as aggressor was more than he'd bargained for. " . . . It's got unsnapped."

"Thanks," I said. "I've got an unruly Adam's apple."

I stepped up to Lennie and took the bag he thrust out in exchange for the one I'd picked first.

"If you're gonna eat 'em, you shoulda taken one from the back row," he instructed me.

"The fresh ones?"

"You got it, mister."

I packed the bag in my armpit while I fixed the tie.

"You know how it is," I soliloquized beneath a sky now nearly black bombazine. "My valet took the afternoon off. Went to see his mother. Visiting day at the pokey."

They snickered. I went past them and crossed the mall to Boylston Street. I shucked and ate a couple of peanuts while waiting for WALK to kayo DON'T WALK. Lennie was right. This batch was fresh. Half raw, maybe, but fresh.

The bells of the Arlington Street Church caroled six peals. Cleon Entigott had told me to be at the Cart-tail Club at six-thirty. I had, I saw, plenty of time to look around for another tie.

In the next ten minutes I covered three blocks walking west toward the Pru. No luck. The posh haberdasheries had closed for the night. So had Brooks Brothers. Friar's Bib & Tuckery, which was open, had one tie, transfixed like a dead bat on a display board, its wing span ample enough to unnerve a night watchman at a Transylvanian mortuary. Certainly nothing like it ever had flapped its way across the threshold of the Cart-tail Club during the whole of its century-long existence. Reconciled to a night of furtive probing attacks to see if the enemy still was entrenched, I jammed my clip job tighter into my collar.

I went back down Boylston, past tiny Carver where Poe was born, and Emerson, in boyhood, came as drover (leading his grandfather's cow to its modest paddock), to Dyer Place where the Cart-tail Club has ignored the caprices of time from its inception.

Built on the site of Bridewell, Boston's first prison for women, the Club took its name from the colonial practice of stripping female transgressors to the waist, tying them to a cart-tail, and whipping them through the streets of the town. Dyer Place had been the starting point for this premier Boston marathon, which, even without a designated Heartbreak Hill, must have had its full quota of heartbreak.

I don't belong to the codfish aristocracy of Massachusetts. In fact the Laymans still were fighting alongside Horatio Nelson when the merchant princes of Salem and Boston were opening up the China trade. Yet lately the Cart-tailers had voted to open their ranks to embrace a few newcomers who, without the resource of pedigree, seemed nonetheless, by temperament, social standing, and accomplishments, likely to be compatible, and Cleon Entigott had put my name in nomination. A glacial courtship, already several weeks under way, had now progressed to the come-to-dinner-and-meet-the-screening-committee stage. While I didn't covet membership, I did realize that an affiliation with the Club would be immediately useful to me. I was writing a biography of one of Boston's immortals—Ralph Waldo Emerson. When he was in England in 1848, Emerson had enjoyed the privileges of two London clubs. On his return home, having resolved to plant the club idea in Boston, he had helped found the Cart-tail. Predictably, given the steadfastness of Boston traditions, more than half the Club members in the present day were descended from the people who had made up Emerson's original literary coterie, many of them still cherishing letters, journals, and manuscripts dating back to Emerson's day. Here was rich pickings.

Dyer Place is paved with cobblestones. They appear to have been there since the event, in 1630, that got Boston started—the docking of the *Arbella*. Even before I noticed them, however, I heard them. A woman in her late forties or early fifties, in thornproof tweeds, escorting a tan corgi on a braided leash, was strutting toward me, the leather heels of her boxy Enna Jetticks colliding like carnival mallets with the stones. She took me in with no sign of approval.

"One of the Queen's corgis?" I suggested brightly. Some people like to be admired through their dogs. This lady was not one of them.

"Isn't there a service entrance to this building?" she asked in a tone as crisp as the one she must have used to make the corgi heel as smartly as he did.

"If you came to see me," I said, "I'd let you in the front door. What are you selling?"

The whole of Louisburg Square was mustered in her reply.

"Young man," she said. "I am Parthenia Wentworth. The Wentworths sell nothing!"

The name, of course, brought instant recognition. Here was the woman who, in sixteen hours, walked forty-seven miles from Boston to Providence, to save the whale; the woman who parachuted into the Fens to feed the Ethiopians; who lived on salads for twelve weeks to cuke the nukes—Miss-into-Everything, Boston's most celebrated reformer. I listened in what I hoped was a reverent posture as she continued.

"A pigeon is trapped in the show window of the Boston Music Company, crooning between *Petrouska* and *Die Entführung Aus Dem Serail*. The store's closed for the night. I want someone to be aware of the situation."

"What happened? Did one of Boston's finest run him off the Common for panhandling?"

Parthenia Wentworth's eyes narrowed to arrow slits of menace.

"*Why* he is there," she said, "is not the point at issue."

"And *how* to spring him is?"

"In a word—though I don't espouse *your* word—yes."

"You want to get him back home, I suppose, before the ladies of the seraglio miss him?"

Parthenia Wentworth gave me a look that would fry ice.

"The window has a drop grill," she said. "Otherwise I'd break it—even though it might be traumatic for the pigeon."

"Not to mention the Boston Music Company."

"Faddle!"

"Or, as Leroy Anderson said to Arthur Fielder, 'Fiddle, Faddle!' But, putting that aside for the moment, why don't you get the SPCA on the job?"

"They're not to be trusted. Haven't you heard they're poisoning gulls at Monomoy to make room for terns?"

"Who's the loser if one pigeon doesn't make bed check tonight?"

"For you 'compassion' is a word in the N.E.D. Is that it?"

I was pretty sure 'compassion' could be found even in

my vest pocket Funk and Wagnalls, but why draw blood when I didn't have to? I took up her query from a different angle.

"I'm not wholly devoid of compassion," I said. "I have a bumper sticker that says I brake for blue dot salamanders."

"Spoken like a diehard Cart-tailer. You are one, aren't you? Why else would you be found in this loathsome shambles, dressed as you are, on a Tuesday night?"

"I'm not a member. I merely have prospects."

"To belong to a club which, in its name, commemorates cruelty to women—despicable! You are as much imperiled as that pigeon."

"I'm not an endangered species," I said. "I'm one of a kind."

"One too many, it seems."

With that parting thrust Parthenia Wentworth allowed loops of leash to uncurl from her hand. The corgi, scarcely believing his good fortune, leaped forward as though the clarions of the hunt had sounded. His mistress, leaning into the wind, struck out after him. Her interest in me had ceased. I should have been relieved, but I wasn't. Somehow I felt I had not seen the last of this formidable champion of worthy causes.

2

I went another fifty feet and ducked into the outer vestibule of the Cart-tail Club. Aided by the burnished surface of a brass escutcheon plate recessed in the dark walnut door, I once again firmed my tie in place, then walked through into the Paul Revere room, so designated because on one wall there hung a series of small, latten-brass lanterns beneath each of which was the name of a current officer of the Club. When an officer was in attendance, the Club steward, Enoch Gookin, lit his lantern to signify his accessibility to other members. Four lamps currently were lit.

The Revere room was permeated by a sharp stable odor. Cleon, who had walked me through the Club one September afternoon when he took me there for lunch, had told me that that circumstance had become a Club joke. The building that housed the Cart-tail Club had once been a mews—the only mews, some insisted, that the Club had any rapport with. Although the Club had succeeded to these premises in the Garfield era, a majority of members supposed the ripe odor had been generated by coach and driving horses long since departed, and was the

Club's equivalent of a resident ghost. Whatever truth there was to this supposition, no one could say the Club's atmosphere lacked that character which taste and tradition engender. Sofas and stuffed chairs were upholstered in red cordovan and traced with brass tacks (antiqued for sake of unobtrusiveness). Desks and tables were mission oak, fumed oak, or carved Jacobean oak. The Moorish wainscotting was black larch, here and there obtruded upon by oils, water colors, or pencil sketches done by a few locals—Copley, Winslow Homer, Whistler, Sargent, Hopper, Prendergast, and Gluyas Williams, the latter represented by the original ink drawing of Calvin Coolidge, bags packed, refusing to vacate the White House till the domestic staff located his left galosh. Cleon had assured me Williams's drawing was looked at more often, with more real enjoyment, than the works of any of the other artists represented in the Club's catch-as-catch-can gallery. There was also a steeple clock, face yellow and sere as that of a gold medallion member, and a tarnished slate plaque, its dimensions those of a child's burial slab (the use, in fact, it had been intended for originally), on which was inscribed a faintly raffish rondeau to which Thomas Gold Appleton had given spontaneous utterance when, in 1879, he had assumed the Club's highest office, that of first magistrate.

I entered the adjacent borning room where there was a row of hooks for hats and coats. A sixtyish man, in evening wear old enough to have taken on a green mossy look, was standing on a deacon's bench hanging a gray twill slouch hat on a hook he was otherwise too short to reach. As I slipped out of my Burberry, he cocked his head toward me, on the alert—like a boy caught stealing plums, though many years must have gone by since he had last raided a plum tree.

"Champney?" he inquired.

"Austin Layman. Entigott's guest."

"Yes, of course. Champney died didn't he? Never ate right. Piccalilli and doughnuts for breakfast. No way to start a day."

"Certainly not my day."

"Cleon's upstairs rehearsing *Nile Bodies*. Where I'd be right now if I hadn't got caught in traffic on the Cottage Farm Bridge."

Though the Cottage Farm has been the B.U. Bridge for decades, to my interlocutor it was still the Cottage Farm. The true Bostonian cottons to change about as readily as the Reverend Mister Mather did.

I went on through the borning room, past a seated figure jackknifed, fetal-fashion, into *Barron's*, and stepped into the library. Several elder statesmen types—tanned heads perched like deep-creased walnuts above limp shirt fronts—sat around the edges of the room in deep-creased, somber crimson cordovan chairs and sofas.

I greeted the crimson-jacketed bar steward, who told me his name was Thaddeus Nebble, and asked for a double Teacher's on the rocks. Because I didn't know where else to look, I kept my eyes fixed on him while he got it ready. He looked as though he hadn't smiled since Sacco and Vanzetti lost their final appeal.

Behind me, reading from left to right, were: Robert Dixwell, who lately had relinquished, after thirty-six years, his seat in the United States Senate; Earl Hallow, the philanthropist who had called Nathan Pusey one Christmas morning to tell him he was giving Harvard twenty-seven million dollars (Harlow's face was as ugly as ever but, with his money, I'm sure years had gone by since anyone asked him if he was born on Earl Hallows Eve); next came Gamaliel Bandine, Secretary of Attractive Industries in President Reagan's cabinet, as handsome and noble as a princeling at prayer; George Belcher, lieutenant governor of the Commonwealth, the Democratic party's show WASP in Massachusetts; Raymond Colesworthy, Episcopal bishop of southeastern Massachusetts, Cape Cod, and the islands, who, as a Harvard junior, had been rusticated for a semester for wedging a cast iron chamberpot underneath the chair of Daniel French's statue of John Harvard; and Richard Allerton, the octogenarian chief justice of the Massachusetts Supreme Court, about whom I knew nothing that wasn't laudable.

It would be presumptuous, I decided, to accost this gathering of Boston Olympians with no one to run interference for me. The only previous encounter I'd had with any of them had occurred when they were being interviewed on TV, in living color, as movers and shakers, and I was watching them, in living black and white, on the eight inch screen of my portable Sony.

Nebble handed me my drink across the library table that was, for the moment, his improvised bar, then bent toward me and said in a confiding whisper, "Some of the other gentlemen will be over to speak to you directly."

He was right. As I turned away, Senator Dixwell loomed up from the seas incarnadine of his leather sofa and offered me a hand that was strong and firm, no doubt because of his well-publicized practice of splitting half a cord of kindling every chance he got.

"One of the baby members?" he asked quietly.

An octogenarian who says that to someone my age, which is thirty-four, isn't indulging a talent for flattery.

"I came to see if someone wanted to bounce me on his knee," I went along. "I'm Austin Layman."

"Oh, dear!" Dixwell said. "My declining ability to dandle drove me from public life. What future is left to the politician whose knees creak when he dandles?"

"He's up the creek," declared a man with a resonant voice who showed up at the senator's elbow.

"My very thought," said the senator.

"Frank Trowbridge," said the newcomer, confronting me.

"Austin Layman."

We shook hands.

Other members were spilling into the library now and Dixwell, with a deferential nod, moved away to greet the Thistlethwaite twins, Lionel and Lawrence, whose ninetieth birthday was the occasion for this black tie turnout. Trowbridge, notwithstanding this influx of cronies, clung to me like a slug to wet cabbage, which, under the circumstances, was ego building. In a club the membership of which is drawn from families that have tailgated together ever since the after-the-game celebration of the Boston Tea Party, an unfamiliar name registers no response at all unless a slackoff in interest counts as one. I found myself managing more easily.

"Cleon tells me you probe enigmas for Bigelow, Sturgis," Trowbridge said.

"When not probing people."

"That's right! Those biographies of Fiske and Beston. Ample and able. Whose life are you taking now?"

"Emerson's."

" 'Consistency's the hobgoblin of little minds.' "

"You left out the qualifying adjective, 'A *foolish* consistency'."

"I ought to have remembered. I'm provost of the Hallowell School. Hence expected to know everything. Standards of the founder."

"Bishop Leverett."

"My paternal grandfather."

"Paternal?"

"Like Fiske I took my mother's maiden name. A thing Bostonians do, as you know, when an old family's daughtering out."

"Walking in the bishop's footsteps . . . a tall order?"

"It is. Nothing's harder to predict than the past."

Another Cart-tailer, who'd been bantering with a lean, raspy neighbor, broke away now to face Trowbridge.

"Storrow Davit says I must do another Clayton Poole story," he began.

"Eliot," Trowbridge replied, "a lot of people are saying that."

"To put myself in Clayton's shoes I must assume the mind set of a thirty-four-year-old. I won't resurrect him, let the petitioners queue up from here to Dacca."

Trowbridge reached for a smoked oyster on a tole tray that a steward, like a wily Arapaho stalking a wagon train, was circling the room with. I found myself watching Eliot Bradstreet with fascination. Here before me, in the flesh, was the creator of Clayton Poole, sleuth nonpareil in thirty-seven novels, the favorite series detective of forty million readers, myself among them.

Bradstreet extended his hand. His clasp was vibrant, the

handshake of a man who could, if he chose, shed thirty years and again be thirty-four.

"Austin Layman!" he exclaimed with pleasure. "Cleon deputized me to look out for you and after you. Said I'd know you because you look like Clayton Poole. And so you do."

"If that's true, how come I'm not mobbed every time I stick my head out the door? Clayton's a superbly fit and functioning guy."

"The fantasy figure I drew when I realized I wouldn't conquer the world with might and main. Yet . . . you could be him!"

"Be thankful you're not a casting director. I'd make a pretty shallow Poole."

"Poole's modest about his exploits. Perhaps, unless an addiction to punning overrules circumspection, you have that in common with him, too?"

"Though often exacerbating, my puns are rarely indiscreet."

Davit now had Trowbridge's ear. They moved off together toward the bar. I helped myself to a hot cheese puff as the steward, prudently without war whoops, orbited again. For the moment I had Bradstreet to myself.

"Tell me," I said, "Did you quit Clayton cold turkey?"

"To quote a discerning lady, 'The only thing anyone can quit cold turkey *is* cold turkey.' "

"Then you've had regrets?"

"Clayton's adventures were the only adventures I ever really had."

"Have you ever been asked to carry out some kind of commission—establish someone's guilt or innocence?"

"I have. Clayton has, too. We decline civilly."

"Yet the temptation to do something is there?"

"There and ever threatening to engulf us."

The steward came back. I took a piece of smoked salmon on which reposed a perky sprig of dill. I wondered if the Cart-tail Club harbored a Swede in the kitchen.

"Have you ever given any thought to trying your own hand at detective work?" Bradstreet asked me now.

"My last year in grade school I set up a detective agency in my grandmother's preserve cellar, fingerprinted all my classmates and sat back to await clients. None showed. I wish I'd saved the prints. Some of those kids didn't turn out too well."

"Lost occasions are best forgot."

"The work I do for Bigelow, Sturgis, sometimes skirts the investigatory, though not of the criminal kind as ordinarily understood. How long has an envelope with a thousand dollars in it lain in a Congressman's safe? Why did a hospital fail to report a patient's claim that she'd been raped during the night by the chief resident?"

"Do such matters intrigue you?"

"Sometimes."

I ate a piece of stuffed egg provided by the indefatigible Arapaho. He had many arrows to his bow. The paprika stung my lips.

"Enough so to make you want to do something about it?"

"The little boy who set up his agency in granny's preserve cellar is still unrequited. Why do you ask?"

"When you've created a successful detective on paper, you find yourself wondering how he would cope in a real life situation."

"So that's it. I look like Poole. Have the proper credentials—WASP, Harvard undergrad degree, graduate degree from M.I.T. Am in a corresponding line of work. So here's your chance to test his credibility while you, without courting ridicule, handle the remote controls. Is that it?"

Dipping his chin slightly, the slack wattles beneath it trembling in mock self-reproach, Bradstreet nodded.

"I feel as though I've been gaffed and hauled aboard," I said.

"You should. Cleon's not implicated, however. I talked it over with him, but so far as he knows, that's all it was—a speculative conversation. Perhaps it should end there."

"In the right circumstances I could be interested."

"Unless Cleon's way off base, the right circumstances already exist. Three Cart-tailers have died recently. While the supposition that the manner of death was, in each case, suspect, began with me, I was merely propounding an hypothesis. When I outlined it to Cleon I expected to get nowhere. On the contrary, he found it plausible. What we have to deal with, he thinks, is three murders, planned and carried out by someone who is either settling a score or is actuated by madness."

"If there's even an outside chance that he's right, I should think the whole business would've become a police matter before now."

"The Club doesn't court notoriety. We'd have to be sure before going to the police." He stopped. Bishop Colesworthy, clutching an empty glass, was edging between us.

"Eliot," he said, "you look younger every time we meet. How do you do it?"

"I pay my friends to tell me, every time we meet, that I look younger. Their compliments rejuvenate me. Your check is in the mail."

"Right now," the bishop said, elevating his glass in misty veneration, "my own waning spirits need replenishment." He looked toward the drinks table and continued, "I see a clear path to the bar. If you'll excuse me, I'll take it."

A rush of people poured through the gap the bishop had opened in the pressed ranks of revelers. The distance between Bradstreet and myself widened.

"I'll get back to you," he called to me over the bald dome of Boylston Huddle, chief of pilopathology at Mass General. "I want to follow up what we've been talking about."

I signaled agreement, at which point the gleaming dome swiveled and confronted me.

3

Although his crown was hairless, hair the color of decaying ivory flourished in abundance on the back of Boylston Huddle's head—snug, narrow waled, like a corduroy cataplasm. A six-footer, he met me at eye level, cold and aloof. I met his eye arrogance for arrogance.

"I haven't seen you here before," he said, in a tone that implied I was either a gatecrasher or had gained admittance as the result of some ghastly blunder.

His stare was a challenge.

I took him on. "You can bag the aerobics. I'm a pimp who blew in from the Common. You know those girls who walk around over there shaking ankle bells to let you know they're available? My crew. Business tonight has been hotter than a smoking pistol. Thought I owed myself a coffee break." If Huddle is devil's advocate for the screening committee, I told myself, let him try advocating that.

"I'm reassured," he said. "I'd taken you for a paid assassin."

"For recreational events of that nature," I replied, "I never accept reimbursement."

"You blend in plausibly here," he went on. "I congratulate you on your versatility."

"Guttermost or uttermost," I said, "I'm at home with either."

Huddle's lips came together in a tight smile. "I prefer," he said, "to be left guessing as to which category you assign the present company." Then he swung away to minister to Lawrence Thistlethwaite who chose that moment to have a coughing spasm.

I jerked my arm aside barely in time to avoid a trickle of Wild Turkey spilling from a passerby's glass. It was Simon Spendlow, inventor extraordinary and, by avocation, fore-edging consultant to the Athenaeum. He halted in his tracks.

"Did I get you?" he wanted to know with an eagerness that could have implied a wager was at stake.

"No, damn it. This jacket could do with some hundred proof moth-proofing."

Spendlow stayed to talk but, unlike Bradstreet, made no offer to shake hands. That was understandable. His right hand lacked three fingers. During his senior year at Harvard, after he'd struck a friend in anger, he'd gone back to his room in Thayer Hall, built a fire in the fireplace, and held his hand over the flames till three fingers were burned away. Six months later he returned to Harvard and graduated with a summa. It was difficult now to relate this urbane, self-possessed man in his mid-sixties with that wilful youth who, repenting folly, had exacted of himself such fierce retribution.

"Have you remarked," he asked, "how many Cart-tailers have to do with books?" For illustration he inclined his head toward Isaac Quelch, watchdog of the *Atlantic*. I'd heard that Quelch, who'd gone not to Harvard but to Hobart—a word which, if mumbled (and sometimes Quelch did deliberately mumble it) sounded like Harvard—had a compulsive need to assert his individualism. Therefore, I wasn't surprised to observe now, in his appearance, a likely confirmation of that fact. He was wearing charcoal gray trousers and a yellow and red blazer, the dress tartan of the Ogilvies. I watched as he enfolded Lionel Thistlethwaite in a bear hug of a greeting. I heard Spendlow's voice, louder now, addressing me anew—"Have you noticed how many people here are book-connected?" I got on track.

"That's Boston for you," I said, affecting nonchalance even as I exhorted my subconscious not to inject any hearthside or digital allusions into the conversation. "Money doesn't make Brahmins. Brains do."

"There you have it," Spendlow said. "Get the first people here together and every one of them either has written a book or intends to."

"They all have a job to get done and a message to impart and give equal weight to both."

"Like John Wesley, they see themselves as brands plucked from the burning fire, and, on that account, owing the world something extra. Survivor's guilt, wouldn't you say?"

So there it was—hearthside with flames leaping, to my dismay, higher than the flames of hell. Yet I hadn't said it. Spendlow had. Had I led him into it? A change of direction was imperative.

"How," I sputtered, "do they get that damn stable odor in here?"

Spendlow grinned and I realized that, for him,

yesterday's tragedy had become today's sport. His lopped fist gestured in blatant contempt of the past in the direction of a thick-set elder dimly visible through a haze of tobacco smoke he himself had generated.

"Bets are it's Sumner Craddock's cigars. We think he smokes horseshit."

"He must have an understanding wife."

"His wife's my sister-in-law. Believe me, she doesn't understand Sumner."

"Something of a Rumpole, is he?"

"He's here more than he's at home. When he's neither place he's off looting pyramids, which is most of the time. And why not? Isn't that what an Egyptologist's supposed to do?"

"He's done a book, hasn't he, about ancient Egypt building up its national myth in consonance with the Nile?"

"Says we've spurned our natural destiny by not making the Mississippi work the same way for us. For Sumner a myth built in consonance with the Cart-tail Club would make more sense. Here, where the old bonding instincts still prevail. Enclaves like this, which exclude women, are becoming rare."

"Is the exclusion total?"

"Women can come to the final rehearsal of the Forefather's Day play."

"A concession to Women's Lib?"

"Men's libido."

"I didn't think Cart-tailers had libidos."

"People think the Puritans had none either. Yet why do you suppose they stripped those women to the waist and whipped them through the streets?"

"That was kinky, I guess."

"When Mark Twain visited the Club in 1902, he urged us to adopt, as our motto, 'the penis mightier than the sword.' "

"And killed his chance of getting elected to membership?"

"He would've become a member by acclamation if a week later, in Manhattan, he hadn't offered the same motto to the Mammoth Cod Club."

The chief justice, Richard Allerton, now showed up at my side. He had Lionel, the smaller Thistlethwaite, in tow. (Though twins, the Thistlethwaites were not a matched set.)

Lionel had a speech on tap, which must have made up the bulk of his conversation throughout the evening. He began with it at once.

"Lawrence and I are not identical twins. As boys, father once brought us to visit a farm he owned in Peterborough. A man named Flavius Rideout, who did a little work about the place in exchange for his keep, told us, 'Lawrence will one day look over the tops of the corn. Lionel will look at the ears.' "

Sonorous vibrations from a bronze gong echoed through the room. With a white rubber mallet, Nathaniel Byfield, director of Harvard's resurrected Institute of Altruistic Love and present first magistrate of the Cart-tail Club, struck the gong twice more. Thus were members urged to ascend the stairs to dinner.

A moment later, leather heels clattering against wood, the four-member cast of *Nile Bodies* came piling down the back stairs from the Club's own Sewall Theater, named impudently for the judge who forbade all theatrical entertainments in seventeenth-century Boston. Once among us they made a sprint for the bar. General Caleb Stoughton was a cinch to pick out. People standing six feet nine usually are. I also recognized Jabez Brattle, perennial cash-keeper of the Boston Symphony Orchestra, busier than ever now that the B.S.O. had begun its second century. The other playmakers, Spendlow told me, were Gideon Mayhew, master of Harvard's Leonard Hoar House (never, at Harvard, alluded to by anything less than its full name), and Cabot Lanyard, the Club's epic mariner. Lanyard was the diminutive plum stealer I'd met on my arrival.

In Lanyard's wake came Cleon, who'd written *Nile Bodies* in three days and was directing it now in six. Although intercepted by Gamaliel Bandine and George Belcher, Cleon broke clean with an instant quip and, shouldering his way past others surging in the opposite direction, perservered till he stood at my side.

"Austin," he said, his voice contrite, "I meant to get here sooner. How are you?"

"I may've set a record for scrapping an acquaintance with half the Club membership in less than an hour."

"I can appreciate what you've been through."

"Can you? Remind me to have you over for a glimpse of my shrunken head collection. It's one short."

4

*N*ow we were upstairs. The intrepid Thistlethwaites were already in their chairs at the center of the long, pinch-waisted rectangular table, backs to a cowled fireplace, which, though massive, had burning in it applewood logs big enough to simmer a nonogenarian's desiccated bones, but no bigger. Cleon, using my elbow as steering apparatus, led me around widdershins to a seat across from the guests of honor. He sat me on his right. Brattle, already seated, was on my right. Bradstreet came and sat on Cleon's left. After a few minutes all the chairs were filled and the stewards began serving the Club's traditional, full cream, lobster bisque.

"What about this?" Brattle said to me, quite as if we were picking up midway an interrupted conversation. "Wendell Leverett turned away one of our people the other day when she approached him for his annual donation to the B.S.O. Said he'd give nothing this year because I'd objected to those flamboyant costumes Sarah Caldwell got from Red China for her production of *Turandot*. Object! Have you seen them?"

I was wondering how to proceed without giving offense when suddenly a *deus ex machina* in the shape of a full dinner plate—beef Wellington, corn pudding, Harvard beets, and a popover—was frisbied in front of Brattle and at once occupied his attention to the exclusion of all else. With equal dexterity other plates were scaled in front of my remaining neighbors and myself. Incredibly, the person serving them was a crackleware crone. Cleon was amused at my slack-jawed amazement.

"Lorna Greenstockings," he said. "A Boston institution. Forty years at Durgin-Park. Since then, nineteen years here."

"On the job since before Lindbergh winged it to Paris?"

"Paces herself easier these days. Comes here only Tuesday nights."

I gave Lorna a closer look. She seemed old enough to have been on hand to brush corn bread crumbs off the cloth at Durgin-Park the day Lafayette dropped in for tiffin.

"The name, Greenstockings," I asked, "is it a put on?"

"Sure. The only color she ever puts on. I think that's how we got her. Manufacturers stopped making her stockings. Senator Dixwell owns a hosiery mill in Leominster. He has three dozen pair run up every year to put in her Christmas box."

"Her choice of color's peculiar."

"Money colored. People here find that reassuring."

Brattle, his plate now clean, passed a half-folded napkin across his lips and abruptly resumed with me. "Layman, is it? Where are the Laymans from? Norfolk, I should think. Unless you're a Lehmann?" He spelled out this version.

I toyed with the idea of announcing that my grandfather

was a butcher from Leipzig. Then, on further consideration, decided to give him a genealogical earful.

"My Laymans were from Ipswich. Before that, from Diss and Kenninghall. And you're right, those places are in Norfolk. Habbakuk Layman, M.D. was buried at Kenninghall in 1699. There's a headstone there that says so. That's as far back as I can get. Before that, I suspect, we were spawned in catch basins. Ben Franklin's Folger kin were from Diss. Maybe Habbakuk birthed some of them."

Brattle hesitated. Was I overdoing it? In his eyes, ties with the Franklins couldn't have counted for much. Hadn't Franklin's grandmother come to America as an indentured servant? Yet, when Brattle spoke again, I found I'd achieved a measure of acceptance.

"None of us here has much occasion to trace his family back beyond the seventeenth century. Common stock. At best, linendrapers and such, like the Sewalls. John Lowell was a shoemaker's son. Emerson sprang from bakers and distillers."

"And a Salem witch."

Before I could comment further, he gave me a finalizing tap on the forearm to seal off the encounter and turned away to talk to Belcher, who sat on his left.

"Cleon," inquired a voice from down the table. "Have you pummeled *Nile Bodies* into shape yet?"

The speaker was Trowbridge.

"Ask Caleb," Cleon answered. "He's rewriting the script."

"A seven-foot Cleopatra should be able to write her own ticket."

"Must he say she sailed down the Nile in 'poop and circumstance'?"

When that brought an explosion of laughter, General Stoughton looked as elated as if basking in the rocket's red glare.

"On the battlefield the general's all blood and thunder," Cleon said. "On stage—all thud and blunder!"

More laughter, led off by Stoughton himself.

Lorna cleared away our plates, leaving in their stead lime sherbet anointed with dribbles of Drambuie. Demitasse cups now moved along the table, along with low pewter pots of steaming coffee.

I was slipping into a mood of complaisant somnolence when, without warning, there was a sudden failing of the lights, till the only light remaining in the room was that coming from the fireplace. The faces around me bobbed with reverent expectation. Then Nathaniel Byfield, who'd exited discreetly some moments before, reentered carrying a silver salver on which reposed a porcupine, carved from wood, save for one gleaming quill which, Cleon whispered, was the work of some ancient Inca goldsmith, recovered by Halversam from the ruins of the great sun temple at Cuzco, and thought to represent the golden rod of Manco.

Belcher and Mayhew, with candles provided by Enoch Gookin, now escorted Byfield to his chair where he held the tiki aloft and declared, "By virtue of the unquenchable golden quill which illumines the manuscripts of all true Cart-tailers, I declare this meeting begun."

He then plucked the gold quill from the porcupine's back and, holding it out before him at arm's length, intoned words of Eleusinian portent: "Without the quill to succeed, we are naught!"

"We are naught!" the assembled gathering echoed with a fervor that would have done proud a witches' coven gathered on the Hampshire heath.

Byfield now handed the quill to the neighbor on his right who called out, "The quill to succeed!" It went then to the waiting hand of the man on his right who repeated the words. In this way it traveled on around the table though, as mere guest, when it came to me I passed it along in silence. A vigorous nod from Brattle told me my instincts had not played me false.

When the quill got back to Byfield, he, with surgical deftness, reinserted it in its proper socket, then, with Yankee matter-of-factness, placed the tiki on the mantel above the fireplace, to glimmer and be forgotten beside the two candles, now thriftily snuffed.

The ceremony was ended and those who participated in it surely imbued with a fresh resolve to confront pencil, pen, tape recorder, SCM typewriter with Change-a-keys, Diablo word processor (the only demon any Cart-tailer had congress with), or North Star Advantage—whatever suited their writing purposes best—with reanimated zeal.

A chair scuffed and Richard Allerton got to his feet, swayed like a Lombardy poplar in a stiff gale, then steadied himself.

"Bear with me," he said, with a judicial calm. "I'm too close to the table."

"After such a meal," Quelch quipped, "so are we all."

This well worn jest was everyone's cue to settle his chair so as to have the speakers in view. Allerton gave a phlegmy cough into a scrolled hand, then spoke.

"The summer after I graduated from Harvard, while

sightseeing at Khartoum, I learned from a Melkite missionary that Lionel Thistlethwaite had set up a medical outpost at Bor, on the Upper Nile, the first of his race to visit there. Nothing would do then but for me to be the second. I won't weary you with the details of how I reached Bor. I'm not certain I knew then. I'm certain I don't know now. But I've never forgotten my first night there. I awoke to a rustling sound coming from under Lionel's cot. With a crooked staff I gaffed out a green mamba—Africa's most lethal snake. Only then did Lionel awaken. He told me: 'I've heard that skitter every night for a week and paid it no heed. I keep my rice under the cot and thought the mice were cutting themselves in for a share.' "

The table rocked with laughter. After a few compliments applicable to both Thistlethwaites, Allerton surrendered his gavel to Gamaliel Bandine.

"A toast," Bandine said, "to Boston's own constellation Gemini!"

All stood. Vintage burgundy, from vineyards at St. Auberge, in which Jabez Brattle owned an interest, was raised aloft in Pepe Hermann crystal and the toast quickly downed. The brothers perked with elation.

Now Bandine paused. Lorna Greenstockings, her legs a green mamba twosome, came at him in a spasm of hurry, her fingers snarled about a telegram. Bandine scanned the yellow half-sheet, then spoke: "I have here a communique from another embattled outpost of modern civilization—sixteen-hundred Pennsylvania Avenue!"

A chase chorus of guffaws and chortles traveled around the table. Clearing his throat with the gusto of a veteran of many New England winters, Bandine began reading:

"Congratulations to the brothers Thistlethwaite on attaining ninety. Have this day placed their names in nomination as joint ambassadors to Pago Pago. If assignment too pulse quickening, will they consider Walla Walla? Sincere best wishes, Ronald Reagan, President of the United States."

Though few men present warmed to the president who had entered the White House by way of "Kings Row" rather than Tory Row, there was an interlude of further hand smacking and, here and there, a grudging admission that when Reagan was right he was supreme. After a minute, Bandine rapped the gavel.

"I'm afraid," he said, with feigned dismay, "Mr. Reagan's appointment, rusticating this pair to the Equator, comes too late to do Boston much good."

During the outpouring of laughter that ensued, Gamaliel got the twins to their feet. Applause soared.

"One truth remains to be told," Lawrence said. "I've never told Lionel this before . . . *I've always rather admired him!*"

An uproar of approval followed.

"I was afraid he'd say that," Lionel said, when the din subsided. "To merit his good opinion I've been exerting myself for ninety years. Tonight, I find I've had it all along."

Byfield rose now and stepped forward to embrace the twins. "Admiration begets admiration," he said. At that moment a log shifted position in the fireplace, throwing off a tumult of sparks. Gasps and exclamations were heard as though the event had been decreed to happen in pleasant confirmation of the speaker's words.

"Wonderful stock, our yeoman stock," Justice Allerton said, nodding his approval.

"Boston's genes surpass her beans," said Byfield. "To illustrate:

> There was once a young Brahmin of means,
> Who doted on the subject of genes.
> 'I'd rather,' he said,
> 'Read Mendel unfed,
> Than breakfast on codfish and beans.'

"Now, gentlemen," he said, raising his voice to be heard over the groans of derision that followed, "downstairs, for those who care to linger, there's Welsh rabbit and Bass ale. As for the rest of you—to your chariots and home!"

5

*B*y ten thirty, after dismissing a roaring motorcycle escort sent around, George Belcher surmised, by Governor McGurk's ever alert aide-de-camp, Dunscotus O'Flaherty, the guests of honor were quietly wending their way back to their Hammond Pond Parkway estate. Most of the Thistlethwaite's well-wishers had departed also, scattering to Beverly, Milton, Sudbury, Dover—those enclaves where Brahmins lived still in measured contentment save when, on town matters, they had to indulge what that failed Bostonian, Arthur Hugh Clough, once described as "the horrible pleasure of pleasing inferior people."

In the library, where I went now with Cleon and Eliot, in a corner I perceived Cyril Outerbridge, Caleb Stoughton, and Isaac Quelch. Cousins all, they were discussing the imminent dissolution of a family trust. From the doorway, Sumner Craddock hailed the lot of us. He was staying the night because, in the morning, he was taking the earlybird flight to Cairo. "Mubarak sent for me," he said. "Wants me to look at a red granite temple they've excavated beneath another temple. Built before the pharoahs. By whom, nobody knows."

"Say what you like," Cleon replied, "we know Mubarak wants you to set up a Cairo engagement for *Nile Bodies*."

Eliot spoke. "The fact is, Sumner's on an annihilation mission for the CIA."

"Would that their money was so well spent," Craddock said. He turned toward the stairs, calling back over his shoulder, "I'm to be trapped on the top floor for the remainder of the night. No way to come down without tripping the security alarm. I hope Mr. Gookin's here to release me at six. Otherwise I'll make my way to the airport with the police hot in pursuit."

"Better stick to grave robbing," Eliot said. "It becomes you more."

Craddock, grinning, disappeared up the stairs.

Throughout this exchange the Outerbridge heirs had, with studied indifference, conveyed to us every assurance any reasonable man could want that they would be miserable till we withdrew and left them in sole possession of the library. Since we also wanted to be by ourselves, their need imposed no hardship. With affable assurances of our reluctance to diminish the circle of camaraderie, we withdrew, toting bottles of Bass ale, to the neighboring east-facing room, or muniment room as lately it had come to be called.

The muniment room, Cleon told me, had been set up when Thayer Dabney, the Club archivist, realized it had become the common practice of members to "loan" family documents—some recording King's Grants dating back to the 1630's, others as inconsequential as A.K.C. papers for long deceased Boston terriers—to the Cart-tail Club, loans made, of course, to save the loaners the expense of a safe deposit box. In time, these file cases so multiplied they began to push off the shelves those numerous limited editions of family memoirs which constitute Brahmin Boston's favorite underground literature. Since, in most instances, restricted usage for these documents had been stipulated, their presence in its library offered the Club no discernible advantage. Hence the inspired alternative of a muniment room. Thayer Dabney may have put his foot down, but, being a true Yankee foot, it had set humming the treadles of another industry.

The muniment room did, however, contain one document that had much to do with the present—a parchment scroll which recorded, in elegant Spenserian whorls (Thayer Dabney's sole achievement with the quill), the name of every person ever advanced for membership. Since the screening committee had found unsuitable many of those put up for consideration, this was, in fact, one of the most interesting documents the room contained. In the course of a hundred years, many eminent Bostonians had learned to their astonishment that the Cart-tail Club had determined it had nothing to gain by admitting them to membership.

Despite its dubious origins, the muniment room had become much more than a repository for obsolescent paper litter. My eyes were drawn to a Heppelwhite breakfront with beveled glass doors, which held an assortment of Revere silver. A companion piece accommodated Franklin memorabilia. Filling the shelves of a third cabinet was an array of Chinese funeral bronzes, dating to the Shang dynasty.

We sat down, sinking into black leather, pliant and hospitable.

After a minute or two had gone by, Eliot, his voice edged in approval, said to me, "Your practiced eye has encompassed everything." He meant I was deepening my identification with Clayton Poole. That should have brought a blush. Clayton hadn't entered my thoughts for a couple of hours.

"Your socks are mismated," I said, taking a leap into the unknown, "one black, one brown. I wonder if Clayton would have noticed that?"

Eliot uttered a bray of self-deprecation. "Without even looking," he said, "I know you're right."

"Austin," Cleon said, "put that in your memory bank. The creator of modern fiction's most colorful detective is color blind!"

"A not very marketable flaw for a novelist," Eliot allowed, "but true nonetheless." He paused, drank the last of his ale, then resumed. "Austin, there's another matter we ought to take up. Something that could really test your mettle."

I confronted Cleon. "Murder times three? Your department?"

"Not any longer. I've gone my limit."

"Well, whatever there is to hear, let's have it."

"Since August, three members of the Club have died. All unexpectedly—an accident, a suicide, another accident. Or so it's been alleged."

"But, in fact, foul play?"

"That's my opinion."

"Nobody here tonight spoke of the departed, not in my hearing anyway. What were the names, again? Tom Hatherly, Silsbee Enright . . . "

"And Dana Champney."

"Champney. Yeah. I take it back. Lanyard mentioned him. Said the lethal weapons were doughnuts and piccalilli."

"Cabot gets carried away sometimes."

"No one mentioned either of the others."

"No one would, believe me. If, by selected acts of murder, you wanted to deplete the membership of some Club you couldn't find one better suited to that purpose than the Cart-tail Club. Instantly, everybody's mind would be at work to pretend it wasn't happening."

"The Cart-tail Club," Eliot contributed, "is an extension of the clubs most of its members belonged to at Harvard. When you come through the front door, you're back in college again. You want no reminders that the years are slipping by and death's stalking you."

"There is," Cleon said, "a tacit conspiracy among Cart-tailers never to hold post mortems on terminated members. Moreover, if you're ailing, you don't come to the Club. If you've been ill and have recovered you don't speak of it when you return. If you intend to drop dead you go elsewhere to do it. No one wants to hear human frailty rehearsed here. Within these ensorcelled walls everyone's immortal."

"One member," Eliot said, "left funds for mint juleps to be drunk in his memory the first Tuesday following his demise. Nobody came."

"Well, acknowledged or not, three members died lately. Who was the first to go?"

"Dana Champney," Cleon said. "Car stolen from his driveway in Wellesley Hills. Found it back there next morning. Drove into Boston. On Storrow Drive the car went haywire, pieces dropping out on the roadbed. Then the car flew headlong into an abutment. One big scrunch. They had to hose him out."

"Hatherly came next?"

"No, Enright. Staying alone at his place on Louis Bay while his wife was abroad. Found frozen to death in a freezer chest. Fingernails broken to bits. Fingers themselves lacerated to shreds. Gore splattered everywhere inside the freezer. Holes actually gouged in the enamel underside of the lid. The police theorize he stripped and climbed into the chest to commit suicide, changed his mind but couldn't force the lock to get out again."

"I can see why nobody brought that into the conversation tonight. And Hatherly?"

"Found under a sun lamp. Glider he was basking on was covered with foil to reflect the light. Heat prostration, they said, or a stroke. Baked to death."

I was queasy.

Cleon rallied me. "Don't quit on us yet, Austin. More to come."

"Go ahead. Whatever it is, let me have it."

"Each died precisely two weeks apart. Tomorrow another two weeks are up."

"And, conceivably . . . " Eliot began.

"The jig's up for another Cart-tailer?"

He nodded. My eyes searched Cleon's face. He had whittled his features to so firm and lean a log of inscrutibility I wanted to take a hand ax to him. I let the temptation pass.

"Seems a shame to make a gift of those two-week intervals to the long arm of coincidence," I said.

"It's a signature of some kind," Cleon said. "Don't ask me what kind. That's as far as my thinking goes on the subject." He leaned forward, took hold of the brass weight at the end of a needlepoint bell pull and gave it a sharp tug. From some distant point I heard the faint tinkle of a responding bell. More ale, I surmised, and settled back in my chair to await its arrival.

"In times past," Eliot said, "to dump on Boston you said, 'Respectability stalks her streets unchecked.' "

"Boston can't get by with that any more," I said.

"Murder's invaded our own enclave," Cleon said, "and the murderer knows us well enough to be one of us. What became of the Boston society John Quincy Adams wrote about? 'The morals of our people are much better . . . our laws are wiser; our religion is superior. . . . ' "

"Wasn't that more or less true in his day?"

"For Adamses perhaps. They're a breed apart. Destiny has deified them."

"I am not a candidate for deification," Eliot announced, hefting himself out of his chair. "I'm all too human. It's as they say, 'You don't buy beer, you rent it.' Nature must be served." He stepped out over the threshold and disappeared into the men's room across the hall.

There was a creak of floorboards and Lorna Greenstockings came into the room balancing a tray containing three bottles of ale, a grasshopper, and half a dozen pieces of what looked like divinity fudge, arranged on a Stridendecker plate. Her attire had curiously altered since dinner. On her feet now were rough cut, mid-length boots from which her green-sheathed legs protruded like gangling amaryllis stalks. Her head was hidden under a bone white, mohair watch cap pulled down well about her ears though the long lobes still could be seen. She refilled our glasses, then lowered herself into a roseback rocker and took a sip of the grasshopper. Cleon's grin told me that what was happening was his doing. I swigged my ale and looked attentive.

"Lorna," Cleon began, "does Durgin Park know what they lost when you left?"

"You can always remind them," she replied.

"Too risky. They might go all out to get you back."

"You've problems enough without that," she said. "Members dropping like horse chestnuts in a September line squall."

"What's to be done about it?"

"A low-density diet, that's what. Something that'll enable a man to stand up under stress." Having said that she got hold of her plate of fudge and nudged it toward us. Cleon and I each took a piece. I bit into mine and thought I had a mouthful of pencil shavings.

"Low-density health food?" I asked, when I was able.

"Potato fudge. My own recipe."

"I never doubted it," I said. I put the rest of my piece on a napkin and it stayed there. Cleon went on nibbling his as though it was some exquisite Viennese confection.

"Is your watch cap part of your regimen?" he asked her when he again had access to his tongue.

"Raises brain temperature by one degree so you can think better. I don't wear it during dinner because Mr. Gookin thinks it wouldn't look right."

"I don't suppose you do any of your major thinking during dinner?"

"You'd be surprised."

Eliot came back and plopped himself down with pleasurable ease in the chair he'd occupied before. He then took a small piece of fudge and popped it into his mouth. From the look on his face I wondered if, caught unawares, he'd bitten through his tongue.

Cleon got up, shoved his chair around, relocating it with a thump in a position bringing him closer to Lorna. This left Eliot and me offside—penalized, I surmised, for not feigning enthusiasm for the fudge. With a downward thrust of his hand, however, he assured us that our presence was wanted. I was sure then that he was after something Lorna had, and willing to bet it wasn't her recipe for potato fudge.

"Lorna," Cleon said, "you've seen Cart-tailers die in clusters before. It's not exactly what you'd call mind boggling. The average member's already outrun the actuarial tables by some years."

"So have I. But not those three. I'm still here. They're not."

"What's your interest in them?"

"The last Tuesday in August they had dinner together— the three of them—upstairs. I set up a table for them in the alcove. They wanted to be by themselves."

"Yet you overheard something?"

"In snatches. When I served them. What it came down to was that someone was making ready to publish something derogatory. Boston could end up place-rated right next to Sodom and Gomorrah, Mr. Champney said, if they didn't squelch him."

"Squelch whom?"

"Never caught the name. Must've been some foreigner though. I did hear them say he was 'over the Atlantic.' "

Forgetting my role as passive listener, I jumped in. "By

any chance could they have said 'over *at* the Atlantic'?"

Lorna thought hard. Finally she answered. "Yes. Could be they said that."

"And maybe," I said, really reaching deep into the stands for this one, " 'Quelch' instead of 'squelch'?"

Her fingers touched lightly the mohair cap, her marvelous thinking cap.

"Isn't Mr. Quelch with the *Atlantic Monthly?*" she asked.

"Yes."

"Then it *was* 'Quelch'! I should've picked up on that. Mr. Quelch is bossy. Needs setting down more often than not. It's gotten so that whenever I hear his name mentioned it automatically comes up 'squelch' in my mind. Odds are that that's what happened that night." She finished her grasshopper in one remorseful gulp.

"Those poor men," she said. "That Quelch must have hounded them right off the face of the earth."

"Perhaps," Cleon said, "he did find out something they wanted kept secret, but he would never have been nasty about it. That's not his way. We'll talk to him. I expect he'll be able to account for himself honorably."

He offered Lorna his hand. Steadying herself she got to her feet. "If it answers your purpose," she said, "tell him I was your source. When you're as old as I am you've got all the reputation you're going to have and could do with less."

Cleon moved with her toward the threshold. "A cab?" he queried.

"No sense in that," she said. "My condo's round the corner, at the old Touraine. If a mugger mugs me, I'll mug him back. I'm just in the mood, too. I'll squelch him! And this time I mean *squelch!*"

She headed down the hall, the tassel on her watch cap bobbing defiantly.

Cleon slid back into his chair, his face luminous.

I confronted Eliot. "Are you sure you don't want Lorna handling this case instead of me? She understands you people through and through."

"No way," he said. "For my money you could out-finesse Clayton Poole any day of the week."

"Nick Carter used to be my ideal," I said. "Keep the applause coming and I may have to upgrade my aspirations."

"Surely you don't mean you're ready to take on Holmes himself?"

"Would you believe Luke Skywalker?"

6

"*I* suppose," Cleon said, "all probability experts rejoice in dazzling others with their analytical powers?"

"Here's one that doesn't," I said. "My thinking's analogical."

"Explain yourself."

"I pair off things—'Squelch'/'Quelch'. And, presto, there's the answer. Computers are of both kinds—analytical, analogical. The analogical ones sometimes come up first with the answers. The brain, like the heart, can do its job without having to be instructed. It only seems to skip steps. It takes them unperceived."

"When you're up against a logician, don't you feel inferior?"

"Whatever for? The analogical thinker's the next development of man—he's suprarational."

"I warn you," Cleon said, "Quelch has a tenacious allegiance to logic. He amasses facts till he's got an ironclad case."

"A blood runner?"

"What?"

"Resolute. The dogged type who'll work out till he has blood in his urine."

"That's Isaac! Last year he cried foul when a lady trustee at the Boston Public Library walked off with Greenough's portrait bust of Fenimore Cooper. Nailed her good. She's since moved to Gibraltar."

"That should distress no one. I understand Gibraltar's well anchored."

"Three years ago he sounded the tocsin when two of the proprietors went looking for a buyer for the Athenaeum's copy of Poe's *Tamerlane*."

"First family peccadillos engross him," Eliot contributed.

"Can he be bought off?"

"Oh, he's incorruptible. It's just that, for a good story, he'd sell his grandmother for dog meat."

"Yet, on this occasion, before breaking the story, he consulted with those who'd be hurt by it. A courtesy to fellow Cart-tailers?"

"Could be he was hoping to add to his information," Cleon said.

"Couldn't they get him to back off with pleas or . . . "

"Threats? No. And the threats that would lead him to commit murder have yet to be devised."

Eliot agreed. "That's right. Besides, what would he have gained? While the three of them still were alive he could have gone to press and brazened it out. Were he to publish his information now, after it's provoked a rash of murders, everyone would be down on him."

"If," Cleon said, "it was Isaac against those three, at least we don't have to worry about another murder, come tomorrow."

"Tomorrow's here," I said. "Two after twelve. What's to say there won't be other victims. Others who we don't know about could be involved in this thing."

At that instant the air was smitten with the clamor of a metal striker hammering against an alarm bell.

Though, by all rights, this clangor ought to have overwhelmed every other sound, surprisingly it was encountering competition—the shouts of a man determined to be heard and endowed with a lung capacity which left no doubt that he would be heard.

"That's Craddock," Cleon said.

"How like Sumner," Eliot exclaimed. "He's tripped the alarm and thinks now he can bellow it into submission."

"He sounds scared," Cleon said. He sprang up.

We ran toward the stairs. Even then new sounds were sundering the night, the whooping of sirens as police cruisers, coming from three directions, converged on the cacophanous premises of the Cart-tail Club.

The sight I saw when we burst into the Revere room made me wonder if the Cart-tail Club did, after all, harbor its own resident spook. On the stairway a bizarre commotion was in progress. In after-hours shirtsleeves, Enoch Gookin was engaged in an indecorous waltz of restraint with a struggling apparition—Sumner Craddock clad in a yellow nightshirt. Actually all the agitation was concentrated in Sumner. He was excited—babbling, flailing. As often as Gookin acted to restrain him, Craddock shoved him away. "Give Enoch a hand," Cleon shouted in my ear. Then he turned and ran back into the borning room.

I leaped up the stairs, Eliot at my heels. "I'll help," he said. "Sumner knows me."

Having gone a couple of rounds with no decision, a flushed Enoch Gookin was glad to relinquish the struggle to us. Yet he'd accomplished more than he guessed. First the thrashing ceased, then the torrent of words, and then, as though by consensual agreement, the alarm itself fell silent.

"Cleon's snuffed it," Eliot explained. "The control panel's in the library."

We led Craddock down the stairs. He was barefoot. At ground level, his eyes widening, he pointed at the Revere lanterns. "Look," he said. "His lantern's lit, yet he's upstairs—dead!"

Cleon, who'd joined us, read off the name below the lantern: "Isaac Quelch—Permanent Chairman, Backgammon Committee."

"Steady," he told Craddock now, and eased him back toward a chair into which, knees buckling, he sank the instant his bare calves made contact with the leather.

At the door to the inner vestibule, the police were strumming the knocker in brisk, staccato thumps. If they had had any idea of bursting in, they were disappointed. At ten thirty, as was his usual practice, Enoch Gookin had sprung the Chubb lock. Until we knew more, admitting the law was unthinkable.

Enoch already was slipping into his jacket. Even with death and hysteria at his elbow he couldn't disillusion outsiders about the standards the Club observed. His eyes met Cleon's. "Stonewall them," Cleon told him, "by whatever means you can." Gookin went straight to his task. Cleon went into action, too.

"Sumner," he asked, "you're certain Isaac's dead?"

"Dead as Amenhotep."

"What happened?"

"I couldn't sleep so I went into the theater to look at your *Nile Bodies* set. No light except a little filtering in from the Troubadour Tavern. I mounted the stage to get a closer look at Cleo's barge. Thought at first that there was a mummy on board." He hesitated.

"It was Quelch?" Cleon prompted.

"In his Ogilvie tartan . . . like a clan chieftan on his bier."

"You're certain he was dead?"

"Blood sopping his shirt front!—All around *it*!"

"It?"

"Our gold quill. Stuck right into his heart." He stopped. His eyes, like sauce thickening, seemed to congeal in a murky gaze. For now we'd heard all we were going to hear.

"Damn!" Eliot said. "Try keeping this out of the papers."

At that moment Gookin emerged from the inner vestibule. "If you please, Mr. Entigott," he said, confronting Cleon.

"Yes, Enoch?" Cleon said. His tone was gentle.

Gookin looked apologetic. "I told the police the alarm was tripped accidentally," he said. "They seemed doubtful. I said we'd accept responsibility. They accepted that."

"And so?"

"Before they could go away, Mr. O'Flaherty arrived—*in his white Lamborghini!*" He paused. O'Flaherty's car, a favorite butt of the *Globe*'s political cartoonist, was notorious. In Gookin's eyes, to have it parked outside cast a shadow on the Club's reputation. He resumed. "He insists on being admitted so as to satisfy himself the Club's come to no harm."

"Horsefeathers!" Eliot said. "He wants to poke his nose in here. Tell him no dice."

Gookin smiled with constraint, mentally struggling to translate "no dice" into gentlemanly parlance. Cleon stayed him. "This time," he said, "our situation may warrant indulging Mr. O'Flaherty's curiosity."

"I see your point," I put in. "If we send him packing and an hour later call homicide to come see a corpse with a stab wound, how do we explain it?"

Cleon turned to the gaping steward. "Mr. Gookin," he said, "Mr. Quelch is dead upstairs in circumstances not easy to explain. Go let Mr. O'Flaherty in. Give us a minute though. Mr. Craddock's still in his nightshirt."

"I'll look after him," Eliot offered.

"Here," I said, "I'll give a hand."

The way Craddock was sunk down in his red leather chair, it seemed that a brace of Morgan horses might be needed to haul him out. We went at it. Out of the corner of my eye I saw Cleon walking ahead of Gookin, into the vestibule, making ready to greet the governor's aide.

Once on his feet, Craddock, to our surprise, shook us off and ran ahead to the elevator. Eliot stepped inside after him. My last glimpse of him was of a man as pale and shaky as Craddock was. Was it possible that Clayton Poole's creator was squeamish about viewing a corpse? Why not? The prospect didn't exactly make me want to turn cartwheels either. The door closed and the ancient mechanism began its climb to the top floor.

7

*T*he ambitious guest was seated now where Craddock had been sitting moments before. He sat forward to the chair's edge and did so intentionally. He was observant and alert.

I'd figured O'Flaherty for early James Cagney—cocky, blustering, assertive—or if that persona was passé, then a present-day John McEnroe—boyish, contentious, intense. He conformed to neither stereotype. He was my height (six feet), lean, ramrod erect. His hair was close cropped and sandy gold, his face open and clean cut. I'd expected him to be wearing docksiders, narrow-wale black corduroys, and a v-neck, magenta cashmere sweater pulled over his bare torso, tufts of coarse black hair and a short gold chain with a claddagh dangling from it, protruding at the gap. Instead he was in black tie; his tie, unlike mine, regulation by Cart-tail standards, and, what was still less forgivable, securely in place. It irked me, too, that his manner, poised and self-assured, conformed to his appearance. When, however, he said he'd heard our alarm as he was pulling away from the Four Seasons where he'd given a slide lecture to the Dante Society, he caught me off guard.

"Can it be," I said, "that the Dante Society finds present-day Massachusetts politics more intriguing than the politics of Dante's times?"

"Oh, I had a holiday from politics this time," O'Flaherty said. "My topic was Dante's likeness in Giotto's Bargello frescos."

"Isn't it unreasonable," I said, retrenching, "to expect the governor's aide to be knowledgeable about twelfth century Italian frescos?"

Looking apologetic, O'Flaherty clarified. "That was one of the things I followed up the year Harvard sent me to I Tatti."

Our encounter was not developing as expected. What the hell, I told myself, deep-sixing the smug preconceptions I'd begun with, I'll take him as I find him and so far he's doing okay.

"I was out of order," O'Flaherty went on, "insisting that your steward admit me. Yet, for all I knew, he might have been talking to me with a .357 Mag pointed at his occiput."

Cleon seemed amused. "And if he had been?"

"No weaponry other than myself. Tae Kwon Do. Black Belt since 1981. I can see, though, that tonight no occasion offers for a trial of martial arts. I can only apologize for my intrusion and get out before your Mr. Gookin bounces me out."

He rose and took a step toward the door. Cleon caught his arm.

"We do have trouble here," he said, "and may well need your help."

"Oh?"

"The security alarm was set off by a member who's staying the night because he has to catch an early flight to Cairo tomorrow. He says there's a murdered man upstairs. One thing's certain. He murdered no one. Not his style."

"Mummies being his style?"

"Ordinarily any corpse more recent than the Ptolemaic dynasty would only rate a yawn from him."

"Your Egyptologist isn't reporting a nightmare?"

"We were making ready to settle that point when you came on the scene."

"Inopportunely, I guess."

"You might think so. I don't. If what we've been told is true, the deceased is someone whose death would not go unnoticed under any circumstances. So we've got trouble and a half. Say the word and we'll cut you in for half, though why you'd want in on such a deal is beyond me."

"If we always stopped to weigh the hazards, nothing would ever get done."

"You didn't ask if the killer's still lurking on the premises."

"Nor would I. Sounds like a sinister refrain from an old Batman script. Once raised, though, the point's valid. Is he?"

"Our informant never said."

"Sumner Craddock?"

"You know Sumner?"

"He directed my honors thesis at Harvard and nominated me for the Hitti Award. I was on the Aswan dig with him. He was famous for his fumigation cigars. At least that's what he called them—said he smoked them to purge the atmosphere of the pyramids. We thought he impregnated them with raw lanolin to get that sheepdip stench."

"You've solved one mystery already."

"Oh?"

"I'll explain someday."

"Now, what about your murderer?"

"My guess is he's long gone."

"What makes you think so?"

"He didn't set off the security alarm. Sumner did. That's one point. There are others."

"What are the odds he's a random maniac who just got lucky?"

"If so, then a fastidious one who chooses his occasions. Does someone bent on whimsical slaughter leave his victims lying in state?"

"That's the case here?"

"Yes."

"I can see why you're both strung out."

"Strung out?" I said. "I'm six shades of indigo."

"Being afraid's normal. Cowardice takes over only when you give in to it."

"Mr. O'Flaherty," Cleon said, "I think you're telling us to get moving and you're right."

"Dunce," said O'Flaherty.

"Dunce?"

"A derivative of Dunscotus. My friends call me that. My foes, too, I guess. That, or worse."

"Does it bother you?"

"I'm stuck with it. I might as well enjoy it."

"Then Dunce it is," Cleon said. "I'm Cleon. I've learned to live with that, too."

They shook.

"Austin," I said, offering my hand. We shook, too.

"And now we set off to conquer the Amazon," said our new ally.

"The Nile," I emended. "This murder has an Egyptian motif."

"Does Professor Craddock supply his own props?"

"Looks that way, doesn't it?" I left it at that.

Our return to the second floor, via the stairs, was uneventful. Not even a riser squeaked off key. The dining room lay huddled under peaks of shadows. No echoes lingered of the recent dinner party. Almost immediately, however, Enoch Gookin called down the stairs from the floor above. "Mr. Entigott? If that's you, come up."

"Can you give us a star to steer by, Mr. Gookin?"

"Power's out up here. Have to make do with this, I'm afraid." He came toward us, a small taper in his hand. As we climbed he reversed direction, mounting backwards till all arrived in the passageway that led to the guest rooms and theater. There Eliot greeted us.

"Where's Craddock?" I asked.

"Gone to bed."

"Not so riled as we took him to be," Gookin contributed.

"And the deceased?"

"A shared experience," Eliot said. "I waited for you."

Guiding Enoch's hand, Cleon tilted the taper till its light picked out a wardrobe trunk standing against the far wall. From it he took four candle stubs which we lit. The passageway blazed with light.

Cleon introduced Dunce and Eliot. Eliot fell back on flippancy. "I feel," he said, "like a superannuated torchbearer in an under-rehearsed Shakespearean matinee."

"If 'Out, out, brief candle' is one of your lines," Dunce told him, "I hope you cut it."

"Our most pressing need right now," Cleon said, "is to

verify the presence of a corpse. So we do need our candles."

Eliot was less sure. "Doesn't a candlelight procession to the bier verge on farce?"

Gookin spoke up. "Can't say as I want to look at a corpse by starlight, candlelight, or daylight. I'd sooner go downstairs and pull the circuit breaker. Then you can look proper-like, for as long as you've a mind to."

"Do that, Enoch," Cleon said.

Gookin needed no coaching. A short, dry laugh from Eliot summed up our opinion of his swift withdrawal. We shuffled toward the doorway of the theater. On entering I saw a room that would hold no more than sixty patrons. The stage, though, was larger than most stages found in public halls. As we drew near, the candles threw dancing lights on the drop encompassing the area beyond. I caught glimpses of distant pyramids and a probable sphinx. Even as these blurred into vagueness an extraordinary spectacle came into focus.

"Is that Cleopatra's fabled barge?" I asked.

"You're looking at it," Cleon replied.

"It's been Bostonized!"

"Who would have it otherwise?"

What we had before us was an Egyptian swan boat as elegant as Paget's swan boats which churn about in the Public Garden, except that it had peacock plumage. The effect was staggering.

Dunce sucked in his breath. "I can see the headlines," he said. " 'LIFE Goes to a Swanboat Murder.' Or 'Death Ascends the Peacock Throne'."

Once on stage we saw Sumner Craddock hadn't been fantasizing after all. Beyond the swan's broad wings, a pair of upended shoes protruded. I tilted my candle forward. Melted wax emitted a low hiss as it struck the cold boards. Cleopatra's "pretty worm of Nilus" sprang to mind. I felt my flesh crawl.

"You don't use a live asp, do you?" I asked.

"Sure," Cleon answered. "Watch your step. There must be a hamper of them crawling around."

"My first appearance on any stage," I said, "and I'm hissed!"

"That's odd," Cleon said, pausing on the top step. "Quelch wore black loafers tonight, not patent leather. Said that crossing the Common he didn't want the dorks there thinking he was a prince of the realm."

The Nile barge had to be mounted from the stage left. Till this was done all we could see of the deceased was his shoes. We all moved forward. On the barge's makeshift fantail someone had pasted a bumper sticker—"I Brake for Asps." Uproarious once. Not now.

The barge's deck consisted of heavy planking, un-secured. Under our tread it emitted a rumble like far off thunder. I hoped Cleon had written this din into the script, otherwise the audience (if *Nile Bodies* ever had one) was going to think cannons were pitching loose.

Up ahead a more immediate reality awaited us. Cleon's candle brought the pants legs of the corpse into view, and then the Ogilvie tartan jacket that Quelch alone would have dared to wear to a Club function.

"No mistaking that jacket," Eliot said.

Elevating his candle, Cleon picked up the glitter of the gold quill implanted in the dead man's chest.

"He took the sharp edge, all right," Dunce said.

Cleon nodded and let the light travel forward. Suddenly

his hand jerked back and I heard the splutter of hot wax on the deck boards. In knee jerk reaction we all recoiled. More wax spilled and the deck hissed as though Cleon's mythical hamper of asps had been trodden awake.

"Sumner never mentioned *that*!" Cleon said. "The basket for the apricots . . . the asp . . . it's covering Quelch's face. . . ."

Just then half a dozen wall lights soared into brilliance. Cleon stepped back and leaned over the gunwale to reach a wall switch behind the bunched, baize curtain. "Let's have the floods, too," he said.

Lights from a set-up in an improvised loge inundated the stage. We turned again to confront the deceased. Cleon lifted aside the basket. It dropped to the deck from his hand to skip along in a macabre frolic. We drew closer. Eliot peered, then jerked away. A second passed before I caught the significance of the ribbed waves of white hair cushioning the corpse's head.

"Huddle!" I said. "Wearing Quelch's jacket!"

Even as I spoke the corpse began to rise up from its royal bier. Almost at once a shuddering rumble followed. I looked down. Eliot had keeled over, his body sprawling across the deck planks that supported Huddle, tilting them so that the corpse inclined toward us. I squatted and lifted Eliot away from the depressed boards. Huddle sank back to the posture he'd formerly held. My breath came in stentorian gasps. Cleon caught Eliot's wrist to monitor his pulse. After a pause he said, "It's coming back. He must've fainted from fright."

"The very thing I meant to do," I said, "if he hadn't pre-empted the part."

8

*T*he press got it all. That is, all that the Club cared to have the press get, which was considerably less than it would have thought was its due. Nothing, for example, was said about the gold quill. Too many Cart-tailers dwelt in high places—including high places in the world of journalism—to let that bit of fraternal tomfoolery get voyeuristic notice in the mainstream press and penny-dreadful treatment in the tabloids. The last scandal touching the Cart-tail Club to have had a public airing dated back to the eve of World War One when the septaugenarian wife of the first magistrate had been taken into custody, at a millinery shop, for concealing in her reticule a burnt ostrich plume. That so trifling a business was the most the press could come up with in recapitulating a hundred years of Cart-tail Club history was fortuitous. As a consequence, suspicion did not center on the Club membership, especially since the adjacent Common offered a generous pool of suspects. During daylight hours the adherents of half a dozen cults roamed its reaches. Few Bostonians doubted that, after dark, their ranks were reenforced by Satanists, warlocks, and necromancers, any one of whom was capable of infiltrating the Cart-tail Club and, for Manson-ish amusement, dispatching its occupants either separately or in batches.

Not a whisper was heard that could link Huddle's murder with the deaths of Champney, Enright, and Hatherly. Best of all, nothing was said about Huddle wearing Quelch's coat. Surely some members were surprised to read that the deceased was wearing a red and yellow tartan jacket but no one was so foolish as to voice his surprise aloud. Even Huddle's widow when, for identification purposes, she viewed the corpse had no comment to make on that fact, supposing, probably, that it signified some hidden side of her husband's life which she would be wise not to inquire into lest it brought with it unbecoming revelations such as the existence of a sybaritic love nest with resident pampered mistress. The Boston way was to not want to know about such things.

Success in keeping much hidden came easily. It hadn't occurred to officialdom to link Huddle's death with the earlier deaths. Nor had the press picked up the scent. There was no reason why it should have. In none of those instances had the possibility of foul play been suggested. Moreover, no one outside the Cart-tail Club realized that all four of the deceased had been linked fraternally as Cart-tailers. Membership in the Club was never acknowledged even in obituaries.

As for Quelch's coat, that was a matter for Quelch, as surely he knew, to explain. As for getting Captain Ultan Mulqueeny, chief of homicide, to enjoin silence on the matter of the quill, all thanks for that went to Dunce. Mulqueeny managed this by characterizing it as a murderer's hallmark and, accordingly, something useful to clasp *in petto* against the day when he struck again or came forward to confess his crime. As a clincher, in addition to suggesting this tactic to Mulqueeny, Dunce had offered himself as sacrificial lamb, proposing to meet the press and take the heat. Nothing could have won Mulqueeny's compliance more quickly. To him, public relations was the snakepit of his operation. His usual method of dealing with the fourth estate was to elbow his way from the scene of the crime, muttering "I'm a coroner, not an orator"—repeating it over and over till he was in his limo and in the clear. For Dunce, this front line, headline exposure involved a sizable risk. For a public official with his potential to acknowledge that he was one of the first on the scene when an eminent man of science was found murdered could be fraught with hazards. To us, the gesture was noble as well as heroic because he had stepped into the part not merely to keep the press from speculating recklessly on the occult rituals of the Cart-tail Club, but to divert the glare of attention from Cleon, Eliot, and myself, and most certainly Craddock who, no questions asked, was allowed to catch his morning flight to Cairo quite as though he'd passed the night in the chaste environs of the Copley Plaza.

With the freedom that goes with anonymity, Dunce saw, we could pursue our own line of inquiry unobstructed. Grateful to him for his intervention, we knew he was in for some slams but counted on them averaging out. Foes would marvel at his gall and remain his foes. Friends would marvel at his resourcefulness and remain his friends. With many his glamour would be enhanced.

Eliot, shaken to a jelly by what had happened, was now more determined than ever to step aside and let me, functioning as Clayton Poole, flush out the demon that had seized the Cart-tail Club by the throat. Cleon and I, therefore, were free to confront, on our own terms, the formidable Quelch.

It was ten after three in the morning when I retrieved my Sun Runner from the Common garage. Jack Cool, gone off toll booth duty since eleven o'clock, had been superseded by a sullen Cambodian so engrossed in studying a computerized mah jong set that he looked up in annoyance when I tapped the horn to gain his attention. Cleon was waiting for me up on the mall as I emerged. Though he looked almost as sullen as the oriental, I knew he wasn't working out mah jong moves.

"I tried calling Quelch," he said. He pointed to a pay phone on the outside wall of the militaristic bunker that housed the comfort stations of a Common under siege. "All I got was his Easa-phone which offered to record my message. I declined in my best robot staccato."

"What next?"

"We'll go back to my place on Pinckney Street, get a little sleep, then try again."

"No point, I suppose, in driving over to his condo on Bowdoin?"

"Whatever he can tell us will keep until morning."

"When he sees the morning papers he'll know he has to talk to someone. Who better than you?"

"The papers will deliver him to my doorstep with the morning milk."

At Pinckney Street I noticed a plaque outside the door which said that Charles Dickens had slept there in 1842. It had rained during the last hour and, coming around from the mews where Cleon had directed me to park, our shoes had picked up flecks of mud. I scrapped mine off on a wrought iron scraper old enough to have been in place when Dickens muddied his boots.

"You're not, by any chance, expecting another visit from Boz?" I asked. "We could use his help with the plotting."

Cleon turned the key in the lock and the door swung inward. "Come on," he said. "If we don't call it a night the only thing to get unraveled tomorrow will be ourselves."

I stepped aside to let him move past me. At that moment, a white Ford van with blue baseboard, which had been parked a few houses above us on the opposite side of the street, shot ahead, then cut toward the curb. I shoved Cleon forward, sprung after him, gripped his shoulders with both hands to brace myself and, without taking time to look behind me, lunged back with both feet to propel the door shut. The slam that resulted was followed instantly by two sharp reports and an anvil-like clang as something impacted against the escutcheon plate of the ancient bronze knocker centered in the upper third of the door. My mule kick had been enough to throw Cleon off balance. He had sprawled forward on hands and knees and I landed on top of him, still gripping his shoulders as though I meant to ride him to perdition. He gasped, the breath knocked out of him. I rolled free, gained my feet, and pulled him to his. Half crouching, he braced himself against the walnut newel post of the staircase which led to the floor above. I could hear the roar of the van as it caromed down Pinckney. I also could hear windows being hauled up, and inquiring voices. For Cleon, no explanations were necessary. He understood everything. Even before he regained his breath, with a gesture he bade me open the door again.

Across the street, a man with his head out the window shouted, "Is anyone hurt? Anyone shot?"

Other heads bobbed in other windows but none added another word. This fellow evidently was their designated spokesman.

His breath back, Cleon declared, "A van backfired. Punks out joyriding. They've come and gone. Go back to bed."

"Never a sign of a cop around when something like this happens," said the spokesman. He pulled his head back in and the window came down with a bang of dismissal.

"Judge Pembroke," Cleon notified me. "Didn't he make that window sound like the rap of his gavel?"

Other windows shut in rapid succession. Cleon and the judge had covered the situation in full review. Nothing more needed to be said.

Cleon looked at the escutcheon plate, then stooped and picked up a mashed bullet which, as it ricocheted from the plate, had been intercepted by the foot scraper.

"Looks like it's from a thirty-eight," he said. "There's probably a second one here somewhere which we needn't stop to retrieve. The message is clear enough. Someone doesn't want us snooping."

"Who could know?"

"We're not going to find out tonight. Come in and go to bed."

The door was shut for a second time, this time without slamming. I followed Cleon up the stairs.

"You all right?" I asked him. "About that shove . . . I never meant . . . "

"Forget it. When someone saves your neck you don't expect him to apologize for necessary roughness. I'm glad to have you for a friend." He clapped me on the shoulder good-naturedly, a gesture that was, from him, the equivalent of a hug of approbation from anybody else.

I said nothing. Yankees are a queer lot, I told myself, stifling themselves as they do. Yet, I had to admit there was something decent in the stifling. There was the puzzler.

9

I awoke at half past eight to the sound of a phone ringing somewhere. Cleon told me afterward that his caller said it rang seven times before he'd answered it. That wasn't because he was asleep. He'd left bacon frying, french toast sizzling, a blender whirring, the microwave purring, and coffee perking while he ran downstairs to scoop up the newspapers. This breakfast ruckus had muffled the sound of the phone. There'd been a further distraction, too. Cleon returned with the second bullet (which disclosed its whereabouts when he tipped up the strawberry jar that, bereft of its summertime drapings of portulaca, stood on the margin of his doorstep). The bullet looked much the same as its companion.

The morning editions, as Dunce had foreseen, confirmed that the press had found his presence at the murder scene an event more interesting than the murder itself. Huddle, pilopathologist extraordinary, tragically slain, simply could not grip the public imagination like the intriguing young man whose professional career was at its very beginning. Later editions would scrutinize the murder more closely. That was inevitable. Meanwhile, Dunce had bought us valuable time.

The real news was the phonecall. Owing to that we were going to be able to put the time accorded us to immediate use. The early caller had been the convivial bishop himself, Raymond Colesworthy. Isaac Quelch was with Colesworthy at Seven Els (by some of the younger clergy disrespectfully yclept "Seven Hells"), the Brookline estate where Colesworthys had lived since the War of 1812 when Captain Jason Colesworthy, U.S.N., used his first prize money to buy the eighteen acres which would, in time, become the epicenter of a much larger estate.

Isaac had shown up at Seven Els at six o'clock and roused the entire household by tolling the fifteenth-century chapel bell that Colesworthy had rescued from the ruins of a Carmelite convent devastated in Barcelona during the civil war of the thirties. Now, more than two hours later, though the bishop had used the interval to make him eat and to expose him to the full range of his counseling skills, Quelch's condition had not noticeably improved. His problems, it seems, were not to be resolved solely, or even mostly, on the spiritual plane. He needed some worldly advice, and Cleon, Colesworthy believed, was the person best able to give it to him. Indeed, a few questions from Cleon drew from Colesworthy the embarrassing admission that Quelch had not come to him for counseling at all but for information.

"Were you able to tell him what he wanted to know?" Cleon asked.

"There are boundaries even a bishop cannot transgress," Colesworthy had answered. This enigmatic utterance, Cleon saw, freely translated to "Somebody told me something which I'm not at liberty to repeat."

"Does Isaac want to see me?" Cleon asked.

"He does."

"Concerning Huddle's murder?"

"That, and the events that led up to it. For his own safety I've persuaded him to stay here for now. Will you come see him?"

"I'll come, but not alone. Austin Layman's offered help. He's qualified and he's discreet."

"I don't know the man."

"Isn't that what St. Peter said to the soldier?"

Colesworthy hesitated, then said, "I take that as a measure of your determination to show up here with Layman in tow. Bring him. Let him know, however, he'll still have Isaac's wariness to deal with when he gets here."

At the breakfast table Cleon repeated this conversation for my benefit. Afterward we ate in near silence. Things were at a stage when they had to be thought about, not speculated upon. As I watched Cleon presently, stacking dishes in the dishwasher, I ran my hand speculatively over my stubble of beard. Did one call on a bishop needing a shave?

"Use my Remington," Cleon said. "Can you be ready in half an hour?"

"I can shave ten off that," I told him.

Cleon brightened.

With a shower I shed the last sluggishness of sleep, jump starting myself for the day. Ten minutes later I was behind the wheel of the Sun Runner, having won my wager with a minute to spare.

"Day well under way and nobody's taken a pot shot at us yet," I said as we moved down Pinckney, picking up speed as we went.

"Life on Beacon Hill moves at Victorian pace," Cleon said. "Even our muggers are late risers."

I slowed as we reached the flat of the hill. A policeman was pacing around a white Ford van with a blue baseboard, parked in the middle of the sidewalk. Cleon touched the steering wheel, indicating that I should stop. With his other hand, he rolled down his window.

"What's up, Brian?" he called to the cop.

"Jig's up, Mr. Entigott. Last night somebody stole a white van on Chestnut Street. And, lo and behold ye, here it is!"

"Shortest joy ride ever."

"You've no idea, I suppose, when they drove down Pinckney?"

"Middle of the night. Lots of gunplay. Better than 'Miami Vice'."

"That's what makes my job so easy. Helpful citizens," Brian said.

Cleon smiled. A tap on the steering wheel told me to get moving again.

"A pity, Brian," he said, "you couldn't pack the wife and kids in the van and take them on a picnic."

"There's five kids," Brian said. "All under seven. Having them out of my hair a few hours is picnic enough."

We found our way back to Beacon Street. From Beacon we made our way to the Chestnut Hill Reservoir where we stopped at my apartment, which looks down on the Res. I changed out of the windrunner Cleon had loaned me, into slacks and a brown houndstooth jacket. In eleven minutes, operation complete, I was ready to go. We went on into Brookline and, finally, to Corey Hill Road. Another world. Not a McDonald's or Burger King in sight.

"That's Colesworthy's estate on the left," Cleon said.

All I could see was woods, mostly conifers. I slowed down for speedbumps put there to inhibit those who like to drag race through posh neighborhoods. I drove on another half mile. Still only woodlands—conifers, getting taller. I thought we'd reached the outskirts of Yosemite.

"All this is Colesworthy's?"

"Yes. The drive leading in is just up ahead. You'll see the stone pillars flanking it."

"Does it extend the same distance in the other direction?"

"No. A little way up ahead is Rosings. Colesworthy's mother's estate."

"How ample is Rosings?"

"Runs on another half mile."

"Right to the edge of the world, eh?"

"For all I know. For all anyone knows. No one gets in there."

"And I thought the human race lost its lease on the garden of Eden years ago."

"Life at Rosings may not be all that great. She never goes anywhere."

"As Boston folk say, 'Why go elsewhere when you're already here?' "

"Raymond's not like his mother. This place . . . " he gestured toward the sprawling English country house that loomed up ahead after we'd been in the drive for some minutes, "he calls his *pied a terre*. He's not here that much. Usually he's at either his episcopal residence at Wellfleet, or his favorite getaway spot, a ranch on the outskirts of Mar del Plata, in Argentina."

A slouching fellow in soiled chinos and faded Harris tweed jacket, out at the elbows, stepped into the road and flagged us down. His shoes were half laced, his hair uncombed. He approached Cleon.

"You're Entigott, aren't you?" he asked. At Cleon's nod he went on, "Figured that. You're wearin' the Cart-tail Club tie. Dad said park over there by his Porsche. Don't brake too briskly though. The ground's spongy and right beyond there's a sunken Italian garden outlined with stations of the cross he got from a deconsecrated church in Palermo. Don't want you catapulting yourself onto the Via Dolorosa."

"You must be Cezanne. . . . "

"Got it right. Cezanne Colesworthy. Born and named when he was into his impressionist phase. Nowadays I'm all of it that survives. Now it's Goya and El Greco with him. Better Cezanne than El Greco, I say." He scratched at one of his torn elbows which led him to give some thought to the matter of his appearance. "Don't mind the way I look," he said. "Shifting compost this morning to a new location. Dressed for it. Once you're parked go right in by that side door, through the greenhouse. He'll be waitin' for you at the far end."

Cezanne turned away with a half wave and went off to wrestle with his manure pile.

Colesworthy was where Cezanne said he'd be—in his conservatory. We found him pinching a cinnamon-scented geranium and pushing food spikes into the soil at the base of the plant. Several neighboring geraniums evidently had received a pinching also. As we moved past them, a blend of fragrances greeted us—apple, lemon, and even chocolate, an impression Colesworthy confirmed when I asked him if it was so.

"I take it," Cleon said, as we entered the house, "your plant pinching activities mean that Isaac's present state of mind gives you no great cause for concern."

"I wish I was that sure of him," Colesworthy replied. "He asked to be alone, to line up his notes on the things he wants to talk to you about."

We passed through a Moorish hallway and by doorways that looked in on a Moorish sitting room and a dining room hung with fretted oak lanterns. Unless I was badly misreading the signs, Colesworthy was deep into a Moroccan phase. I looked in vain for artifacts that would confirm he was a high ranking Christian churchman, then decided they must all be on view at his episcopal seat or at Mar del Plata. I saw no sign of the Goyas or El Grecos.

As we penetrated farther into this half world of East and West, I was beginning to wonder if we'd presently be asked to remove our shoes and don a burnoose when Colesworthy paused, turned the porcelain handle of a Honduras mahogany door and, stepping aside, bade us enter his library. Here was a surprise—a room, at last, which attested that Charles Martel had indeed stopped the Moors at Tours. The first thing to catch my eye was a French mantelclock, wrought in the likeness of Mephistopheles. In his lap he caressed the world. The bishop must have found it an excellent joke. The clock, however, was an anomaly unto itself. Otherwise we were in a room traditional by British standards—floor to ceiling built-in walnut bookshelves; leather-bound books in pro-fusion, the leather pliant and rich as only well cared for bindings can be. On the wall to the left, on entering, the shelves came only to shoulder level, the space above them being allotted to oil portraits in filigreed, goldleaf frames. Still no El Grecos, no Goyas. Not even a Valesquez. Three Copleys instead—all three subjects identifiable at a glance as Colesworthys. Incongruously, the books from four shelves beneath a broad casement window were laid out on sheets of polyethylene stretched over a section of the Kazvin.

"We've lately had a flood," the bishop explained. "My serene haven violated by a burst pipe. And we fancy ourselves impervious to the slings and arrows of . . . a sea of troubles . . . "

"Yet," I chimed in without thinking, "you've taken up arms against . . . outrageous fortune!"

Colesworthy laughed. "Serves me right," he said. "Yet I wasn't trying to make Shakespeare's mixed metaphor apply to my flood. I reached for 'outrageous fortune' and it wasn't there."

"It's there all right," said Isaac Quelch, rising up from a brocade covered wing back chair where he'd been sitting, by evident intent, out of sight. "There's no snug harbor—at Seven Els, at the Cart-tail Club, anywhere!"

Cleon, who'd been scrutinizing the salvaged Barsetshire Chronicles, not at all put off by Quelch's baleful declaration, now broke his silence. "Good leather and gilt edging saved them from serious harm." As convincing proof he held *The Warden* aloft.

"Good," I said, "Mr. Harding survives yet another crisis."

"Quality things," Colesworthy said, "like quality men, are survivors."

"Too bad," Quelch said, "no one got the word to Huddle, Enright . . . and the others . . . "

A youth entered with a tray of sandwiches and set it on a cork mat temporarily covering the leather inlay of Colesworthy's desk. He was dressed in a double pinstriped polo shirt, stonewashed denims, and red Reeboks. Another son? Utrillo? Gauguin? Then I heard Colesworthy address him as Standish. Not a son, then. Standish Hegarty, a graduate student in the School of Management at neighboring Boston College, a friend of Cezanne's who, for his room and board, helped out part time. Standish soon brought in a pot of coffee and left us. By then we'd pushed chairs close to one another and close to the desk and were seated.

"Where shall we begin?" Cleon asked after we ate in silence for a while.

"It's last night that brought you here," Quelch said. "Let's begin there."

That was the first move in what I saw could be a long, drawn out game. I countered with a move to curtail it.

"You're wondering if the police realize Huddle had on your jacket. We never told them. If we did we'd have had to tell them about Enright, Champney, and Hatherly, and about those papers that came to light lately."

Quelch was caught up short. He directed a glance at Cleon, who had been making steeples with his fingers while he listened, but now cupped his hands as though resigned to the inevitable. Only the bishop looked pleased, and not because he saw steeples. He was, I surmised, privy to most of what Quelch knew and relieved to know that it wasn't going to be left to him to decide how much was to be told and how much left unsaid.

Quelch wasn't long in making up his mind. "I doubt," he said, "if you're going to like what you hear, and I doubt if, by the time I'm done, you're going to like me very much either."

Cleon said, "You've been in a tight corner for a long time."

"I blame myself for most of what's happened."

"You have no cause for remorse," Colesworthy said. "You did what any responsible editor would have done in the same situation. Your motives were valid."

Quelch drank his remaining mouthful of coffee, shifted his posture so as to have us all in view, and addressed us, his words crisp and precise.

"Last August someone sent me an anonymous letter. It instructed me to examine the Smedley Barlow papers at the Athenaeum and, if I saw fit, remove them with a view to publishing them. This would not constitute a theft since they were not the property of the library anyway, having been deposited there unofficially. I was to take the elevator to the basement, then descend, unobserved, to the sub-basement by the iron staircase that leads down to that level. Few Athenaeum proprietors realize the building has a sub-basement, supposing there's only a furnace room and storage area down there. But the Athenaeum's spread over a large plot of land and the sub-basement has as many square feet as any of the six floors above."

Quelch poured more coffee and went on. "The letter pinpointed the exact location of the shagreen file containing the Smedley Barlow papers. I went straight to them. One glance was enough to tell me I had Boston's scoop of the century."

I interrupted. "Who was Smedley Barlow?"

"That's a pen name used by a woman who wrote for the true confession magazines back in their heyday in the twenties and thirties. Not wanting to tip my hand I made only limited inquiries about her actual identity. I drew a blank. All I can tell you is that she was someone who knew Boston society from top to bottom and, because she wrote about it without inhibition, took elaborate care to conceal her actual identity. Contact between her publishers and herself was maintained entirely through the mails. Even Fulton Oursler, who ran the confessionals for Bernarr MacFadden, thought her success in preserving her anonymity was phenomenal. She dropped out of sight during World War Two and no one's heard of her since, until now!"

"A Boston Brahmin lady who, on the sly, supports herself writing lurid tales for the pulps," Cleon said. "Then, if the facts got out, that would have destroyed her. Today she'd be the darling of the talk shows."

10

"The forty-two articles Smedley Barlow wrote for the confessionals between nineteen twenty-nine and nineteen forty-three," Quelch continued, "are about as sordid as anything published in that era. When her name appeared on the cover of *Lurid Confessions* her publisher had to quadruple the size of the run to meet the demand. Smedley Barlow was porn with class, what everyone wanted to read about—how toplofty families vented their passions behind closed doors."

"What gave her the edge over the competition?" I asked.

"See for yourself," Quelch said, producing some papers from the inside pocket of his suit coat. He held aloft the top sheet. "Here, for example, is one of her resources, an abstract from the Plymouth Colony records for sixteen fifty-five: 'We the grand jury present Richard Enright for lascivious carriage toward Anne Turtall, the wife of John Turtall, in taking hold of her coat and enticing her by words, as also by taking out his Instrument of nature, that he might prevail to lye with her in her own house.' "

"Given the time and place, a painful incident," Cleon

conceded, "but something an Enright did three centuries ago hardly besmirches the character of the family today."

"Ah, you can say that because you're not reckoning with Smedley Barlow's insidiousness. Here's another item, dated seventeen hundred and six. Brewer Enright, accused of adultery and of murdering his infant son, escaped hanging by throwing himself into the sea from the cliff at Gurnet's Nose. Nor does it end there: Smedley was able to enumerate scandals touching every generation of Enrights down to the present. Using a fictitious name, usually a mere anagram, in place of the actual surname of the family she was traducing, she began each of her narratives with a pithy almanac of offenses, arranged to suggest the family thus chronicled had a hereditary taint. Once she established the motif, she launched into a narrative set in our own day, purportedly fiction but founded on fact. The idea was for the reader to try to figure out which of the many sins blackening his family's reputation over three centuries would be repeated by the modern Bostonian. In a sense, you might say, Smedley anticipated some of our modern computer games. Smedley was skillful enough to raise a lot of expectations. She kept you guessing up to the last. That was her gimmick and she worked it with consummate skill. And when you came to the answer it was a shocker."

"Let me get this straight," I said. "The epigraphs that led off each story—her bill of fare as it were—all had a common theme and all were historically verifiable in the annals of existent families?"

"Exactly."

"How could she hit upon characteristic failings for each family? Over three centuries you'd think they'd have varied widely."

"Elsewhere they might. In Boston you're dealing with families heavily inbred."

"It's still hard to credit."

"Let me illustrate. Take the Hatherlys. In the first generation we have Thomas Hatherly, put to death in sixteen forty-two for 'buggery.' 'A very sade spectakle,' says the Plymouth records. A whole barnyard shared Tom's fate: 'First the mare, and then the cowe, and the rest of the lesser catle, were kild before his face, according to the law, Leviticus: twenty, fifteen, and he him selfe was executed.' Fortunately Leviticus said nothing that applied to Tom's sister, Prudence, who bore his child, a son, progenitor of the next generation of Hatherlys, seven months after Tom's hanging. Incest was a still bigger problem two generations later when Isaiah Hatherly sired six children by 'his two willing sisters.' A refreshing interlude came in sixteen ninety-four when Margaret Hatherly, after a sensational trial, was expelled from Massachusetts Bay Colony 'with both her lovers.' They were, however, her father's nephews. In seventeen forty-nine the Hatherlys were back in form when Benjamin Hatherly was expelled from Harvard when a proctor, paying an unscheduled visit to Ben's room, found 'five beastly sodomiticall boys in one bed.' The nineteenth century had nothing worse to report than that Andrew Hatherly posed in the nude for Fred Holland Day. Since both plates and prints were destroyed when Day's studio in the Harcourt Building burned, it serves no purpose to conjecture on the propriety of Andrew's behavior. Still, from other Day plates that do survive, we can surmise."

"Smedley found yet another way to individuate the Champneys?"

"Dull stuff compared to the foregoing. The Champneys

were basically bullies and vandals. Things quite usable though to someone with Smedley's agile pen. She began with Nathaniel Champney, Harvard's executive head in its swaddling days. With his wife's help he beat his usher 'over the head and shoulders with a club.' Both were dismissed 'excommunicated, and driven from the colony.' Nonetheless, a grown son stayed behind to establish the Champney line in Boston. Intermittent episodes of incendiary bombing and malicious destruction of property piece out the family's subsequent history. A Champney was behind the group of men who disguised themselves as ministers and tore down Fanueil Hall in the seventeen-forties. His son took a lead, more for mischief than for patriotic reasons, in the Boston Tea Party. In eighteen seventeen, a grandson piled 'sticks and other debris in the doorway of the Hebrew School and set it afire.' In Teddy Roosevelt's time, another Champney blew up a rival's room in Hollis Hall, by stuffing the keyhole with gunpowder and touching it off. Sophomoric stuff. Nevertheless, Smedley made the most of it."

"What perplexes me," Cleon said, "is why the actual identity of the families Smedley wrote about didn't become common knowledge at the time her articles were appearing. Surely her capsulated compendiums of transgressions must have made it simple to get the range of those families?"

"Several things kept that from happening. She worked from unpublished records gathered from the archives at the Old State House, the Mass Historical Society, the New England Historic Genealogical Society, Widener, and the Athenaeum. Remember, too, the sensation-craving readership she addressed lacked the initiative to put out the effort she did to get results. And, finally, there was obviously a conspiracy among Boston's first families to minimize the impact of what she wrote by feigning indifference. Incidentally, Smedley said she did all her actual writing at a location where it was commonly believed she was working on a documentary history of crime and punishment in early Massachusetts—evidently the Athenaeum itself. Apparently that gave her an added fillip."

"How the devil did she have the run of places like the Athenaeum anyway?" I asked.

"Impeccable credentials," Colesworthy proposed.

"It's a truism of the porno trade," Cleon offered, "that the heavy breathers burn themselves out in two months. Smedley kept the flames leaping high for over a dozen years. How did she manage that?"

"A need for money isn't enough of an explanation," I said. "There had to be something more."

"There was, and we've got it. Item one in the files: the articles themselves—not only the printed texts but the manuscripts they were printed from. Enough material to make a hefty book. Item two in the files: complete documentation for each of the forty-two articles, establishing beyond possible cavil or complaint that she wrote about actual episodes garnered from the histories of three certified Boston Brahmin families—the Enrights, Champneys, and Hatherlys."

"And," I contributed, "by extension, every other family of substance in Boston, since those are the families everyone schemed to marry into."

"My paternal grandmother was a Hatherly," Quelch conceded.

"Mine," Cleon said, "was an Enright."

Colesworthy put the final stone in place. "Father had blood ties with the Champneys. Mother with both Hatherlys and Enrights." With a smile he then addressed me. "Now that you've got us all to admit that we have tainted blood, would you like us to disqualify ourselves from considering this matter further?"

"If respectable families have so much to hide," I said, "what about families like mine that never dared to keep records?"

"Something tells me," Colesworthy said, "that when you chose your present vocation, diplomacy lost an able spokesman."

"There's one thing I still don't understand," I went on. "Since Smedley Barlow never told anybody where she got her information from, why didn't she save herself the sweat and make up her stories out of whole cloth?"

"In the shagreen file," Quelch said, "there's a declaration of intent that answers that question. Smedley, it seems, was a latter day Hester Prynne, with one notable difference. Instead of letting the community punish her, she set out to punish the community."

"The modern touch!" I said. "Only thing is, how could she have said that much without giving herself away?"

"You fail to reckon with her ingenuity. Let me fill you in. Smedley grew up taking as gospel Doctor Holmes's declaration that 'Boston is the thinking center of the continent, and therefore of the planet.' She could never recall a time when the subject of Boston didn't fascinate her. For a while, previous to her marriage, she worked as a volunteer doing research at what she tantalizingly identifies as 'one of Boston's five major cultural institutions.' "

"Tantalizing is right. It tells you nothing," Cleon said. "No two people who know Boston would narrow down their choices to the same five."

"At least," I said, "it tells us Smedley had a sense of humor."

"As warped as her moral sense," Quelch complained.

"Oh, all right, irony, then," I emended.

"The man she married," Quelch resumed, "was a widower with a daughter Smedley's age, one of those men who fitted Holmes's phrase, 'the type and head of the Brahmins of America'."

"A description," the bishop pointed out, "that, in Boston, fits many men in every era."

"Her husband," Quelch went on, "was the last male member of his family. He hoped for a son to keep the line going. Prospects for that were good since Smedley, when she married him, was already pregnant by his sister's son."

"Did he know that at the time?"

"Smedley never says. All she does say is that the actual father assumed no responsibility for her condition."

"She did have a son?"

"Yes."

"That ought to narrow things down."

"Not necessarily," Cleon said. "To safeguard her anonymity Smedley could have doctored the facts. She was adept at that as we are aware. Storyteller's art."

Quelch began again. "Smedley's husband was delighted to have a son. His daughter wasn't. In her estimation he'd been hoodwinked. That mightn't have mattered if he hadn't died. His estate had consisted mostly of a spendthrift trust that had become accessible to him through his first marriage. While it had assured him an income to meet his essential needs, he had had no power of appointment of capital. On his death, it passed, in its entirety, to his alienated daughter. She, on the condition that Smedley would legally change her son's surname and leave Boston, offered Smedley a survival allowance, terms that Smedley would not accept."

"At this point," I said, "shouldn't she have appealed for support to her son's actual father?"

"Bitterness ruled that out."

"So the stage was set," Cleon said.

"I've got here," Quelch said, pulling more folded sheets from his pocket, "a xerographic copy of Smedley's statement. I'll read you an excerpt." He spread open the pages and began to read:

Almost at once I saw what I had to do. At the Athenaeum I began to gather the materials I would need. At home, in the evenings, I passed a lively apprenticeship perusing the full range of confessional magazines. It didn't take me long to recognize that they contained little that carried conviction. I was sure that with my motivation, standards, and resources I could do better. Success came sooner than I believed possible. My first piece, "I Married a Transvestite," won accolades from everyone in the field. My second piece, "Tales of a Boston Sporting House," secured Smedley Barlow's fame. It dealt with a South Shore resort hotel where Brahmin males sojourned purportedly for brant shooting. Though one staff member was kept fully employed shooting brants so that no guest need depart without a leash of them to attest to a profitable stay, the place was, in fact, a sumptuous bordello which gave unprecedented prosperity to its actual owners, the Champneys.

Thereafter there was a market for everything Smedley Barlow wrote. The circulation of **Lurid Confessions** *soared. Even Henry Miller took out a subscription. I myself made sure that certain Bostonians anathema to me received complimentary copies of those issues which dealt with loathsome passages in their own family histories.*

I was not concerned about libel suits. The general reader, I knew, was too lethargic to track down my documentation. Those who knew better would, I was confident, remain silent so as not to swell a private annoyance into a public scandal. No one disappointed my expectations. On several occasions, however, to give currency to my materials, I actually engineered scandals. For example, I once recruited an exotic dancer to lure a founder of the Watch and Ward Society into the dunes at Wingaershek Beach and depart with his clothes precisely at the moment two busloads of children from the Home for Little Wanderers (and how they did wander through those dunes), arrived for a clambake. Usually, though, such measures were not necessary. I never really lacked material. Besides, I was anxious that nothing should thwart my plans to publish, in good time, **A Key to the Smedley Barlow Papers** *which would contain not only all my confessional pieces but the documentation hitherto withheld.*

Quelch returned the sheets to his pocket. "The statement breaks off there . . . unfinished," he said. "My examination of the contents of the shagreen file satisfied me, however, that the *Key* was completed and ready to be handed over to the publisher. Why it never was is anybody's guess."

"We can rule out a belated encounter with the Great Awakening," Cleon said. "An onrush of piety would have led her to destroy her cache. Yet, forty years later, it's still around, still capable of generating hatred in men's hearts."

"It's all been awful," Quelch said. "Enright, Champney, Hatherly . . . and now . . . Huddle . . . who got . . . what I was supposed to get."

"Then you saw it as we did," I said. "Are you going to tell us now how it happened?"

"Yes. And I'll keep it simple, bare bones simple. The papers are even more appalling than you might imagine. After I went through them I decided to do an article not on Smedley's disclosures but on Smedley herself. Who was she? What motivated her to do what she did? That sort of thing. Nothing barbaric. I wasn't even going to mention the *Key*, or her declaration of intent—just discuss, in general terms, the psyche of a person who's impelled by revenge to denigrate and destroy. I thought it only common decency to take into my confidence those fellow Cart-tailers against whose families she had nurtured her greatest grievances. That's when I ran into trouble."

"They wanted the story squelched?" I offered brightly, taking care to ignore Cleon's look of dismay.

"Hardly!" Quelch exclaimed to our surprise. "The fact is, they wanted the *Key* itself published, wanted to be interviewed on the subject, and wanted to be paid handsomely for the trouble. All they could think of actually was the money that it would bring in. They said the scandal didn't matter any more."

"Did you show a willingness to compromise?" Cleon wanted to know.

"I didn't. I couldn't. I held firm, thinking they'd come to their senses. That didn't happen. Things were at an impasse when, one by one, they began dropping off. Hatherly must have thought it was a ghastly coincidence to lose his team mates that way. Still he didn't come to me. He must have found he had some pride after all. For my part, I was more resolved than ever to suppress the papers. They frightened me now. I even thought of torching them. Yet I never quite believed there was anything deliberate about the three of them dying as they did, when they did. Then last night, Huddle was killed and I had to face facts, the worst fact, of course, being the realization that someone wanted me dead."

"Who wants you dead?" I asked. "Do you know?"

"Isn't it obvious? That person who put me on to the Smedley Barlow papers and wants me to publish them. Somehow he found out the others wanted to exploit the papers to their own gain and he killed them. Now he's found out I want nothing more to do with Smedley Barlow and he wants to murder me too."

"How would he know your present intentions?" I said.

"I don't know. I'm not sure . . . unless maybe when he found I'd returned the papers . . ."

"What?"

"I got rid of them. Put them back where I found them."

"And they're there now? In the Athenaeum's sub-basement?"

"They are. And, so far as I'm concerned, they can stay there till kingdom come. Sub-basement. Aisle twenty-three. On the right."

This was a stunner.

"Isaac," Cleon said after a silence. "Boylston Huddle died because his killer mistook him for you. How did Boylston end up wearing your jacket?"

"Isn't it enough to say there was a reason?"

"No, it's not," I said. "We've covered for you. We can't go on doing that without knowing for sure that it doesn't benefit Huddle's murderer. Maybe you don't think it does. That's something we've got to determine for ourselves."

Quelch weighed the odds. Finally he spoke. "I asked Boylston to swap jackets because I . . . well I wanted to walk down to the Combat Zone, have a couple of drinks at Moors-el-Dorado, and watch the strippers do their midnight show. I was punked-out. I needed a lift."

"The midnight show," Colesworthy repeated in hollow tones, understanding, yet not understanding.

"By then, after several drinks, the patrons have loosened up some," Quelch continued, the tightness in his own voice lessening. "Their enthusiasm soars and the performers catch the contagion of it. You never know what'll happen. Why, once. . . . " He broke off. What happened once, he saw, had in this company best be forgotten.

"What contribution did Huddle's jacket make to your outing?" Cleon inquired.

"Waiters, musicians, theater people, off duty by that time of night, drop into Moors-el-Dorado for a nightcap and a chance to unwind. With a black jacket I blended in. The tartan would've made me a shining mark."

Quelch's voice broke as he ended his statement. Because of his self-indulgence, death had found its shining mark in Huddle. That wasn't a pleasant realization to live with. That fact didn't need to be elaborated on, however. Hence we were glad when Quelch suddenly resumed. "One other thing Smedley Barlow said, which I forgot to mention—something in her declaration of intent—flaunting her invulnerability, I suppose."

"What was it?" I said.

"This: 'Some would find it fitting that my name is that of she who, in colonial times, accused others of Satanic deeds and brought poor Richard grief.' "

"What did you make of it?"

"Much and little. It's a taunt and a riddle, of course. I tried to crack it. John Richards came to mind first—one of the presiding magistrates at the Salem witchcraft trials. If, like Samuel Sewall, he felt remorse for any of his judgements, however, news of it never came down to us."

"Anyone else?"

"Sir Richard Saltonstall. It wasn't Richard, though, but his son, Nathaniel, who refused to serve on the tribunal that condemned the witches. Richard, earlier, had opposed persecuting Quakers. By the time of the witchcraft hysteria, however, he was dead. So that's no help."

"Where does that leave us?"

"Nowhere. Richards were in short supply in the Bible Commonwealth."

"If the solution to Smedley's riddle was ready to hand," Cleon owned, "she'd never have propounded it."

"All she gave us," Quelch said, "was another stickler. Who was poor Richard? Add it to the list. Who was Smedley Barlow? Why didn't she publish her *Key*? Where has the *Key* been for the past forty years plus? What caused it to come to light now? Who, to get it before the public, hasn't stopped short of murder?"

"She didn't publish it," Colesworthy said suddenly, "because she couldn't."

"How can we be sure of that?" Quelch asked, catching apparently, in the bishop's voice, a speculative emphasis the bishop never intended.

Colesworthy stared at us in silence, a world of sorrow in his eyes. When he spoke his words came in a piercing whisper. "I confessed her murderer," he said.

11

*W*e now had some crucial decisions to make and made them sensibly and without delay. Someone had to go to the Athenaeum and repossess the Smedley Barlow papers. As a hunted man, Quelch was not the one to do it. His job was to keep out of sight. Colesworthy was all for having him stay on at Seven Els. Quelch said no, he'd be better off if he went home where he had work he could do. On one point he compromised. He'd let Cleon and me tail him home to his condo in the old Bellevue, the same suite JFK had had when he first ran for Congress. Since the Athenaeum was right around the corner from the Bellevue, he reminded us, as an added inducement, he could provide us with a parking space while we went to fetch the papers. Falling in with our plans, Bishop Colesworthy produced a large, lizard-skin bag, roomy enough to accommodate the peregrinating shagreen file.

Before we set out, Standish Hegarty, at Colesworthy's behest, laid a substantial American buffet for us in the Moorish dining room—six cold sliced meats; cheeses in still greater profusion; compotes of melon and fruit marinated in brandy; red and white wine from the Colesworthy vineyards in upstate New York. A hint to the bishop before I pitched in, and he offered me the hospitality of his library so that I could call Ladonna. Logic urged me to tell her to move the Smedley Barlow papers to some out of the way nook till I could come for them. Since there was no way I was going to send Ladonna down into that dark lazarette alone, however, I told logic to go take a walk. I got her on the first ring.

"Alma-Tadema calling," I said. "Is it true the Athenaeum wants to hold me over?"

"Yes. Over a pit of broiling charcoal."

"While you're at it, toast me a few marshmallows."

"Oh, you're coming by?"

"Yes."

"Austin! Are you all right?"

"Right as rain after a prolonged drought."

"I've been worried. I read the papers."

"An occupational hazard that goes with working in a library."

"I thought you might call sooner."

"Couldn't. Allowed only one call to my lawyer. They beat me on the soles of my feet all night with bamboo sticks, and zapped me in the kidneys with a stun gun. I never folded till they got out the taser."

"You told them everything?"

"Yup. Told them I love you like crazy."

"Do I see proof of that when you get here?"

"Sure. I'll zap you with my lips. Fifty thousand volts, give or take a volt."

"I do believe you *are* crazy."

"Is this a private line?"

"Yes."

"If I need help in smuggling something out of the Athenaeum can I count on you?"

"Sure. Even George Washington's personal library."

"Why not? They've already shipped out George and Martha themselves."

"Cries of pillage and rapine. Oh dear!"

"What I want actually is something the Athenaeum doesn't know it has."

"If it's me you're after, darling, that's hardly flattering."

"Oh, I'm after you all right. After hours."

"Does that mean I can stop glancing over my shoulder to make sure you're still in pursuit?"

"Better than that. You can throw me a come hither look."

"There. I just did. Now when are you coming hither?"

"It's one thirty. Give me an hour. Oh! One other thing. Is there any staffer there old enough to remember who some of the Athenaeum's habitués were during the nineteen thirties?"

"Someone ninety years old, you mean? A few of them look it. Several of them act it. But no, I don't think so. Parthenia's records might show who was drawing out books then, if that's any help."

"Parthenia Wentworth?"

"The very same. You know her?"

"We've had a brief encounter."

"Sounds romantic."

"It wasn't."

"Knowing Parthenia, I doubted that it would be."

"I've never seen her around the Athenaeum. Do you file her under 'Restricted Access'?"

"She's our volunteer archivist. Spends most of her time here in her cubby hole."

"Wise planning on somebody's part."

"That's not very chivalrous."

"Wasn't meant to be. No one ever looked less like a damsel in distress."

"I'd be untruthful if I didn't admit that Parthenia tends to have that effect on some men . . . most men."

"Get on her port side or starboard, whichever way she's listing, and find out what you can. Only don't tell her why you want to know."

"What if she's insistent?"

"Tell her you're trying to run down rumors that, in those days, the Athenaeum was a rendezvous point for Beacon Hill matrons and French sailors."

"I think you're trying to get me run out of the Athenaeum."

"Do what you can. Be discreet. Tell Parthenia that you love corgis. That'll make her your slave."

"Don't say that. She looks like she might be into bondage."

"You've got me enslaved and I like it."

"I wish you were more devious. Parthenia isn't easily bilked."

"Tell her you've heard that, in that era, Marquand's most passionate love scenes were rehearsed at the Athenaeum."

"I think you're trying to get me run out of Boston!"

"That William Burroughs came there looking for new insights into pruriency."

" . . . out of Massachusetts!"

"I love talking to you."

"Finally you're making some sense."

"That's because I'm about to go into my heavy breathing routine."

"Save that till you get here," she said. The connection went.

As I settled the phone into its cradle, it purred. I was purring too. Instinctively I went for it in some vague expectation that Ladonna was still there. What I heard instead was Eliot Bradstreet's voice asking for Raymond Colesworthy.

"I'll have him for you in a second," I said. "Eliot, this is your Clayton Poole–designate, Austin Layman."

"My God, it is, isn't it? Well, forget about Raymond for the moment. I've been calling around trying to get some news. Tried Cleon half a dozen times. Even his answering service isn't answering."

"He's here with me."

"There? What's the story? I hope you aren't seeking spiritual guidance from Raymond. He needs counseling himself. I thought you fellows would be on the job by now."

"Oh, we are. Believe me."

"Any progress?"

"Plenty, in a way. Can't give much of it to you over the phone though. Tell you what. Are you at home?"

"Yes. Lime Street. Where else would I be? A circum-spect old gentleman who's already had his night on the town? And some night. Even so, that doesn't mean I don't want to be filled in on what's happening."

"Tell you what. Cleon and I are heading uptown now. When we get there, Cleon will stop around and tell you what there is to tell. Only first let's get Isaac safely deposited on his doorstep." I stopped. Last night had taught me that doorsteps aren't all that safe. "Or . . . better still . . . tossed in over his transom."

"Quelch is there with you?"

"Beelined it here impelled by the rosy breath of dawn."

"A revolting spectacle."

"I'll bet it was."

"What's Raymond staging out there? A full-fledged camp meeting? Does he think he's a Methodist?"

"I doubt they'd have him. He owns too many vineyards."

"Stay out of those vineyards. You won't be able to function."

"Don't kid yourself. I'm working hard. It's no sinecure. You should pay Clayton Poole more money."

"He supports me. I don't support him."

"Cleon will be there an hour from now. Will that suit you?"

"Yes. Only tell him not to come unless he can explain why Huddle was wearing Isaac's jacket. Damnedest thing I ever saw."

Colesworthy's repast, I saw, when I rejoined the others, was largely unfinished. I ate some of the stuffed shoulder, a little of the fruit compote, and managed a couple of swallows of coffee before telling the others we should push off. They were as ready to go as I was. Colesworthy understood that and made no effort to detain us. Yet he seemed uneasy. He was sending us away handicapped for lack of information which he had but was powerless to impart. I saw him chewing on his lower lip as, mechanically, he poured from the coffee pot, into a clean cup, the half cup of coffee remaining, and passed it to Standish, telling him to put it in the refrigerator.

" 'Waste not, want not'—Benjamin Franklin!" he said, mostly to himself, as though reaffirming advice drummed into him early in life. I broke in on his reflections to thank him for the use of both his phone and his satchel.

"I'm glad you mentioned the satchel," he said, recollecting himself. "I've a favor to ask of you. Reorganizing my library, after the inundation, I came across two Merrymount Press editions I'd promised to the Athenaeum some time ago. They came through the flood unscathed. Another time, perhaps, they wouldn't fare as well. If I put them in the satchel will you remember to give them to the acquisitions librarian?"

"A trade off?" I said. "The Athenaeum's coming out ahead in this deal."

Colesworthy smiled. His hand came out for the satchel. I passed it to him and soon had it back again, only a particle heavier than it had been before, an easy item to store behind my seat in the Sun Runner.

We followed Quelch down the unprepossessing dirt road that led back to the highway. En route we passed Cezanne pushing a wheelbarrow pungent with fresh manure.

"Long conflab," he called out. "Father been holding a consistory?"

"We've only been blowing smoke," I said.

"Didn't you see that puff of white smoke?" Cleon asked. "We elected him pope!"

Cezanne laughed. "A comedown for him," he said. "He thinks he's God." He waved us on.

12

*H*ad it been later in the afternoon we would have had trouble keeping Quelch's Honda in view over the distance covered between Brookline and Beacon Hill. He drove as though he wanted to ditch us. At Cleveland Circle we almost lost him and again at Brighton Center. By running a light we kept him in view over the length of Market Street. Packed into the next five minutes was a hectic spin down Soldiers Field Road, so intense I barely had time to throw my usual salute to Henry James, buried on the summit of the Cambridge Cemetery across the silver ribbon of the Charles fluttering along beside us. Then came a breakneck race along Storrow, soaring up its wending overpasses, plunging through its meandering underpasses, exiting at last at Charles Street to thread through a snarl at Government Centre where, in front of the JFK building, a Greenpeace demonstration was under way. Finally, a hairbreadth skittering up Somerset Street and down Ashburton Place till we pulled into Bowdoin Street.

Despite the moves Quelch put on us, I filled Cleon in on Eliot's call. He gave the matter thought.

"Eliot insists he's sent Clayton Poole to the showers. Still, old habits die hard. He may construe everything we tell him to conform to the expectations of the people who read his books."

"Reality isn't that accommodating."

"That's the point. We can't let ourselves be carried away by his speculations."

"On the other hand, we can't hold his imagination in contempt. He was the first one to think there was something peculiar about the way Club members were dropping off."

"And it was his idea that you should conceptualize yourself as Clayton Poole and fathom the mystery as Poole would fathom it."

"Even if I could assume the unreality of being a character in fiction, I knew events weren't going to assume the unreality of fiction to oblige me."

"Since fiction's routed reality, aren't you impressed enough to buy the rest of Eliot's package—to approach, in a fictional persona, a situation that's assumed larger-than-life dimensions?"

"Once I realized we were playing for keeps, I saw I'd have my hands full drawing on my validated resources without trying to cultivate hypothetical ones."

"Have you told Eliot that?"

"If he needs to be told then he's not ready to be told. You saw what happened to him last night when we found Huddle. Perhaps he's sojourned in the world of make-believe so long he can't handle reality. If it's solace to him to think Clayton's on the job, why deprive him of the illusion?"

"Trouble is, if he thinks of you as his surrogate, he'll want to know everything you know."

"Every minute particular! I agree."

"I don't think that's wise."

"Neither do I. That's why I told him you'd look in on him when we got to town and brief him on what's been happening. I figured you'd know what not to say."

"There are things to hold back, certainly. How much do we tell him about the Smedley Barlow papers? If we get hold of them do we tell him? Incidentally, how do we go about fetching them if I've got to go directly to Lime Street? I can't bilocate."

"Two of us, traipsing into the Athenaeum like a pair of footpads, would only call attention to our mission. I'll do it solo. Ladonna can cover my moves. She'll do it, no questions asked."

Not till we saw that Quelch was secure within his condo and had his promise that he'd barricade himself in and stay there till he heard from us further, did we leave him. With his usual brisk stride Cleon struck out for Lime Street. I, in contrast, practicing the deception of toting a light satchel as though it was a heavy one, rounded Joe Twiss Corner, crossed through the stalled traffic, and labored a block up Beacon to where 10½ proclaimed the presence of the Athenaeum.

At the entrance I paused a moment beneath one of the two laurel trees which, by some act of horticultural legerdemain, seemed to be growing where no tree, save the ailanthus (misnamed the tree of heaven unless it thought Beacon Hill was heaven), ever had grown before. But it wasn't trees now that I thought about. How, I wondered, had the Alma-Tademas been carried into the Athenaeum and out again? No freight entrance was apparent, unless the steep flight of steps, to the right of the main entrance, that led down to a narrow door in a narrow well, was one. It was absurd to suppose Alma-Tadema's huge epics came and went by that route. Equally improbable was the freight elevator abutting this stairway, hidden below ground under a wide slab of metal weathered to a bleakness as melancholy as the soot coated sandstone that formed the Italianate facade of the building itself. I passed in through the padded, red leather doors. Continuing to consider the problem I put it to an intense young man sitting at the checkpoint.

Color flowed into his cheeks with a suddenness that made me think of a corpse reanimating. Days must have passed since he had last been noticed by anybody. He spoke up eagerly. "Beyond the next building there's a narrow alley with two locked gates, one above the other. It extends to the back of our building. What fits goes in and out through there." A smile broadened on his face. "Though we don't advertise the fact, bigger things are taken in and out through the burying ground."

"The Old Granary?"

"The Athenaeum backs up to it. Our biggest freight door opens out on to it."

"Surely they don't let trucks come and go through that hallowed spot, rattling the bones of Franklin's parents, Judge Sewall, Sam Adams, Paul Revere, John Hancock, Mother Goose?"

"That's not possible. The burying ground has to be entered by steps leading up from Park Street and a gate that's padlocked after four. It has only foot paths, none wide enough for a vehicle. Things have to be carried in and out, coolie style."

"That must be disillusioning to visitors treading the Freedom Trail."

"It's done after dark, when the tourists have quit and maintenance people have taken over—circumspectly, no loud hallooing or audible cursing. It's tolerated because it's been going on that way since the last century and there's no other way to go. We have the key to the gate."

"It's surprising what Boston tolerates," I said.

"In the eighteen thirties," the youth went on recklessly, "Josiah Quincy let his cows graze in the Old Granary. He was mayor of Boston. Then president of Harvard. No one objected."

"All flesh is grass," I offered in a shrewd insight.

My informant shook his head in silent acknowledgment, satisfied the subject itself had been laid to rest. Then I had another thought.

"Did Alma-Tadema take his departure through the Old Granary?"

"Oh, I think so. Before I went off duty, yesterday, Apthorp Morison—he's periodicals librarian—asked me to tell the chief of maintenance, Liam Cool, to leave the Granary door unlocked for Muldoon's Trucking."

"Is Cool from County Fermanagh?"

"Somewhere over there. He has a lilt."

"And a lilting brother, Jack, as well?"

"Jack fills in on days Liam can't come. You know Jack?"

"We have some slight acquaintance."

By now I was on such a solid footing with Checkpoint Charlie that I could have left ten minutes later with the *Bay Psalm Book* and been waved out with a cheery "Good day!"

I took the elevator to the fifth floor and found Ladonna in her office. Open before her on her desk was a ledger big enough to stagger Bob Cratchet. Her right index finger was moving steadily down the page and she didn't look up till I spoke. Then she jumped up and came to me and put her arms around me in a quick hug that seemed to have as much to do with some gleeful excitement over her work as it did with her being glad to see me. I gave her a gleeful peck on the cheek and she at once released me and moved back behind the desk, beckoning for me to follow. I set my satchel on the desk's front side and came around to stand next to her.

"Austin," she said, "Parthenia took a late lunch and has gone back to Brimmer Street to walk her corgi. I caught her as she was leaving. She gave me this ledger from the thirties and said that from it I should be able to compile a reliable list of those people who were steady users of the Athenaeum back then."

"It could be a long list. Remember, those were the Depression years. Probably every proprietor turned down the heat at home and came here to keep warm."

"Many still do. Yankee thrift hasn't gone out of fashion."

"What's the ledger consist of? A record of handouts to Brahmin bag ladies?"

"Austin!" Ladonna said. "It's a record of the library's special events programs through the thirties, together with the names of volunteers who supported the programs by chairing them, compiling program notes, soliciting the loan of art works, or even pouring tea at the preview receptions. For the Jane Austen exhibit, for example,

Mark deWolfe Howe loaned us an original Jane Austen letter. Another time, when the Athenaeum was observing the Emily Dickinson centenary, Bathsheba Spendlow made a fruitcake from Emily's own recipe. It was a great success. Each slice had the potency of two martinis. Emily steeped her fruits in brandy for two months before making the cake. Admiral Byrd came once and talked about the fate of the snowmobile he took to Antarctica."

"Didn't anyone ever just come here and read a book?"

"That's just the point. They drew the regulars into these programs—the people who came every day."

"Okay. Have you come up with a list shrewdly winnowed?"

"A long list. Still growing. Only thing is, most of the people on it are dead now—John Marquand, Cynthia Lanyard, Samuel McChord Crothers, Olive Higgins Prouty, Mary Caroline Crawford, Robert Cutler, Samuel Eliot Morison, Addie Bemis Rowe, Allan Forbes . . . "

"Forbes? Wasn't he the banker?"

"Yes. An exemplary one, too. He led a double life, however."

"Just the person we're looking for, though, come to think of it, he can't be, unless he was a transvestite."

"He researched and wrote many of the historical booklets published by the State Street Trust, though he was reluctant to take credit for them. Also, he wrote the rule book for bicycle polo."

"This gets more and more amazing. Probably worked here, cheek by jowl with my mystery user and saw her as a kindred soul. Who else is on your list?"

"Abigail Adams Homans, Bathsheba Spendlow, Bertha Harding Temple, Mark Howe, of course, and Daniel

Sargent—Dan's still on the scene, by the way, and still very much with it. He may be the only one of them left. Does that matter?"

"To them it probably does. Not to me. The one I want to connect up with has been dead for some time."

"Sounds chummy."

"Right now the names that sound chummiest to me are Lanyard, Spendlow, and Temple. What can you tell me about Cynthia Lanyard?"

"She's one I wasn't sure I should include on the list. Her husband gave the Athenaeum a bust of Catullus in her memory—she published a translation of some of his poetry—and her dates are eighteen eighty-six to nineteen thirty-four. So she wasn't here for the last part of the thirties."

"Scrub her. How about Bathsheba?"

"Oh, there, I meant to tell you. I've made a discovery." She took my hand and led me out through the reading room. The sight of a young man and woman holding hands in the reading room of the Athenaeum is not an every-year occurrence. We were watched by several pairs of eyes as we sauntered toward the stairs and we enjoyed every daring second of it. Ladonna led me past a bust of George Stillman Hillard, who bankrolled Hawthorne while he wrote *The Scarlet Letter* (I gave George an approving leer as I went by), down to the fourth floor, and up to a bronze wall plaque secured to the wall above a rosewood secretary.

"Read what the plaque says," Ladonna told me.

My parents had done a good job raising me. I did as I was told.

BATHSHEBA AMBLER SPENDLOW
(1890-1943)
SCHOLAR AND FRIEND OF THE ATHENAEUM
A GRACIOUS LADY
FOR FIFTEEN YEARS SHE WORKED DAILY AT THIS DESK
HER GENTLE SPIRIT
FROM LONG ASSOCIATION LINGERS HERE STILL

Ladonna linked her arm in mine, gazing rapturously at the plaque.

"There," she said, "we've pinpointed her work area for you—right next to the alcove on Salem witchcraft. Only one or two other people who've used the Athenaeum over the years ever have merited a plaque. Is she the one you want?"

"The dates are right," I said. "I don't know, though. She sounds all peaches and cream. Too nice for my purposes."

Ladonna withdrew her arm. "You didn't tell me," she said, "you were looking for Lizzie Borden!"

"I'm not. Wrong dates. Anyway, I never believed Lizzie did it."

"Tell me about it some day!" She went ahead of me and began to climb the stairs to the fifth floor, heels clicking sharply on the treads. I'd spoiled her surprise. The patrons in the reading room stared anew. We didn't look like a couple who'd recently been holding hands.

Back in Ladonna's office she passed me my satchel.

"What is it you're here to do?" she asked me. From the chill in her voice I had the feeling she might rat on me when I tried to get past the checkpoint—and after all the bother I'd gone to to make a pal of Charlie.

All at once I remembered Colesworthy's gift to the Athenaeum. I opened the satchel and pulled the books out.

"Here's a present for this establishment," I said.

"Beware of Greeks bearing gifts," Ladonna replied.

"Not my gift. Bishop Colesworthy's. Two nice books from the nice Merrymount Press." My nices were meant to coax her out of the sulks. Both books were works by Ben Franklin—*The Way to Wealth* and *Poor Richard's Almanac*. I handed her the first and glanced through the second. Everything was perfection but the color work was almost overwhelming. I held the book open to an illustration I wanted Ladonna to look at—then it suddenly hit me like the avalanche that buried Hawthorne's ambitious guest at Crawford Notch. I slapped myself on the forehead to jar my memory into action. What was it Smedley Barlow had said? "My name is that of she who, in colonial times, accused others of Satanic deeds and brought poor Richard grief." I almost shouted the phrase in Ladonna's ear.

"Why I do believe old King Colesworthy credits me with a modicum of intelligence," I said, bursting with satisfaction. What he couldn't tell me straight out he thought maybe, with a little nudge, I could tell myself. "Ladonna," I said, "we're within an ace of finding out if Bathsheba Spendlow's our quarry."

Though her interest quickened, a wary look hovered in the back of her eyes. She didn't want to look foolish twice over the same issue.

"The Athenaeum must have some reliable biographies of Franklin," I said. "How long will it take you to locate three of the best?"

"If they're on the shelves, not very long. They're on the

gallery level below." She went out the door without asking any questions.

I looked at the color prints in Updikes's two Franklin volumes. They were great. I couldn't have cared less. Ladonna was gone five minutes. I felt an hour ticked by. Anxiety can do that to you.

"Sorry," she said, when she got back. "Van Doren's out. I got the others I wanted, and two more besides."

"Let's concentrate on the indexes," I said. "We're looking for someone in Franklin's life whose first name was Bathsheba." For ten minutes we flipped pages furiously. It seemed impossible that Franklin knew so many people whose first name wasn't Bathsheba. Even Hawthorne's Dimmesdale had in his study a tapestry of David and Bathsheba, and he hardly got around at all. Finally only John LaFarge's *Franklin, Friend and Forebear* was left.

"Ho!" said Ladonna after a minute. "Here's a Bathsheba Pope!"

"I didn't think the popes would touch a Bathsheba with a ten foot crozier," I said.

"Page forty-three," Ladonna said, ignoring my giddy idiocy.

I smothered my excitement as she leaped back, through clumps of pages, to page forty-three.

"Does this help?" she asked, and read:

"Franklin's cousin, Bathsheba Pope, was one of the instigators of the Salem witchcraft hysteria. She claimed that Mary Perkins Bradbury set demons on her. In sixteen ninety-two, Bradbury was tried for and found guilty of witchcraft on spectral evidence offered by Bathsheba, and sentenced to be hanged on Gallows Hill. The court that condemned Bradbury was presided over by John Hawthorne, great grandfather of Nathaniel Hawthorne. Bradbury herself was a great grandmother of Ralph Waldo Emerson. Speaking at a later time, in the character of Poor Richard, Franklin said of his overwrought kinswoman, 'She who pleases only herself in youth will, in age, have only a legacy of displeasure to leave to others.' "

"That's it, isn't it?" Ladonna said, jumping up from her seat.

I threw my arms around her and gave her a clamorous smack that must have reverberated through the reading room and made George Stillman Hillard blush. I didn't care. "It's got to be," I said. "Only thing now is, whoever supplied the wording for that plaque really sold the Athenaeum a bill of goods."

13

"*I*'d send out for Dom Pérignon," Ladonna said, "only I'm not sure what it is we're celebrating."

"Send out for Friar Lawrence and I'll marry you," I said.

"How can I marry a man who doesn't take me into his confidence?"

"I could say I'm chivalrous and trying to keep you out of harm's way. That would be just talk, though. Working here, you've been closer to the source of danger than most of the people involved in this business."

"I see you have a high opinion of the Athenaeum. Do you think we serve strychnine with our occasional cups of Earl Grey?"

"I haven't given you the facts because there's a lot of them and most of them are new to me, too. Tell you what, I'll give you some highlights now and amplify over dinner at the Maison Robert."

I undertook a quick run through on the history of the Smedley Barlow papers without getting down to the nitty gritty. When I finished she had one question.

"Is that why Boylston Huddle was murdered?"

"The killer mistook him for Isaac Quelch. Who the killer is we don't know yet. Finding out who Smedley was, however, is a big step forward. Even her publishers didn't know. Apparently her peaches and cream reputation fooled more people than me."

"Bishop Colesworthy knew."

"He wasn't at liberty to tell others."

"He found a way."

"With her riddle Bathsheba showed him what to do. He played by her rules."

"Why do you have to fetch the papers? Can't the police handle it from here?"

"That would mean too much embarrassment for too many people—not to mention the Athenaeum."

"If anything happens to you I'll be so furious with everything old Boston stands for I'll kick the cornerstone out from under the Bunker Hill monument!"

"That would make a pretty footnote to history."

"On further reflection I think you need a kick more than the monument does."

"Is that all the gratitude I get for paying you a compliment?"

I might as well have said that to the wall. Ladonna's thoughts had already traveled elsewhere.

"I remember now," she said, "last summer Parthenia asked me if I'd ever seen the name Smedley Barlow in our records. I told her I hadn't. It was an offhand inquiry, never repeated. I guess that's why I forgot about it till now."

"It seems we have some business with Parthenia."

"You don't think . . . ?"

"That's right. I don't. Despite appearances her thrust is

all humanitarian. Without realizing it, though, she may have been used."

"She should be back shortly from running that corgi around the block." Ladonna paused, listened, then got up and opened the door a crack and stuck out her head. She pulled it in again. "She is back. I just heard her slam a file drawer."

"That's our girl. Slam 'em whether they need it or not. Show them who's boss."

"I'll bring you in and introduce you—out of slamming distance. You can take it from there."

We found Parthenia sitting on a Carver-Brewster chair beneath a Benjamin Russell painting of a whaling ship. Legs crossed, she was leaning back, smoking a tiparillo and thumbing through a typed and stapled brochure. A thin copper wire, fastened to her right ankle, stretched, like a traveler's clothesline, across the room to where it was secured to a radiator. Was she in the habit of tethering herself to make herself companionable to her corgi? I hoped things hadn't progressed to that point. I like dogs but there are limits that oughtn't to be exceeded.

"Watch out for Parthenia's grounding wire," Ladonna said, an archness in her voice that got past Parthenia's ears but not past mine.

"A mere precaution," Parthenia said, matter-of-factly. "In ordinary circumstances I convey a good deal of static electricity."

"Join the club," I said. "I'm a long standing victim of static cling myself."

"You're Layman, aren't you?" she observed. "In mufti you don't look quite so hostile or seem so brash." She stood up before I could stop her, took a deep breath so that her bosom seemed to approximate the size of the prow of the ocean liner whose name she bore, and offered me her hand. It was good to know that when we made contact the sparks wouldn't fly. The hand closed firmly around mine.

"Did you find someone to release your pigeon?"

"No. I called Boston Music this morning. They said they found it dead. It got into a packet of cactus phonograph needles, World War Two vintage, and ate them. Punctured its gullet."

"It seems, then, that you had reason to be concerned."

"A pigeon's a pigeon—to some people, only a rat with wings," she said with a degree of resignation that surprised me. "Boylston Huddle's another matter. Such an occurrence reflects not only on a Boston institution—and the Cart-tail Club, whatever its imperfections, is a Boston institution—it brings discredit on the community."

"Hard on the sifted few," I clarified, knowing that was the community she meant.

"Dr. Holmes's apt phrase."

"Probably much invoked on a similar lamentable occasion—when Webster killed Parkman."

"When a subscription was taken up for Professor Webster's wife and daughters after he was hanged, Mrs. Parkman's name led off the list of contributors. If she really believed Webster murdered Doctor Parkman could she . . . ?"

"Of course she could," I said. "That's the Boston thing to do."

I had her. She all but dissolved in preening contentment. "True! Dryden says forgiveness belongs to the wronged. We see so little of it . . . elsewhere."

"The wronged can't always speak for themselves."

"If Dr. Huddle's death prompts that remark, isn't it premature to talk about forgiving anybody?"

"My candidate right now isn't Huddle—it's Smedley Barlow." There it was. I saw a chance and took it. A shot across her bow. Or was it? Quelch's informant had a staff member's familiarity with the layout and routines of the Athenaeum. Parthenia had that knowledge. That fact, when considered in conjunction with her zeal for worthy causes, made her a prime candidate. To her credit she didn't retreat behind denials.

"Why should you care about Smedley Barlow?" she ventured.

I closed in fast. "For the same reason you care about Bathsheba Spendlow."

That did it. She seemed almost glad matters were past concealment.

"It was easier to find out who Smedley Barlow was than Bathsheba Spendlow could ever have imagined. She hadn't reckoned with the plaque, you see. We have her dates. The name ending in 'low,' and the initials—Smedley's were the same. Merely reversed. People deliberately dropping from sight always cling to some part of their real identity. To clinch it I looked up Simon Spendlow's obit in the *Transcript* microfilms. I suppose none of this is news to you?"

"Our methods were convoluted compared to yours. You know your way around. We got there the hard way."

Parthenia was on a roll. "Smedley's declaration of intent gave her away . . . " she said. She stopped, realizing her pride in investigative methodology had played her false.

I clarified. "You've seen the Smedley Barlow papers."

"Yes . . . I might as well have said so to start with."

"And, under the cloak of anonymity, brought them to the attention of Isaac Quelch?"

"Since you know so much, who brought them to my attention?"

"I suppose you found them where Bathsheba left them, turned them up accidentally when you were looking for something else."

"A bad guess. New shelving was installed in the sub-basement only six months ago. An anonymous letter told me where to find them. That was in August. They couldn't have been there long. There was no dust on them."

"Did your informant say what he had in mind?"

"He wanted me to let the public know what extremes Boston women were put to, as recently as forty years ago, in pursuit of common justice. He wanted the whole story to come out."

"No doubt about it, Bathsheba was ridden over roughshod. You realize, though, that you've opened a monstrous can of worms?"

"All I know is that I'm disappointed in Isaac. What became of his reputation for fearless journalism? As far as I can see, he's done nothing."

"I thought your overriding concern was to safeguard the reputation of the community?"

"Not at the cost of compounding an injustice."

"There's the larger matter of murder."

"Boylston Huddle's? What's that got to do with it?"

"Three other men have been murdered, too, evidently because they threw a spanner into Quelch's plans for handling the story."

"Isaac would never have . . . "

"No one's laying the blame on Isaac. In fact Huddle's dead because the murderer mistook him for Isaac."

"If he's put himself at serious risk to do what I'd hoped he'd do, then I've misjudged him."

"Till lately we've been assuming that his anonymous informant was the murderer. I take it that your annoyance fell short of that?"

"However facetious, your question is ill-timed. You've just told me four murders resulted from the initiative I took. How am I to live with that?"

"The blame doesn't rest with you," Ladonna said, intervening, I suspect, because she thought I was bearing down too hard. "The true instigator is the anonymous letter writer who told you where to find the papers."

"Simon Spendlow?"

"Spendlow?" I said. "What makes you think it was Simon?"

"He was no cleverer than his mother in concealing his identity. He'd never kill anyone, however. Too much control for that."

"If it was Spendlow why would he have brought you in on it at all? Why wouldn't he have packed the stuff off directly to Isaac?"

"He knows me and must have thought that, as a feminist and idealist—the terms, regrettably, aren't entirely synonymous—I'd make the right moves. He's not a young man any longer. I suspect he's come to that time in his life when he wants to know the truth about what happened to his mother that morning, and to see her vindicated."

"There are blanks we haven't filled in yet," I said. "What morning are you talking about?"

"I thought you knew. It's ugly to talk about."

"Try us. We've been taking ugly lessons lately."

"Bathsheba Spendlow was killed when she fell into the subway pit at Park Street Station. Worse than that, in fact. She was literally compacted by the train, scrunched up so that later, when they removed her, they thought at first it was a child's body. Until they found . . . the head."

I swallowed hard. "She . . . fell in?"

"Well, no. A crowd was waiting there on the platform for the train. There was the usual jostling, but three people said that just as the train was pulling in a man rushed past her and shoved her forward, pitching her into its path."

"This was in nineteen forty-three?"

"In late May, the twenty-third, I believe. No one has ever found out who pushed her. The fellow got away before anyone had the presence of mind to intercept him."

A classical education had given Parthenia's word sense a precision edge. Her "ugly" had been incisive and apt. A minute passed during which none of us found anything more to say. Then Ladonna stood up and exclaimed, "I suggest three strong cups of tea."

"Under the circumstances," I said, "a beverage more appropriate than Dom Pérignon. My mother taught me never to pop corks in a hearse."

Ladonna's eyes narrowed to Dragon Lady slits. "It might," she said, "save us a lot of time if you told us what contingencies your mother failed to cover in the course of rearing you. There can't be many of them."

"I have," Parthenia said, "some Caravan tea."

A few minutes later, with an assist from an electric kettle, we were sipping, from export porcelain cups, tea poured from a teapot with a bamboo-turned spout, and eating Yoku Moku almond flower cookies which Ladonna had produced out of nowhere. They do things well at the Athenaeum.

It was Parthenia who brought our topic into view again.

"I suppose," she said, "my visit to Dyer Place last night has advanced me to the top of your list of prime suspects?"

"Never considered it," I said. "Till Ladonna told me you'd asked her if she'd ever heard of Smedley Barlow, you never even came into the picture."

Parthenia could do the Dragon Lady look, too. She leveled it at Ladonna now. "How resourceful of you to have remembered," she said.

"A librarian without a memory is like nachos sauce without the beer, as Austin's mother used to say," Ladonna lied, with a nonchalance that would have floored my mother, who detested beer.

"If you didn't come to the Athenaeum this afternoon to interrogate me," Parthenia went on, "why did you come?"

"To loot the place. To carry off a certain shagreen file."

Parthenia's eyes widened. "The tea's muddled your brain. The Smedley Barlow papers left here weeks ago!"

"When they got too combustible, Quelch put them back. For a week, at least, the Athenaeum once more has been their happy domicile."

Parthenia reached down with both hands and gripped the wire encircling her ankle. For a fragment of a second I wondered if I was about to see her duplicate the feat of Samson, and, with brute strength, burst her chains. Instead, she merely used one hand to slip off her shoe while the other guided the loop of wire passively over her instep. It was not a sight to drive Paris wild. Released, the wire skittered across the floor—energized no doubt by Parthenia's surplus of static electricity—to coil itself anew in the vicinity of the radiator. She now reattached her shoe and stood, brushing almond flecks from tweed pleats into a leather fire bucket which, judging from the other accoutrements of her office, was the wastebasket of her choice.

"I decided," she said, "to bring the Smedley Barlow papers to Isaac's notice because I believed that, within the bounds of discretion, he would tell Smedley Barlow's story fairly. Within her limits I found Bathsheba Spendlow admirable. Fifty years ago, in a male-dominated society, it was possible in Boston even for a woman of good family to be exploited as she was. She had the courage to act in behalf of her own interests. If her conduct was in some ways deplorable, we can only take it as the measure of her hurt and desperation. Though I had no doubt Isaac would be resourceful enough to determine Smedley's actual identity, I counted on him to suppress such details as would make it possible for others to identify her. Her motivation could be hinted at and the point conceded that the parallel lives she wrote about—both ancient and modern—were rooted in fact. I didn't want him to publish Smedley's *Key* and was confident he wouldn't. I expected him to portray her as a woman whose stunning manipulation of a despised sub-genre was a cry for help. I thought he'd end his account, again without providing revelatory details, with the disclosure that she was struck down by a murderer to keep her from playing her final card. From what you've told me, it's apparent he wasn't allowed to follow his inclinations."

I jumped in with the requisite elucidations.

"Why didn't we hear about these other murders before now?" Parthenia demanded when I was done.

"Two were reported as accidents. One as a suicide. After the third death, Quelch got uneasy and decided to return the papers to the Athenaeum and be quit of the whole business."

"All things considered, I can't fault him."

"Nor can I. Only the murderer dissents."

"And now you intend to make yourself a target?"

"If the murderer doesn't know the papers have been returned here, he won't know I took them."

"If we don't know who the murderer is, we can't know what he knows."

"You've stood surety for Spendlow. Unless someone sent him an anonymous letter—a possibility as improbable as it is tiresome—we've run out of suspects. We have none. We have only a murderer."

"Could Quelch be our quarry?" Ladonna asked. "Editors have hot tempers."

"He brought back the papers," Parthenia said.

"A subterfuge!"

"There's Huddle—murdered in his stead."

"Or made to appear that way."

I clanged my spoon on the side of my export cup. The women stopped their bickering and stared at me. "We're forgetting," I said, "Bathsheba was murdered, too. Forty-three years ago, Quelch, barely out of Hobart, can have had no interest in the Smedley Barlow papers."

"Is it less absurd," Ladonna said, "to suppose we have two murderers, forty-three years apart, independently incited to murder by the same parcel of papers?"

"There are certain jewels that people kill for every generation," Parthenia reminded her.

"What we need," I said, "is a clear link between then and now. Someone who had a vital interest in the Smedley Barlow papers in nineteen forty-three and who still has a vital interest in them now. That there is such a person we know already."

"Simon Spendlow."

Parthenia interrupted. "He'd never have shoved his mother into the pit. And, if he did, why would he have held on to her papers all these years, only to produce them now? There were others threatened by the papers then who still have a vital interest in them today. Why aren't they suspects?"

"The fact remains, Simon's the only person with a continuing interest in them of whom we're definitely aware. You yourself think he's the one who notified you of their whereabouts."

"The letter I got was typewritten. When my suspicions centered on him, I checked back in our files for correspondence we've had with him on fore-edging. Some of the letters were typed on the same machine. That fact, in itself, wasn't conclusive. It's a machine we have here, reserved for the use of the proprietors. Simon has . . . you know about that . . . fingers missing. He strikes some keys with less force than others. The spacing's also idiosyncratic."

"Yet you haven't confronted him?"

"What was I to say? I knew what he wanted and why. Besides, when crossed he can be raw edged."

"Raw edged or fore-edged, he's his mother's son. When

life handed Bathsheba a raw deal, she took action. Her tragedy was his also. And, don't forget, even Bathsheba didn't experience the trauma of having a parent murdered. Sooner or later, all this could come out in his behavior. He's got to be confronted. That's the next order of business."

"Your next business," Parthenia emended, "is to go get the papers. Give them to Simon. We can't publish anything about them now. The press would distort the whole thing. Bathsheba would come off looking like the Blood Countess of Transylvania."

"Elizabeth Bathory," I told Ladonna, whose atrocity reading had been skimpy.

"Elizabeth bathed in the blood of seven hundred virgins, in the seventeenth century, to preserve her own youth," Parthenia elucidated.

"Yet Dracula gets all the kudos. That's male chauvinism for you. Maybe you can make her your next cause."

"Austin," Ladonna said, fearful I was about to detonate a feminist explosion, "I'll show you where the sub-basement is. It's spooky down there."

Parthenia interrupted. "Where did Isaac say he put the papers?"

"Aisle twenty-three."

"He's consistent. That's where he found them. Stay here, Ladonna. I can show Austin exactly where to look. A procession of people trooping down there would attract unwanted notice."

Parthenia's emphatic tones left no room for negotiation. Ladonna squeezed my hand. "I'll meet you at ground level," she said. "Try not to be long. Or is that what Penelope said to Ulysses?"

Parthenia snorted and stepped out into the now all but deserted reading room. I gave Ladonna a peck on the cheek. "The Sirens are calling," I said, and followed in Parthenia's wake.

A solitary elderly lady was seated at one of the long cherrywood tables perusing a Latin incunabulum. She was one of the people who had stared at me earlier when I held Ladonna's hand. I wondered if I should accord her a further thrill and squeeze Parthenia's hand while waiting for the elevator. I decided it wouldn't be fair to heighten Parthenia's expectations. Besides, she looked like she was capable of a mean left hook.

The elevator carried us down to B level, which was as far as it went. Iron stairs, painted beige, led down to the sub-basement. They were unlit and stayed unlit till we reached the bottom of the flight where Parthenia found a switch that illuminated the room beyond. When I looked in I thought I was in an abandoned warehouse. Rows of free standing steel bookcases stretched before us for half an acre. Many shelves contained bundles of old *Boston Transcripts* flaking off onto the floor (they had been transfered to microfilm, Parthenia owned, but nobody could bear to throw them out) or stacks of old reports.

I began to count down twenty-three bookcases on the right. Counting to herself, Parthenia took the lead. The clump of her broad-heeled shoes striking the bluestone floor resounded in my ears with Gothic eeriness.

"This place is none too wholesome," Parthenia volunteered. "I'm sure there are brown recluse spiders in every cranny, only waiting to be roused into action."

"Any bug that bunks down here should be classified as a recluse," I opined.

"Twenty-three," Parthenia said, coming to the end of her silent count.

"And so, with the psalmist," I said, "we come to still waters and pastures shagreen."

We looked down the dim aisle at rows of empty shelves. Nothing as big as a recluse spider in view.

"Quelch could have been off on his count," Parthenia proposed.

"Why not?"

We inspected shelves several aisles in each direction with no better results. One flat, irrefutable statement covered the situation. The papers were not there.

"You're quite certain," Parthenia asked, "that Isaac said he *had* returned the papers, not that he *intended* to return them?"

"As sure as I am that my mother put beer in her nachos sauce," I said.

"None of the staff would have moved them. Nonetheless, we should be thorough."

Lips set in determination, she began looking down aisle after aisle. I tagged along, covering the left as she covered the right, keeping pace with her till we found ourselves at the far end of the vast room—a spot so remote even the recluse spiders probably hadn't found it yet. In a corner a darkened doorway caught my eye.

"What lies beyond?" I said. "The river Styx?"

"The chamber of horrors."

"Of course. Every library has one."

"This one does. That's where we store hideous works of art, paintings and statuary mostly, donated to the Athenaeum by shareholders soliciting immortality for things they can't stand themselves."

"Or looking for tax deductions."

"That too. Go in and see for yourself if, with you, seeing is believing."

"I'm one of the blessed who believes without seeing. Besides I may recognize something I grew up with. That could damage my psyche."

At the rear of the room nothing else was to be seen except sixteen wooden boxes, the size and appearance of pine coffins, stacked against the wall, two to a stack. Since they looked new, I figured they'd been brought in for use in some project the Athenaeum had planned for converting their dungeon into a functional part of the library. The directors could hardly go on ignoring this cubic footage forever, not at the price floor space in downtown Boston currently commanded.

I tapped one of the boxes. "Dracula gone condo?" I suggested.

Parthenia moved closer. "I've never seen these before," she said. She shoved at one of them with her foot. It didn't budge. She tried to pull it forward. It stayed put. Her forehead corrugated in cogitation. "We can't very well pry them open to determine their contents," she said finally, "but I certainly can ask Liam Cool what they're doing here."

"Or," said another voice, "you can ask me, since I'm better informed on the subject."

I turned at a half angle to see the ubiquitous Jack Cool standing in the doorway of the chamber of horrors.

"Good day to you, Mr. Austin Layman, sir," he said. "Is it to be our fate always to meet below ground? Surely the nether world can have no serious interest in either of us?"

I felt Parthenia's hand close around my left wrist like a

steel clamp. Without taking my eyes off Cool I patted her fingers, rather to my own astonishment, to reassure her. "I know this fellow," I said. "There's no harm in him."

"I know him well enough," Parthenia retorted. "Don't you see though what he's got?"

To accommodate us, Jack held out before him an object which hitherto had been held snugly against his hip. It was a shagreen file case.

"Oh, this?" Jack said. "It's only an infernal machine of sorts. Don't concern yourself. It won't blow the Athenaeum off its foundations—not tonight anyway. You know its contents, I believe, as the Smedley Barlow papers?"

14

On Jack Cool's insistent invitation we'd gone back through the empty vastness of the warehouse room and were seated now, more or less comfortably, allowing for the circumstances, around a dressing table that had a satinwood veneer and holly inlay—the actual dressing table, Parthenia told me later, at which Lydia Sigourney had written "The Crushed Mouse." That it was stored in the sub-basement gave me some idea of the value the Athenaeum placed on "The Crushed Mouse" and its eulogist, "the sweet singer of Hartford."

Jack, the shagreen file flat on the table in front of him, his elbows resting on it, sat forward like a veteran jurist at his tribunal. "I am," he said, "Cool by name and cool by nature. I might say I have on my person an adequate pistol—a Colt automatic with full clip—which I can produce on short notice. I don't think that that's necessary. We can talk, I'm sure, as people of good sense."

"As an interloper, who's added theft to the offense of illegal entry," Parthenia said, "you've already shown a want of good sense. Since you mean to speak anyway, go ahead. Let's hear what you have to say."

"The charge of theft ascribes, I suppose, to my possession of this file. Since you yourself are here to whisk it away, I'll give that accusation the scant attention it deserves."

"Jack," I said, "you're either an accomplished keyhole peeper or in league with the prince of darkness."

"Sometimes one, sometimes the other, as serves my turn."

"What else can you tell us?"

"This much. Your Smedley Barlow papers have become a plaguy nuisance of late to a growing number of people."

"It's possible to exaggerate their importance," I said, testing the waters.

"True! In the great sweep of global events, several cosy murders within the cold roast Boston set can count for little. Still, Boston people don't readily court the glare of public notice. There are those elsewhere whom it would suit well to be told Bostonians are no better than themselves."

"Spare us the homily," Parthenia said. "Get on with what you have to say."

"As for those cases that caught your notice, there in the next room—two contain twelve-gauge shotguns—pump-action I'm told, though what that means I'm yet no wiser than yourself."

I held up one hand, by way of demur.

"There, you'd know that. And Viet Nam, too!" Jack said. "Forgive my presumption."

I nodded. He resumed.

"Four cases each of AK-47s and Armalites. These are long arms. The other six cases have only bulletproof jackets in them. Those surely, no one would begrudge the boyos. The Pope himself wears one now, I'm told. There are rounds for the weapons, of course, but not in those cases. Those are stored elsewhere. We're not utter galoots. It would be a desecration to bring explosives into the Athenaeum."

"An IRA consignment?" I conjectured.

"A happy insight. Yes. Unfortunately your coast guard has of late stepped up its vigiliance, intercepting marijuana cargoes, kilos of cocaine, heroin, and such, and, by merest chance, some of our boys, transporting arms, have been caught up in the sweep. Faced with the unforeseen task of recruiting a new vessel, we needed, meantime, a stopover place for this shipment which otherwise would now be on the high seas. Brother Liam had the happy thought that the Athenaeum's sub-basement would suit us well."

"They were carried in through the Old Granary as coffins," I said.

"Sixteen coffins! In broad daylight?"

"Early evening. When the Alma-Tademas came out, they came in."

"And so it was," Jack said. "J. N. Muldoon Trucking Service, Boston's oldest, delivered the one and collected the other. Not, of course, that Muldoon's knew the nature of the transaction. A shipment to the Athenaeum's always respectable. Liam coordinated it all."

"New coffins in the Old Granary!" Parthenia gasped. "That's preposterous. I doubt if there's been a burial there this century."

"Who's to dispute a coffin's right to come into a graveyard?" Jack asked. "People take it ill to intrude on such solemnities. Even the curious look the other way."

"Where were the police?" Parthenia insisted, "that

they'd let Muldoon's block up Tremont Street while all this traipsing in and out of the Old Granary was going on?"

"You don't read the papers then? Only last week three of Boston's finest were caught redhanded in what the press called 'an IRA arms running operation'," I said.

"The middle part of our shipment," Jack interjected. "We've had some trying days."

"You mean that was coming here too?" Parthenia's cheeks quavered with indignation.

"Where else? Your sub-basement here is a fine convenience—ample, empty, centrally located and seldom visited."

"Think of the Athenaeum's books and manuscripts—things that a king's ransom couldn't buy. And you, piling up explosives under them!"

"Not at all. That would be a breach of hospitality. The combustibles go elsewhere. The boys in blue who covered our delivery were set on that—two of them great book lovers and a third taking extension courses at Harvard itself. They were right, too. I gave them no grief."

"To convert the Athenaeum into an arms depot. How vile!"

"As a warrior at war I can't be held accountable to civilian rules."

"What's all this got to do with the Smedley Barlow papers?" I said. "Do we buy them back to pay for your next shipment of SAM-7s?"

"It's a matter of barter. We've no idea how long those cases must stay where they are before they can be moved. As of the present there's an all points out and our shipments are at a standstill. It struck us that, if, for the while, your papers were in our keeping, the Athenaeum might, in exchange, be willing to allot us a bit of storage space."

"If you hadn't taken the papers we'd never have found your boxes."

"Not then. Maybe later. We don't know how much longer they must stay there. If we let you abscond with the papers today what would be left for us to bargain with tomorrow?"

"This is monstrous," Parthenia said, adding her shoulders to her quivers of indignation.

"Since this is monstrous as well," Cool said, tipping up the shagreen file till it stood on end before him, "I guess we've arrived at a standoff."

I weighed matters for the full second called for, then said. "If we pledge our silence we have your word that you won't make any vicious use of the papers while they're in your possession?"

"You have my word and, with such a man as yourself, it's a good word."

"And your cases contain nothing explosive or combustible?"

"They do not."

Parthenia's eyes met mine. "The deputy director, John Craig-Jeffries, should make this decision," she said.

"Then he was in on your decision, last August, to loan out the Smedley Barlow papers to Quelch?"

Parthenia's lips tightened. Finally her chin bobbled in a little nod. "Very well," she said, "make your commitment."

"Jack," I said, "I think we can live with your terms."

"I have your word, you'll keep your counsel about those

cases and won't speak against my brother, now or later?"

"If you'll assure us this is a one-time arrangement—not to be repeated."

"That's no great hardship. Not every shipment can be accommodated in coffins. You have the word you wanted."

"And I'll tell you what. Neither will I snitch on your informant."

"An informant is it? The devil's own henchman would it be?"

"Close enough. From Seven Hells."

"Wait now. It doesn't become you to bad-mouth the bishop. For someone living in error, he's a good man."

"In error?"

"A left hander. A Protestant."

"He also may have shown himself fallible in his choice of part-time help."

"Could you be meaning Standish Hegarty? He's a darling boy. A Boston Osgood on his mother's side. A grand-nephew of Erskine Childers himself. Easter Rebellion Irish on his father's side."

"A fine listener, too."

"That wouldn't surprise me at all. He was brought up to pay a mind to his elders. I'm glad you think well of him. I'll tell him so."

"We have a deal, it seems."

"I thank you for that and for not making me show the Colt pistol. I wouldn't want to have alarmed the lady." As he spoke, he backed away, the shagreen file once again hugging his hip. From the doorway that led out to the Old Granary, he bowed in Parthenia's direction and said, "Fact of the matter is, on this occasion I came without my pistol." With a boyish bounce in his step he slipped from view.

It was during our ascent on the elevator that Parthenia briefed me on "The Crushed Mouse." Since I felt like a crushed mouse myself I was able to feign no more than a mild interest. I got off the elevator at the first level. Parthenia stayed aboard. "Tell Ladonna what you like," she said. "I want to go back to my office and connect up. I'm full of static electricity."

I found Ladonna in the room that once housed the Athenaeum's collection of statuary, now a periodical room with its art objects diminished to a couple of busts of founders and a life-size plaster replica of the Discus Thrower, presumably not a founder. At his feet was a placard which said that members of the American Academy of Arts and Sciences had sat there, on 10 May 1876, to listen to Alexander Graham Bell play a parlor organ over the telephone from some place on Beacon Street. Competing with the placard for a foothold was an elderly Brahmin, who'd moved his chair within range and propped his feet on the base of the statue.

"A Prop-er Bostonian?" I asked Ladonna, out of earshot.

"Ouch!" she said. "That's awful." She reached out and took my satchel from me to get some notion of its heft.

Surprise heightened the flush in her cheeks. "Traveling light, aren't you?"

"Very. We don't have the papers."

"Where are they?"

"It's a long story which I'll recount in full over dinner. Can you wait?"

"Yes. I'm not Pandora."

"Is there a phone here I can use? I'll call Cleon and tell him not to expect me."

She found one for me in Winslow Tilley's office. Winslow, the Athenaeum's bookkeeper, lived in Plymouth, as his family had for twelve generations. He'd already set out for home and now was somewhere on the Southeast Expressway, battling traffic. There was no one to monitor me. If there had been he wouldn't have learned much anyway. I told Cleon almost nothing.

"The file wasn't where Isaac left it," I said. "I can't think of anything we can do about it tonight. I'm going to buy Ladonna dinner and then go home to bed. We'll talk about it tomorrow." He thought I was playing at being Clayton Poole. I couldn't wait to see his face when I told him I'd broken the case.

Ladonna came out of the ladies room. She'd put on fresh lipstick and patted into place the one hair that was awry when she'd left me five minutes before. The Maison Robert was in for a treat. She halted at the circulation desk to say good night to a young man who'd just called out, in mortician's baritone, that closing time was in ten minutes. At the door to the foyer she stopped to say good night to Checkpoint Charlie, whom I'd buttered up to no purpose. We were still standing there when a rumble, a startled cry, and a crash which sounded as though the building was collapsing into rubble, almost deafened us. Everyone rushed into the periodical room. Plaster dust was rising from the floor like a twister gathering strength on the plains. Our Bostonian prop-er was standing bewildered in the middle of the room plucking at his clothes, trying to detach dust at one millionth the speed it was settling on him.

"Poor man's shoved the Discus Thrower off his

pedestal," Ladonna said. Sympathetically, she stepped forward, along with Charlie, to guide the old man out of the debris. Less sympathetically, I backed away.

Rotten timing, I thought. What a splendid diversion to have exited by if only I'd had the shagreen file. Just then, looking around, I saw a cool Jack Cool walking toward the forsaken checkpoint, carrying the file case in open view. He halted and gave me a slight bow.

"I thought yours was the Granary route," I said.

"It was," he said, "till it occurred to me it'd be more my style to go out with the Frisbee Catcher. Prudent, as well, since lately I've been tasked with entering illegally."

"Frisbee Catcher? The Discus Thrower?"

"That's it. The very same."

"Demolished at your behest?"

"Few things happen by chance, and never so opportunely."

"But how?"

"Everybody has something he wants kept hidden." To illustrate he tilted the file in my direction. "Oh, here," he said, "give this a glance when a moment offers." He handed me a folded sheet of paper.

"The recipe for poteen?"

Jack laughed. As he went out he pointed to a brass plaque, his parting jest. "Here remains," it read, "a retreat for those who enjoy the humanity of books." I knew it well.

The man who'd dislodged the statue was as authentic looking a Brahmin as any I'd ever seen. I decided against asking Ladonna who he was. I'd been the recipient of as many disclosures as I could handle in one day and still was trying hard to believe in the humanity of books.

15

*W*e never went to the Maison Robert after all. Ladonna was sure she was enveloped in a miasma of plaster dust and could imagine the elegant garde mange swooning into his cauldrons if she passed within ten feet of his sauces. We ended up instead at Luella's on Charles Street.

You can get fish and chicken at Luella's but with its salads and vegetable plates it draws a lot of vegetarians. They can be an odd lot. If they saw any plaster dust on us they'd probably think we put it there to ward off a hex or arthritis.

We were in luck. We got a table without the usual half-hour wait. It was next to a window. Charles Street is no longer the desirable address it was when Annie Adams Fields played hostess there to every celebrity who passed through town but the view still was better than the one we would have had at the Maison Robert which looks out on King's Chapel Burying Ground.

Ladonna ordered the curried-squash-and-mushroom soup and vegetable Stroganoff. I ordered the succotash chowder and Scheherazade casserole, wondering if perhaps it had a thousand and one ingredients, one of which, at least, might awaken in me a yearning to spend the night in a harem and the capacity to profit from it. It turned out to be a blend of ground soybeans, bulgur, green peppers, onions, parsley, tomatoes, cumin and basil, infiltrated with feta cheese—a combination calculated to make louts rather than Lotharios. Had Scheherazade served it to the sultan the first night, her storytelling career might have been cut short by a thousand nights and his days cut short by acute gastroenteritis. I suppose, considering the mood I was in, if Scheherazade herself had served it I would have found fault with it. It says something that I managed to clean my plate over the next half hour.

I waited until we were into the lemon-honey mousse before I acquainted Ladonna with the subterranean conference Parthenia and I had had with Coolhand Cool and the terms he'd pressured us to accept.

I had coffee. The steaming fragrance of Ladonna's chamomile tea, inundating the area between us, made me glad that I did. You can carry this herbs and berries stuff too far.

"Cool can be relied on?" Ladonna asked after awhile.

"Sure. He hasn't a smidgin of animosity toward his Boston hosts, and needs their good will to remain the IRA's Boston connection."

"Would you like that?"

"No. They're a bunch of damn terrorists who'd be out of business tomorrow if they couldn't count on money from misguided patriots and from the same people who bankroll terrorists around the world, neither of whom would speak to the other if ever they came face to face."

"If that's what you believe, why did you accept his terms?"

"Expediency. His guns, in the wrong hands, mean a lot of trouble for people somewhere else—people we know nothing about. The Smedley Barlow papers, in the wrong hands, mean a lot of trouble here for people we care a lot about. It's human nature to put your own interests first. I know it's lousy, but that's the way it is."

"I'm glad Cool took the papers. For me expediency means having you safe and letting someone else run the risks. I guess neither one of us would pass an ethics test."

"We'd do okay on a human nature test. We can't be good at everything."

I felt in my pocket for a roll of mints, and my fingers closed on the slip of paper Jack Cool had given me. I hadn't thought of it since. I glanced down the page. Immediately I had a question for Ladonna.

"What's a scruple room?"

"At the Athenaeum it's a place where objectionable books are kept under lock and key."

"Objectionable?"

"To someone—maybe only one scrupulous proprietor. *All Quiet on the Western Front* was in the scruple room for twenty-five years because one person thought it belonged there. Why this sudden interest?"

"This note Jack passed to me. He says that browsing in the scruple room he came across a book we should read— *Boston Inside Out! The Sins of a Great City*, by the Reverend Henry Morgan."

"Why the scruple room's impregnable! No one browses there. Your Mr. Cool must be Houdini."

"Don't make a miracle man out of him. His brother Liam must have the keys. Anyway, here's what the Reverend Morgan has to say, pages forty-one through forty-four of his five hundred page epic. 'Boston is more immoral than Paris. . . . Boston is the most corrupt city in the world. . . . Puritanism teaches concealment. . . . In Boston you must cover up your shortcomings, play a part, wear a mask, assume a virtue if you have it not.' Those are only the headliners. There's lots more."

"Oh dear, it sounds as though the Reverend's been dipping into Smedley Barlow."

"Dipping into something maybe, but not Smedley Barlow. On the other hand, Smedley may have dipped into *Boston Inside Out!* It was published in eighteen eighty. In Boston, too! Before year's end, heading for a sale of fifty thousand, it reached a twelfth printing!"

"Poor Smedley! Had she survived to publish her *Key* she might have reaped a fortune."

"Poor Henry Morgan! According to Jack, Henry claimed he could document every one of his case histories. No matter. He was maligned by the press, harassed by blackmailers, dragged into court on libel charges, scandalously traduced, mugged on the street, and finally felled by a stroke. I think Jack Cool's trying to tell us something."

"That anyone who tries to turn Boston inside out gets turned inside out himself. For himself read herself."

"In a nutshell."

"Is that enough to put you on the run?"

"From what? My aim's never been to get Smedley's papers before the public. That's somebody else's ball of wax. I'm looking for a murderer. If having the papers in my possession would recommend me to his notice I'd be all for having them. Not being in my confidence, Jack doesn't know what I'm up to."

"Probably he's got you pegged as the vigilante type, striving, singlehandedly, to restore virtue to Gotham City."

"Thank you, Robin. We do our best."

"It would seem that, with or without Smedley Barlow, you're determined to walk into danger?"

" 'Laymans never lie low in languid lassitude,' as mother used to say."

"Mother!"

"You make that sound like an obscenity. You may yet make the Guinness book as the only single girl in the world with mother-in-law problems."

"You told me your mother's dead."

"She lives on in my heart."

"Leaving her there for the moment, is it too much to ask where her son's heading next?"

"Not to the Athenaeum. Much too dangerous there. Arms shipments. Terrorist desperados. Scruple rooms. Statue topplers. Archivists chained to radiators. Seductive women."

"Aren't you ever serious?"

"That last part was serious. Only trouble is, your seductiveness isn't confined to the Athenaeum. It stays with you after hours."

"What I need is a Mata Hari routine to go with it. How would it be if I work one out tonight, and tomorrow morning drop in on Simon Spendlow to put it to the test?"

"From what I've seen of Simon Spendlow he's about as vulnerable to the wiles of a Mata Hari as Gibraltar would be to a mailed fist."

"Is Cleon going with you when you go to see Spendlow?"

"I never told him about Spendlow. I want this one to myself."

"Well you can't have it to yourself."

"Who says so?"

"Spendlow's an odd fish. He won't see you unless someone smooths the way."

"I met him last night. I won't deny it. He is an odd fish. A sun-cured cod. I still think he'll see me, though, without clearance from Cleon."

"He'll see you sooner if Parthenia accompanies you."

"Parthenia?"

"Where Spendlow's concerned, it comes down to a matter of protocol. He can't avoid discussing the papers with her, since she was his designated go-between. He made no approach to you. And it does involve discussing his mother, something he'd be reluctant to do with an outsider."

"Would Parthenia's say-so be enough to ge me past the mastiffs?"

"He's trusted her judgement before."

"What about Parthenia herself? Would she go for this?"

"She'd never forgive you if you tried to see him without relying on her intercession, especially after the humiliation she suffered today, thwarted by Jack Cool on her own turf."

"Spendlow will want to know where the papers are now. I'm pledged not to tell. I intend to tell him they're in safe hands and not elaborate further. Will Parthenia go along with that?"

"You told me."

"Telling you is like telling my own face in the mirror. With Spendlow it wouldn't end there. Maybe even he'd bring Mulqueeny in on it."

"Parthenia will see things this way—though the papers aren't in your actual physical possession their fate still rests with you, and that, therefore, comes to the same thing. She'll back you up."

"What a stunt it is to be so devious."

"I haul you out of the quicksand and that's the thanks I get?"

"I could buy you a second dessert if that's what you're hinting at."

"No, you couldn't. And no I'm not. If I wasn't in the booster phase of my metabolic diet I couldn't even read about the meal I've just eaten. One more calorie and weeks of effort will be undone."

"Do you realize what a couple of innocents we are? Probably half the people around us are counting the minutes before they jump into the sack together, and what are we counting? Calories!"

"If they could read our lips do you think they'd decide we're a couple of prudes?"

"Move your knee closer and I'll run my hand over it a few times. That should reassure them."

"Let's settle for footsie. Anything else may distract you from more important things."

I felt her foot come down hard on the toe of my left shoe. That, I guessed, was to be the footsie part. No one at the neighboring tables stirred. So much for public love making.

"If people do think we're prudes," I said, "they're mistaken. I can't spare the time to reshape their morals.

It's full-time employment trying to live up to my expectations for myself. I can't even say I've got the hang of that yet. I've made plenty of mistakes along the way."

"If you said anything else I'd've been surprised. Today mutual interdependence is a condition of survival. In a sense, every man is his brother's keeper. Yet that doesn't mean the kind of keeping that goes on at a zoo. We were never meant to lock up everyone else in moral cages and shove them a daily ration of virtue through the bars. All we can do is set standards in our own lives and hope they make enough sense for others to respect them."

"These days there are bars up nowhere. Whatever example we set is probably going to get overlooked in the general scramble for freedom. There's nothing we can do about that. Anyone made aware of how things stand between us probably would say we both should go into analysis. All I know is that I can face myself when I get up every morning and I like that feeling. Do you feel any differently?"

"No, I don't. I love you and I love your respect for me."

"Even so, what was it Emily Dickinson said? 'Who never wanted, Maddest joy, Remains to him unknown.' Right now I'm feeling a little of that lunatic elation myself. . . . " By way of illustration I gave a low growl and pawed the tablecloth. The woman at the next table, who'd been letting the man with her rest his hand on her thigh, moved her chair, breaking contact. Watching me, evidently, she decided there was something more to the wooing process than she was getting. Chalk up another one for Emily. Ladonna was less inclined to give my Oscar-winning performance the same plaudits.

"To see you now," she said, "nobody would ever guess you had a sensible side."

"I fake that. This is the real me."

"It's a weird world when two people who decide not to sleep together before marriage find themselves discussing it furtively, as though it was unwholesome. What were the results of that survey Simmons did recently? The class of nineteen seventy, I think. Fifteen percent of the respondents have slept with more than twenty men."

"That's reassuring."

"It is?"

"Right. Who's going to be scandalized by the Smedley Barlow papers? What's there that they haven't already tried out themselves?"

"We're not two kids just emerging from monastic surroundings. I don't have a duenna hovering over me. You haven't been formed for the contemplative life by a Zen master."

"The plain facts are pretty dull, aren't they? I come home from Viet Nam and find that my wife has taken up with someone else. You wait for a guy who never comes back because he's blasted out of existence by a car bomb in Beirut . . . "

"Chad and I never dated anyone else the whole time we were in college. Losing him seemed like losing life itself. I thought to myself, this is what happened to Catherine Barkley and I wondered how she could pretend, even for a moment, that Frederic Henry was her lost love. And you . . . "

"Don't go easy on me. I didn't know when I was well off."

"Bitterness is sometimes the appropriate response."

"Those summers Chad worked at Bigelow, Sturgis, in our internship program . . . I came to know him and value him."

"You weren't the only one he worked with. None of the others came and told me that."

"I realized you were going through a rough time."

"There was another reason. You knew what it was like to lose someone you'd waited for. Only for you it was a sullied experience."

"To be with someone who'd been faithful unto death was, well . . . uh . . . a sort of purification."

"You idealized me. At first I hated it. I thought of what Chad and I had never had, and I told myself I'd been a fool. You brought me through that. I saw I could keep the ideal, that anything else would have been ashes for me."

"It's funny where love comes from. We felt sorry for one another. I'm sure we both thought it was nothing more than that."

"Merely a perfect sympathy for one another, forgetting ourselves altogether in its attaining. Yet isn't that what love is?"

"Whatever it is, I wouldn't settle for anything else," I said.

"If we were characters in a modern detective novel, along about now we'd be crawling into bed together for the umpteenth time."

"A detective who's not a boudoir athlete might be a real novelty."

"Especially one who's trying to disentangle the twisted lines of corruption in sinful old Boston. It would be hypocrisy for him to be cavorting like a satyr while trying to give Boston back its virtuous image."

"I'll say this much. People could accept a wholesome Boston detective even if they doubted there was another community in the U.S. that could produce one. Boston's done a pretty good job of selling itself as spotless. What was it Kipling said? 'I never got over the wonder of a people who, having extirpated the aboriginals of their continent more completely than any modern race had ever done, honestly believed that they were a godly little New England community, setting examples to brutal mankind.' That's something to think about."

"It makes me uncomfortable to think about it."

"Whether people would find a wholesome detective credible in a novel which depicts a struggle to conceal Boston's sins remains to be seen."

"By somebody else. It's not our problem."

The dinner crowd had thinned out, gone away, no doubt, passions roused to inferno pitch by chicory, endive, black mushrooms, tamari, and tofu (surely at least one of these things must have aphrodisiacal properties), to love nests, penthouses, bordellos, and the occasional singles bar.

We'd hit Luella's at the right hour. They hadn't needed our table and we hadn't had to order six rounds of Rolling Rock to hold it. We didn't even have to fill an ashtray molehill high with cigarette butts. That was a break since neither of us smoke. Luella's isn't the sort of place where you should smoke anyway. How can you savor a dish if everything tastes like Lucky Strikes? As for the Rolling Rock, they have that, and I've drunk my share of it, but does it really go with succotash chowder, bulgur, and lem-on-honey mousse?

If Luella's left us unmolested while we talked, our rapport with Diantha may have had something to do with it. We always ate at her table when we could. She liked us and knew we always tipped recklessly. In fact, that could be why she liked us. I made semaphore motions at her now and told her to bring the check. Ladonna got up.

"The little girls room," she said. "And practice custody of the eyes while I'm gone. No looking out the window at perfect tens."

"Not even Susan Silverman?"

"Especially not, unless she's under safe escort."

"Spenser?"

"Brady Coyne."

"Brady Coyne?"

Ladonna's reply was brief and direct—a low purring growl.

"Your day's winding down," I said to Diantha when she came with the check.

"None too soon," she said. "I haven't eaten since lunch time."

"Luella doesn't feed you?"

"Sure. If you don't care what goes into your stomach. If I see another alfalfa sprout I'll go bonkers. As fast as I can I'm gonna hie me over to McDonald's and have the biggest cheeseburger they've got. I could eat a heifer."

"Heifers are vegetarians."

"Maybe that's why they're dumb enough to end up as hamburgers."

Ladonna returned.

"See," I said. "A perfect ten and I didn't even have to look out the window."

"As lovely as her name," Ladonna said.

"It's an awful name," Diantha said. "Growing up, the kids on the block always were yelling 'Diantha the Panther.' I hated my folks for calling me that. My mother got the name out of a Barbara Cartland novel. She dressed me in pink for years."

"You never changed it? The name, I mean."

"It's my name. In the end you have to accept what you get."

"I know a few people who'd be a lot happier if they had your outlook," Ladonna told her.

"I can't accept everything," Diantha said. "Like for instance alfalfa sprouts." She smiled and moved away.

"If Smedley Barlow had seen things Diantha's way," I said, "it might have saved the twentieth century a lot of grief."

"You mean," Ladonna said, "she liked alfafa sprouts?"

I got up. "I think you're running out of small talk," I said. "It's been that kind of day. Before the screen goes blank altogether, however, tell me one thing. How do I get in touch with Parthenia?"

"Then you will ask her to go with you tomorrow?"

"Yeah. It makes sense."

"Pick her up, at ten o'clock, at fifty-four A Brimmer Street. I just talked with her on the phone. She said she's got an appointment with Spendlow for ten thirty tomorrow morning and that, given the understanding that you let her do the talking, you're welcome to tag along."

16

I woke up at six-fifteen. By seven-thirty I'd jogged twice around the Chestnut Hill Reservoir and was back in my apartment where I ate two Scottish oatcakes, one smeared with Nelson's black currant preserve, and the other with Nelson's lemon curd—Nelson's not a purveyor to the queen (at least it didn't say so on the jar), but, what mattered more, a purveyor to me—and drank a cup of Pero, also black. I didn't need anything more. The jogging had been enough to hot wire me for the day, that and a hot shower followed by a quicker cold one. At eight o'clock I called Bigelow, Sturgis, and left a message for the other members of my think tank: "My mind, at present, is operating at a little distance from my body. If it returns in my absence please hold it till I get back." That would keep the tank roiling for at least a couple of days. By then body and mind would be back if ever they were going to be.

At eight-ten Eliot Bradstreet called, eager for information. "You slept well?" he began.

"Like I was slaughtered."

He hesitated, then resumed. "Cleon said you were on

165

the ropes. Down to words of one syllable."

"Some days will do that to you."

"That's where I flubbed it with Clayton. Never allowed for the possibility he could get fatigued."

"It goes with the territory. Fictional detectives always are getting their clocks cleaned, then leaping up to resume the chase. They've even got one now who sutures his own wounds and sets bones. Skips all those boring overnights in intensive care."

"You sound as though you could do that."

"So far I haven't been run over by a steamroller. That could change things."

"You left us with a cliffhanger. The brown file case gone? Carried off by God knows who. Isaac's certain he left it where he said he did."

"In the valley of shadows."

"Valley . . . ? Oh, I see. Twenty-third psalm. What's your next move?"

"For a starter," I said, determined not to dribble out information and lessen the impact later of a full disclosure, "I'll try to nail down Smedley Barlow's identity. There's an archivist at the Athenaeum, a prickly type, who could give me some leads if I handle her right."

"That would be Parthenia Wentworth. She won't let up on you till you've told her everything. Give her a wide berth."

"Sounds like she's made to order for our purposes."

"No. Believe me! Don't go near her!"

At some point, obviously, Eliot had crossed swords with Parthenia. I shifted my ground. "What would you suggest?"

"Can't we confer? The three of us—Cleon, too?"

"Pick a time."

"This morning's out. There's a memorial service for Huddle at the Old North, at eleven. Cleon and I are representing the Club. That was inevitable. People won't linger for chitchat, so the afternoon should be wide open. Shall we try for then?"

"Sure. I've got something going this morning anyway."

"Oh?"

"I still have to work for a living," I lied.

"One forgets. A writer need answer only to his moods."

"Don't tell me Eliot Bradstreet answers to moods?"

"Even Hawthorne said the devil sometimes got into his inkwell."

"It must be nice to retire from all that."

"One retires only from fantasy to reality."

"And that's a loss?"

"You can't control reality."

"I'll call around two. By then, with good luck, we may have figured out a way to make reality submissive to reason."

"A bargain at any price," Eliot said, and rang off.

I'd had enough drill in evasions for one morning so, when I hung up, I switched on my Easa-phone. If Cleon called he could talk to that. Fed up looking for places to park the Sun Runner, at nine o'clock I hopped on the T. When I got out at Park Street I went around and looked into the pit but didn't throw in a wreath. Smedley was going to have to wait a while longer for that. I hadn't made up my mind about her yet.

Once upstairs I cut across the Common. Winos,

sprawled on the grass, were already cagily at work, at nine-thirty, on quart bottles of port or, for all I know, pinot blanc, wrapped in brown paper bags fluted at the neck to catch the spillage. Maybe, I told myself, they've been there all night and that's their way of warming up. October was cold for sleeping on park benches. When one of the imbibers hit me up for a buck I gave it to him. My own breakfast cost me less, but I didn't have to start from as far back as he did. God knows when he'd last had a bowl of succotash chowder or stew Scheherazade.

The previous year, when the Florence Crittenton League had raised funds by arranging a tour of the hidden gardens of Beacon Hill, the *Globe* had singled out as highlight of the day the tour of Parthenia Wentworth's Brimmer Street garden which contains fifty-six distinct varieties of spirea, each of which she identified for visitors. I was thankful autumn was too far advanced to make a repetition of that feat possible. Nonetheless, I made sure I didn't arrive with time to spare. For all I knew, Parthenia might have minored in briars and a briar collection could be shown year round.

By stopping to peer through the latticed panes of several antique shops along the way, I paced myself to reach 54A Brimmer at one minute before ten. As I paused to let the second hand on my Omega ride out the minute, a red van which had been moving along the street below me began to accelerate. My muscles grew taut. My last experience of housecalling on Beacon Hill wasn't calculated to reassure me. The van halted two doors away and the driver got out with a pot of gloxinias for number 50. Muscles still tense, I grabbed the brass knocker (a likeness of Old Sol scowling) and let it thud against the door. One thud was enough to bring Parthenia into view, also scowling. She was dressed to set forth, and, to a chorus of yelps from the corgi whom the blast of the knocker had roused into action, she pulled the door shut behind her. Though muffled by that walnut barricade, the corgi's yelps still drummed on our ears as we moved up the street, until he handed us over to a confraternity of yelpers strategically located in the adjacent row houses. Fortunately, most of the barking was smothered by the festoons of ivy which, climbing up two stories and beyond, grew in thick profusion on the red brick facings. Brimmer Street, I gathered, was a corgi neighborhood and an ivy neighborhood, too. I wondered which house had been Admiral Byrd's. I would have figured the Byrds for Samoyeds.

"You came on foot?" Parthenia asked.

"Both feet. The last mile."

"No alternative really. Where on Beacon Hill does one park a car?"

"I surmised you'd want to go to Louisburg Square by Shank's mare."

"I go everywhere by pedal extremity," she replied, scorning my Shank's mare. I let her do the talking.

"Tell me something about Spendlow," I said. "If Bathsheba left him no legacy, how come he's living in Louisburg Square these days?"

"He's an inventor. No one's sure what he invents but his patents have made him a Croesus. One rumor has it that he invented the machine that punches out Cheerios. What's certain is that his inventions bring in money—unlimited lots of it."

"Not Cheerios. Maxfield Parrish, Jr., gets the credit for that."

"Oh, dear. Probably made more from it than his father did sketching."

"Parrish pere lived to be almost a hundred, so I guess he was content with his winnings."

"Fruit Loops, then. Or some such foolishness."

At first I thought Parthenia was indulging herself in a rare expletive, then realized she was auditioning breakfast cereals again.

"Spendlow didn't marry money?"

"A prosperous bride's rescued more than one Boston family from hard circumstances—the Adamses, the Eliots, even the Cabots. That wasn't Simon's way. We spoke yesterday of his hand . . . How he put it in the fire after a quarrel with a friend."

I nodded. Parthenia went on.

"The circumstances are less well known. They had quarreled over a girl they both liked. Four years later, though her parents did all they could to discourage it— Grand Tour treatment—she married Simon. There was no money in that marriage."

"You have a reason, obviously, for not naming the friend."

"I was waiting to see if you could supply the omission. Obviously you can't. To spare you some awkward moments, I must tell you; Simon's rival for Letitia Hallowell was Eliot Bradstreet."

"God, yes! If I didn't know that I could really stumble badly."

"There's more. Eliot's mother was Lydia Spendlow."

"Bathsheba's difficult step-daughter?"

"None other. And, so far as the world knows, Simon's half-sister, which makes Simon and Eliot uncle and nephew even though they're about the same age. The full significance of that relationship hit me only in the last day."

"How did a friendship develop between Eliot and Simon when there was such hard feeling between their mothers?"

"That they were contemporaries was obviously a factor. Otherwise, put it down to chance and, oh, let's say genetics. They went to the same schools, played the same sports—lacrosse and bicycle polo—shared the same academic interests. At Harvard, between them, they monopolized the Bowdoin and Boylston prizes. Circumstance threw them together. Furthermore, Spendlow's a near genius. He does everything to perfection. It probably gave Eliot a perverse satisfaction to believe they were uncle and nephew. Geneticists say we tend to resemble aunts and uncles more than we do parents. Spendlow's somebody whom Eliot would have wanted to be like. That his mother repudiated the relationship must have made it all the more enticing to him. He had no other male role model to identify with. His own father died when he was six."

"That's quite an earful," I said. What else could I say?"

Parthenia went on. "I know you told Ladonna what became of the shagreen file. I'm not sure that that was a wise thing to do. Still, I suppose there was no helping it. She was in on everything else."

I nodded, saying nothing. We reached the corner of Brimmer and Mount Vernon, crossed over and continued up Mount Vernon, past the Church of the Advent where ivy covered the lawn, past the Charles Street Meeting House, which has no lawn at all, past the now decommissioned firehouse where television's Spenser was domiciled. Across the street I spied a house with a winged griffin situated triumphantly above the doorway, and, above that, just below the apex of the roof, two flamboyant sunflowers. I half expected the doors to burst open and a throng of Tyrolean revelers to stream out lustily singing "Edelweiss." I peered down little Cedar Lane Way, narrow as a bicycle path and tidy as Rapunzel's ribbon drawer. It looked like a street out of medieval York, tidied for a royal visitation. I told myself that one day I'd come back and explore it. We walked a block in silence. Parthenia broke it.

"Have you told others about the file? Or anything at all?"

"I haven't. Cleon and Eliot know the papers weren't where Isaac said he left them. That's all they know."

"They were willing to let it go at that?"

"Cleon more so than Eliot. You can forget them both, though, for the time being. They're at Huddle's memorial service."

"I'm surprised Eliot went. He loathes funerals."

"A mystery writer who loathes funerals? That's like a zoo keeper who loathes animals."

"That's precisely the point. Over the years it's been the butt of endless gibes among us. Eliot faints at funerals."

"He fainted when we found Huddle. I thought it was the circumstances."

"He would've fainted anyway. Twenty years ago, at his mother's funeral, he fainted into my arms. He's never forgiven me for that."

"You'd think he'd have been glad you were there to catch him?"

"I believe I may have slapped him to bring him around.

It's the sort of thing I'd do. Eliot cherishes his humiliations. I suppose that's why he writes what he writes—to experience those triumphs life has denied him."

"He urged me to interest myself in this case—to adopt the Clayton Poole persona—before we were even sure it was a case."

"Before Huddle was murdered?"

"Yes. He's had a watchful eye on me ever since. To let him think I was making headway, I told him I was going to ask your help in finding out who Smedley Barlow was. He doesn't know I already know."

"He wasn't pleased, was he?"

"As a matter of fact, he wasn't. He said if you tumbled to anything he wouldn't vouch for your discretion."

"He knows that's nonsense. He wants everything his own way."

"Does that annoy you?"

"Not in the least. Especially since I'm several steps ahead of him. Wouldn't it gall him to know that!"

We turned a corner to confront the even, red brick row houses of Louisburg Square—twenty-two exactly—and the uneven red brick sidewalks that rippled past them. As usual, the park that stood between the intermittently cobbled roadways of the square lay tranquil and secure within its sturdy, wrought iron enclosure, its elms as majestic and sure of themselves as if the Dutch elm disease had been stopped in its tracks by the awesome reputation of this Boston sanctum sanctorum. Since none of the proprietors had seen fit to come with a key at that hour to let himself in, the park was, for the moment, a mere aviary and game preserve; the habitat of trilling and scolding birds and of two Spanish brown squirrels which, amusing themselves with a prenuptial chase around shaggy trunks and up swaying, tiptop branches, were a major cause of the songbird commotion. Only the statues of Aristides the Just and Christopher Columbus, stationed at opposite ends of the park and staring off into the uncertain world beyond their blissful bower, as they had done for a hundred and thirty-seven years, seemed confident that peace would, in time, reign again. "Twin exemplars of the assurances of Justice and the adventures of Discovery," Mark deWolfe Howe had called them. I looked up at Uncle Louisburg, as Aristides sometimes has been referred to by irreverent youth. In 1850 Joseph Iasigi had laid out $94.63 for Aristides—surely a bargain. To put him on his pedestal, however, had cost the proprietors $136.65, a fact recorded in the annals of the Square under the notation, "Mr. Pike's enormous bill for erection." To many, however, since Aristides' erection has already endured for well over a century, the sum does not seem exorbitant.

Simon Spendlow was a resident of the Square only in the sense that his house at 90B Mount Vernon Street stood at the east end of the Square, centering on the very apex of the park and giving him, from his living room windows, a better view of Uncle Louisburg than was had by any actual resident of the Square. By courtesy he was accounted a proprietor, given a key to the park, and the further privilege of being assessed annually for its upkeep. In addition, he chaired the committee formed to watch over the park's welfare which, of course, included warding off the Dutch elm disease. All this we learned in the first minutes of our visit. No sooner had Parthenia climbed the two granite steps to enter the sheltered alcove before the door and rattle the bronze knocker, then Spendlow himself flung open the door and stepped out to invite us to turn and confront the view it was his daily lot to contemplate.

"You see, Layman," he said, "you don't have to live in the country to have all its advantages."

Though I could never recall observing such symmetry in a rural landscape, or Nature so compacted, I was not there to dispute Spendlow's judgement. Accordingly, I marveled at his success in bringing the bucolic scene almost into his living room, with the added bonus of having Aristides there to call the world to order.

"Damnedest thing," Spendlow said, "last spring the prostitutes down on Charles Street—they've colonized it, you know—had a bake sale for PUMA. That's the organization they've formed to look out for their *rights*. Ha! 'Prostitutes United' et cetera. Can't remember what the 'MA' stand for. Certainly not motherhood!" He gave a laugh that rattled as loud as had his bronze knocker a moment before, and went on. "The reporters came and talked to them and asked them about their services. They said they charged fifty dollars for a conventional encounter; a hundred dollars for a trip around the world, whatever that is; and two hundred dollars for 'a night in Louisburg Square'! Think of that, will you! Thunderation, I said, what's going on at night in Louisburg Square that I don't know about?"

"The Naiad in the Mist," said Parthenia, "gave the park notoriety enough without the press inflaming imaginations further—yours included."

"Somebody found the Naiad last year in a barn in

Beverly and asked us if we wanted her back. Hell, no, I told them."

"I can't place the Naiad," I admitted.

"A fountain, donated by Mrs. Arlo Bates," Parthenia said. "Located, for many years, in the center of the park."

"A nude nymph, taking her repose in a scallop shell," said Spendlow. "We had another name for it—Mrs. Bates on the half shell."

"Decency won out finally," Parthenia said. "It was removed."

"The flow of water wore it away," Spendlow insisted, "that's why it was taken out of there."

"And now," I said, "more eroded than erotic, somebody wants it back."

"People might want to look at her again to see what the fuss was all about," Spendlow said, holding the door ajar so we could pass into the house. "A waste of time. To today's heathens she'd have as much sex appeal as a rutabaga."

17

We passed down a hallway along which stood a birdseye maple Victorian coat rack with a plate glass mirror insert, a porcelain umbrella stand with a pink sprig design, and one of those brass-strapped oak rum casks made in the West Indies from decommissioned British battleships, adapted now to hold a collection of walking sticks that were fitted with impala horn or walrus tusk crooked handles or fleur-de-lis silver knobs. To the right were two flights of stairs, one leading up, the other down.

We followed a Kermanshah runner the length of the hall to the broad doorway leading into a high ceilinged library which lay directly behind the living room and seemed a continuation of it. The living room itself was a kind of ante-library with bookshelves floor to ceiling, accommodating a thousand books. Every wall of the library had bookshelves save the fireplace wall. The fireplace itself was white marble, combined with black marble veined in red, with caryatid supports, typical of the English Regency. Though the room was warm no fire was burning on the grate, which explained why two Eastlake side chairs stood so close to the fender. On the mantel above were three fine Derby bisque figures. Over that was an oil painting, after Benjamin West, of a Spendlow ancestor, a fact that, in different circumstances, might have amused me. Much of the floor of the library was covered by a Persian geometric carpet, some twenty by thirty feet. While the colors were bright and appealing, only segments of the whole could be glimpsed because so many handsome pieces of furniture were placed here and there throughout the room. Near the hall entrance there was a Chippendale serpentine front desk, with ball and claw feet where, it appeared, Spendlow had been working when we arrived, since the saber-leg, late Federal chair in front of it was pulled out at an awkward angle. Adjacent to this was a Sheraton work table with rosette drawer pulls. On top of that stood a rose medalion bowl.

At the far end of the room, where a broad, sweeping archway announced that the library left off and the living room began, stood a nest of Sheraton tables with round, delicate reeded legs and, beside that, a comfortable, comb-back Winslow. Beyond was a tapestry screen. The walls of both rooms were, where visible, not papered but painted a synthesizing coral which seemed to give harmony to this typical eclectic Boston gathering of belongings. How Spendlow had come by such an authentic environment I could only guess. The one incongruity was a huge marble fist that looked as though it had been hacked from one of the gargantuan statues in Mussolini's Foro Italica. This rested, in clenched defiance, on a teakwood trivet, by the far side of the fireplace. It was, I noticed, a right hand.

At our end of the room we settled into cosy wingback

and barrel chairs upholstered in cheerful flame stitch or acres of diamond patterns compatible with the geometry beneath our feet. A housekeeper, a woman in her seventies, brought in coffee in a Beleeck service, Oliver's Bath biscuits, Tiptree's ginger preserves, and withdrew. A bumbling housefly settled on the rim of the cream pitcher, then toppled in. I watched in amusement as Spendlow, with painstaking care, reclaimed it with his spoon and set it down on the hearth to recover from its ordeal.

"You're another Uncle Toby," Parthenia said. "Somewhere in *Tristram Shandy* doesn't he open a window to let a fly out?"

"If I did that," Spendlow said, "while I had the sash up, another six would fly in."

I watched the housekeeper, summoned by Spendlow, replace the cream pitcher.

"Keats is in your corner," I said, and I quoted:

> "A fly is in the milk-pot. Must he die
> Circled by a humane society?
> . . . Werter takes his spoon,
> . . . and lo! soon
> The little struggler, sav'd from perils dark,
> Across the teaboard draws a long wet mark."

"Not on my teaboard!" Spendlow said. "Tolerance has its limits."

After incidental remarks about the state of the season and a polite try at diminishing the quantity of coffee and biscuits, we were ready to come to the business at hand. I was curious to see how things would go. Our visit, I thought, had begun oddly. Spendlow's comments on his park had been those of a conservative moralist. I found it hard to reconcile this stance with the presumption that allowed him to flourish the Smedley Barlow papers before the world.

After scarfing down a last fragment of Bath biscuit, which he devoured with the appetite of a healthy young terrier, and taking a last swallow of coffee, Spendlow set down his cup and addressed me now directly for the first time since we'd entered the room. "Layman," he said, "Parthenia hasn't told me yet why she's come here, dragging you with her. I'll wager it has nothing to do with fore-edging. Suppose you tell me the real reason."

"Please," Parthenia said, "I can tell you in one sentence. We want to know, firstly, what you hoped to achieve by leaving the Smedley Barlow papers at the Athenaeum and then bringing them to my notice; and, secondly, if you foresaw the chaos that would come about as a consequence of your actions."

Spendlow half got up, then dropped back into his chair. There was no ease in his motions. Parthenia arose and walked over to him. I remembered what she'd said about slapping Eliot and hoped that that wasn't her standard therapy for dealing with gentlemen in distress.

"You have no idea what I'm talking about, do you?" she said.

Spendlow shook his head. "The last person to mention those papers to me was my mother . . . the day before she was . . . shoved under that train."

"Can you tell us what she said?" I asked.

"It's more than forty years ago. That whole while I've never said anything to anyone. You feel you've got to know?"

"Huddle's dead because of those papers . . . and Champney, Enright, and Hatherly. Your mother, too, apparently . . . "

Spendlow's eyes went to Parthenia, who had resumed her chair. She nodded in confirmation. Over the next several minutes she briefed him. As she spoke, the fingers of Spendlow's left hand tangled with the stubs of his right, to make a ruined cathedral.

"I see," he said, when she concluded, "that the time has come to tell you what I know. I'd heard, of course, about the things Smedley Barlow wrote, when I was at Milton Academy. What boy hadn't? They were the *Playboys* of that era. Though they were rated as smutters and we weren't supposed to see them—'s-m-u-t,' the headmaster used to say, 'small minds use this!'—we passed them around among ourselves. I wouldn't even mention them to mother, though one day, when I was looking for a button to sew on my blazer before a fellowship interview, I saw one in her Martha Washington sewing cabinet. Even then I said nothing to her. In those days you just . . . didn't!"

Spendlow's throat seemed to go dry. He swallowed more coffee and resumed.

"The day before she was killed, mother was in a state of elation. She had to talk to someone, it seemed, and fixed on me, I guess because she knew it would go no further. Men can't be blabbermouths she said. She told me she was . . . " He stopped again as if trying to decide something, then began over with a change in direction. "She told me Smedley Barlow was going to make us a lot of money."

"And," Parthenia said, her voice low but insistent, "she told you she was Smedley Barlow."

"I found it hard to tell you that. A betrayal. Yet it's not a betrayal, is it, if you already know? She said someone had been negotiating with her, to bring about publication of those papers. Since it was vital to her to retain her anonymity, she'd agreed to leave the manuscript in a security locker at Park Street Station and to mail the key to the other party. Originally, he mailed the key to her. It was for a locker marked 'Out of Order' though in fact it was functional. In that locker, he said, she'd find a key to a locker at Kendall Station. She was to take the subway to Kendall and open that locker where she'd find a shoebox containing fifty thousand dollars in cash, her initial royalty payment. Since she wasn't to mail the key to the first locker to her benefactor till she'd collected the contents of the second, any risk involved seemed to be entirely on his side. As a further assurance that her desire for anonymity would be respected, she was told she could carry out the exchange at any time she chose during a ten day interval."

"To be doubly certain that she wouldn't be spotted," I said, "couldn't she have sent you to make the swap?"

"I couldn't have gone," Spendlow said. "It was right after . . . " He held out his maimed hand to say it for him.

"Your mother took the manuscript to Park Street Station?"

"The first day of the specified interval, at the earliest hour possible. That was typical of her. She never was slow to act."

"If her killer was counting on that, he knew something of her habits."

"So it would seem. Yet how can we know for sure?"

"What else?"

"Nothing else. That was it. I've never heard of the manuscript again till now. And no key. No fifty thousand. Whoever gave her that shove must have taken her purse with the key in it."

"How much of this did you tell the police?"

"None of it. How could I without telling them my mother was Smedley Barlow? I didn't want her name to become an obscenity. Besides, it was a fantastic story. They probably would have dismissed it as further evidence of my instability—as if I hadn't been in the news enough that week."

"Simon," Parthenia said, "we can't stop there. Whoever brought the papers into view again has tried to throw suspicion on you. The typed note I got was done with your . . . mannerisms."

"The telltale trail our follies leave behind."

"Who'd do such a thing?"

"I've no idea."

"What about your father?" I asked. "His family?"

"He died when . . . " He stopped. I was shaking my head. "I see," he said. "You're asking about the man mother loved before she married Simon Spendlow."

"Could he have known your mother was Smedley Barlow and resented it?"

"That man's dead," Spendlow replied. "He had a single heir. She knows even less about this than I do."

"Can you be sure?" Parthenia said. "Have you confronted her?"

"No. Nor do I intend to."

"We need to know. If what you tell us is irrelevant, as you say, it will never be repeated by either of us."

"Gospel truth," I affirmed.

"You've given me a few shocks this morning," Spendlow said. "Now here's one for you. The man my mother selected for my father was Singleton Wentworth."

Parthenia's hands flew up from her lap in annoyance. "Simon," she said, "that's in poor taste. One scarcely looks for amusement . . . " She broke off. Simon, she saw, meant what he'd said.

Spendlow turned to me. "Singleton Wentworth," he told me, "was Parthenia's father."

Over the next moments the intricacies of her dilemma stood out on Parthenia's face like contoured trails on a hiker's map.

"Your mother told you this?"

"She showed me the document of intent she was including with her Smedley Barlow papers. I insisted on knowing who the unnamed man was. Given the state of my nerves, she was afraid to refuse me. It was a shock to discover I wasn't a Spendlow. In effect, I lost my father one day, my mother the next."

"It was something to be a Wentworth," Parthenia suggested gamely.

"Not an unacknowledged Wentworth. Besides, I was attached to the idea of being a Spendlow."

"Were you, in time, reconciled to being a Wentworth?" I asked.

"No. I rid myself of the idea instead."

"I could use the name of your analyst."

"I needed no analyst. When I was on my feet again I called on Singleton. I put it to him directly. Was he my father? He told me, man to man, the only person who could answer that question to my satisfaction was Lionel Thistlethwaite, mother's doctor over many years."

"I thought Lionel's grand passion was tropical medicine?"

"His avocation. Lionel could never bring himself to forsake Boston for the tropics for more than an occasional hit and run mission. His practice was here."

"Was he able to help?"

"Lionel told me I'd been a seven-months child, born two months prematurely, seven months after my mother married Simon Spendlow. That was the start of the trouble. Lydia Spendlow found it easier to believe my mother tricked Simon into marrying her than to believe he was capable at sixty-two of siring a child, a son, moreover, who, in her eyes, usurped the place in his heart that belonged to her son, Eliot, born a month earlier. Lydia's treatment of my mother subsequent to Simon's death gave rise, of course, to mother's scheme of revenge. Part of that scheme was to let Lydia go on thinking I was a changeling—not a Spendlow at all. Mother even pressed this idea on Lionel Thistlethwaite. He was afraid her mind was in a precarious balance so he spoke privately to Singleton Wentworth about it."

"Father was one of his patients," Parthenia supplied. I could see she was coming alive again, the shock passing.

"Singleton confirmed what Lionel already surmised. He'd never made love to my mother. The blood types bore him out. Simon's was compatible. Singleton's was not. He couldn't have been my father."

"Your mother was a troubled woman," Parthenia said.

"Parthenia," I said, "had your father come into the picture sooner, we'd all have been spared a lot of grief."

"Why do you say that?"

"Would you have wanted Smedley's story aired if you'd

known she claimed to have been seduced and abandoned by your father?"

"She was a victim," Parthenia insisted. "Lydia had a lot to answer for."

"Not, however, a victim of the masculine establishment."

"If the laws you men make were more sensible, she wouldn't have been cut out of Simon's estate."

"After a while," Spendlow said, "mother couldn't distinguish between fantasy and reality. Maybe her writing led to that. She began to think Singleton Wentworth was my father."

"Unfortunately," I said, "the fantasy destroyed her before the reality could reemerge and give her peace."

"Dreams aren't that abrasive," Spendlow said. "Nothing erodes like reality. Ask the Naiad of the Mists."

"That squares with something Eliot Bradstreet said to me earlier today—'you can't control reality'."

"That's not surprising. He's heard it often enough from me."

"I'd forgotten. You're uncle and nephew; the nephew a month senior to the uncle."

"Yes. We're that. This Spendlow business put a strain on my relations with some of the Bradburys but Eliot and I have stayed close friends over the years. We were reconciled after my, eh . . . accident and . . . my loss. . . . Mother's death, that is. I've helped him with plotting through the years. I'm no writer. I do have, however, like my father, an inventive turn of mind—as perhaps you've heard?"

"I've heard rumors. Cheerios? Fruit Loops?"

"Scriggles. The Early Bird Breakfast Cereal. Early bird catches the worm, you know? That idea."

Those ghastly Scriggles! I shuddered. I tried them once. A bowl of crispy little earthworms made from gluten, rice germ and barley. Guaranteed to writhe when you pour on the milk. Revolting! Yet, incredibly, they had caught on.

"My sympathies always have gone with the early worm," I said.

Spendlow laughed. "I must remember that. Every worm must have its turn—T-E-R-N, that is!"

With lines like that I could see why Spendlow said he was no writer.

"Has Clayton Poole solved the 'Breakfast Cereal Murders'?" I asked. "If he has, I've missed that one."

"Eliot's not devious enough. That's his undoing. He gets Clayton into straits, then comes to me to get him out of them. Or did, until I quit on him."

"Quit?"

"Yes. Eliot was finding it harder all the time to hold up his end—literally so. Increasingly the burden fell on me. I never took any compensation for my contributions. That was all right. I didn't need it. I have other commitments, however, and didn't have time to nursemaid Eliot through endless—actually endless, if you take my meaning—books."

"And that's why the series was terminated?"

"Oh, absolutely. Eliot would have carried it into the twenty-first century had I been willing to continue."

"How did he take your defection?"

"Or disaffection? Peeved, of course. In time he'll see it was better to call a halt than to let the series drag on to a lackluster finish."

"This comes as a surprise. Eliot's never mentioned it to anyone."

"Nor would he ever. Forget that I mentioned it. This

187

has been a confessional morning, with one confidence shading into another. And no shield law to cover us. It wasn't my intention to snitch on Eliot. I can't deny that I've found it amusing, through the years, extricating him from his difficulties—rather like teaching chess to someone who'll never understand the rules. It's been a sore point with him, I suspect, that the Spendlow inventiveness passed to me. I have a son, you know, who's senior physicist at CERN—the European Center for Nuclear Research—at Geneva."

"I dare say Eliot knows enough about you to get even if he feels you've betrayed his secret?"

"No betrayal could hurt me today. Anyway, he knows the extent to which he's obligated to me. There should be no lasting ill-feeling."

"I suppose you told him what you'd learned from Lionel Thistlethwaite?"

"In confidence. He'd grown up with family rumors about my origin. I owed it to us both, to clear things up, to confirm our kinship."

"Was it a part-way disclosure—a confession of your mother's panic but not of her success in getting even?"

"Look, Layman. I'm not comfortable telling you all this. If it wasn't that I saw you knew so damned much already I wouldn't have told you anything. You are discreet, aren't you?"

"It's a little late to ask that. If I'm not, your goose is cooked. Now, listen, I'm not pulling things out of you because I'm morbid. If I can forget tomorrow everything I've heard today it'll be fine with me. What I'm after is information that can put a stop to all this hell that's been going on and do it in a way that will hurt the fewest people possible."

"What Austin's asking you," Parthenia said, "what we need to know is, did you tell Eliot your mother was Smedley Barlow?"

"Oh, I wouldn't have done that. No . . . Wait! When Eliot first ran into plotting snags he came to me because, as he put it, it probably was innate in me to hack my way through a dense underbrush of complications to emerge, at last, on the summit of pure enlightenment. I thought at first that he was talking about my inventive streak, then I saw he could only mean the things my mother wrote as Smedley Barlow. I know I said nothing to him about the circumstances of her death. Until today I've spoken about them to no one. Did I tell him mother was Smedley Barlow? I would have had to, wouldn't I?"

Parthenia turned to me. "Austin, did Eliot in any way intimate to you that he knew who Smedley Barlow was?"

"Not a whisper. Not an inkling."

"That's understandable. He wasn't at liberty to say anything. Still, Simon, it's curious he never told you those papers were behind the succession of tragedies we've had over the last several weeks. Could he have thought you were in some way involved?"

"He knows me better than that."

A glance at her watch and Parthenia concluded, "We seem to have run this discussion out to its limits."

"That's so," I said. "Another five minutes and we'd be down to discussing Eliot's mixed socks."

Parthenia looked puzzled till Simon said, "Eliot's color blindness."

"Right," I said. "So far as Eliot's concerned, colors are interchangeable. This morning, for example, he told me Smedley Barlow's file case was brown. Actually, it's green."

"No," Parthenia said, "You never saw it in a good light. It is brown. Shagreen's a rough-textured leather. Though usually it's dyed green, it needn't be. This time it's brown."

"The joke's on me," I said.

"It's easy to mistake green for brown when you're color blind," Spendlow remarked.

"Hold on," I said. "I just remembered something. So far as we know, Eliot's never seen the file case."

"Since he's been told it's a shagreen case," Parthenia said, "wouldn't it be logical for him to assume it's green?"

"He didn't, however, which means that he's either seen it or knows somebody who did. That's the likelihood, anyway."

"If this was one of Eliot's plots," Spendlow said, "I'd say we've added a third color. Red, for the red herring, throwing suspicion in the wrong direction. That makes it a great joke. Eliot's color blindness makes him a suspect!"

"I suppose it is absurd," I said. I stood. Parthenia was right. Everything had been said. It was time to be on the move.

"Unfortunately," another voice said now, "it's not absurd. Eliot Bradstreet's capable of anything."

I looked around. The voice I'd heard was a woman's, yet not Parthenia's. It's tone was soft and flowing—the mood of the speaker was one of plaintiveness, something Parthenia held in contempt. She was up out of her chair, too, now, as much surprised as I was. Spendlow arose last, extending his arms out above him in an attitude of surrender.

"I'm sorry if I've deceived you," he said. "There's been a fourth person present throughout our conversation—by her own wishes, till now, not apparent to you." He stepped to the edge of the living room and lifted aside the high Flemish needlepoint screen. There before us was a tiny, dainty woman in a wheelchair, a heather hued Kerry rug flung over her lap. As soon as the screen was put aside she manipulated the motorized chair to roll forward toward us.

"Letitia Spendlow," she said, making her own introduction. "I don't see people because I want people to remember me as I was before this happened." Her fingers fled along the arms of the wheelchair, pecking nervously. "I couldn't let that conversation end where it was ending, however," she said. "You underestimate Eliot. Anything's possible with him. My husband wouldn't say so. I would." Then, before he could stop her, she grabbed Simon's maimed hand and held it out to us. "You see this?" she said. "That's his doing. He drove Simon to that! I've hated him ever since."

Spendlow slipped his hand out of hers, making placating gestures. Letitia would have none of it.

"Ask Simon to tell you how I came to be the way I am," she said. She waited.

"Being confined as she is has been hard on Letitia," Spendlow said. "Her wonderful fund of life was a contagion that spread through the whole family—to be deprived of that!"

"That's not what I wanted you to tell them," she said, her voice querulous. "I'll tell them myself. We'd gone to Switzerland to visit John, our son, and his family. We went climbing. I love to climb mountains. Simon doesn't climb. His hand, of course." She patted his arm, shushing him as he tried to speak. "Eliot climbs. We were linked. A false crust gave way under me and I went over a ledge. I don't weigh much. He said I'd pull him over too, and cut me loose. They came for me six hours later at the bottom of the gorge where I'd fallen, both legs fractured, my spine too. I lived though, lived to curse Eliot Bradstreet."

"A terrible accident," Simon said. "I know it's weighed heavily on Eliot."

Letitia looked scornful. "Nothing," she said, "weighs heavily on Eliot Bradstreet. Certainly not me, neither now, nor then, above the gorge."

18

*T*he subject of the Athenaeum's newest retrospective, which would carry through the holidays, was "Boston: as Engraved in Wood by Rudolph Ruzicka." Although the public wouldn't be allowed in to see it until Friday, there was to be a Thursday preview showing, from five thirty to seven thirty, and a wine and Stilton party for the proprietors and their guests. Since Parthenia had stayed late Wednesday night, to aid in deploying the prints in their glass cases, she had planned to get back to her archival duties no earlier than noon.

It was ten to twelve when we came down the steps at 90B Mount Vernon. We crossed Louisburg Square and together turned up Pinckney Street. If, in our absence, Aristides had descended from his pedestal or the Dutch elm disease had arrived in force, we wouldn't have noticed. The subject of Eliot Bradstreet obsessed us. Even a vigorous polemic mounted on his behalf by Spendlow, in the last minutes of our stay, failed to convince us that Eliot was as much a bystander as he affected to be. To me, Eliot, as a Grand Master of Mystery, had hitherto stood on an unassailable pinnacle. Now that I knew that he was unable to sustain his plots, I was no longer intimidated by his reputation. He was subject to the same scrutiny other mortals were obliged to undergo in their daily doings.

"When Simon gets to thinking about it some more," Parthenia said, "he'll decide his first loyalty's to Eliot. If he gets to him before we do, we'll have lost our chance of taking him unawares."

"I promised to phone him around two," I said.

"I'm against that. A confrontation's needed and it should be on our ground."

"What do you suggest?"

"Tell him to come to the preview at five thirty . . . Tell him the present possessor of the shagreen file wants to meet him there and turn it over to him. Say . . . oh, that he venerates Clayton Poole and thinks it'd be a red letter day in his life to meet Clayton's creator and render him a service."

"The bait's right. It'll drive Eliot nuts wondering who this enthusiast is and how he came into the picture. Won't he find the circumstances odd though? Why would anyone want to make the transfer with so many people milling around?"

"Tell him that's taken care of, that the gathering's an asset not an incumbrance. The library usually closes at five. For the exhibit and reception only the ground and second floors will be open to visitors. In the elevator, on the stairways, and elsewhere, there'll be printed notices stating that only those two floors are accessible, the others being secured for the night by the electronic protection system. I'll deactivate the system, however, so we can visit the other floors. Since the Athenaeum draws a law-abiding crowd, no one will violate the off-limit areas so no one except ourselves will know it can be done with impunity."

"What then?"

"After observing the amenities, you both can step out the side door, ostensibly to visit the men's room. Instead, take the stairs to the fifth floor. When you get there you'll find me waiting for you."

"I want Ladonna there, too."

"I thought as much. I've no objections. I intend to eat lunch with her in the staff room on the third floor. I'll tell her then what we've learned this morning."

"Cleon should be in on this as well."

"You have a lot to tell him. Has he anything to tell you?"

"There you've got me. Perhaps he picked up something this morning at Huddle's obsequies."

"Every occasion has its uses."

Had the Brahmin matron who'd seen me, on Monday night, at the threshold of the Athenaeum, taking leave of Ladonna, seen me now, parting with Parthenia at the same site, she would've been justified in assuming I was someone from an escort service whose luck had run out. Yet, if she did think that, she would have been wrong, for more reasons than one. Not only had I learned to respect Parthenia's intelligence and resourcefulness, I'd even come to like her. When we separated, we shook hands cordially. Nonetheless, as she moved away, I felt no pangs of separation. Feats, such as winning the Boston to Buffalo bike race and negotiating the whole of the Appalachian trail, had given to her physique a robustness that made one doubt the distinction of the sexes. That consideration alone was reason enough for not lingering till she vanished from view. There was a better reason. As the day advanced, clouds announced that we were finally going to be visited by the tail end of the hurricane that had been toiling up the Atlantic coast for a week. The first spitting drops that spun down now suggested we weren't many minutes from a downpour. Since I had to make it back to Park Street Station before that happened, I was away in a sprint. At the corner of Beacon and Park I was brought to a halt, however. Someone had blocked off the sidewalk with construction horses to allow a camera crew to photograph a surrealistic scene. Propped at an angle against the bumper of a red Jaguar was a large oil painting of Nathaniel Bowditch. In the gutter, to the left of the portrait, stood a mammoth transfer-printed creamware pitcher from which protruded a burst of oriental poppies. A young woman in lace pantaloons and matching chemise, with ornate Spanish sidecombs in her hair, was leaning forward before Bowditch's portrait, swinging, as though it was a sacred thurible, a brass parrot cage within which fluttered a highly irate parrot. With each swing the bird flailed its wings and squawked.

The producer of this epic, in a frenzy to get done before the rain stiffened, shouted out commands urging the censer-swinger to lessen the arc of her swing. An elderly man in Turkish festival dress, wearing a fake white moustache, stood next to him, waiting impatiently to be blended in with these bizarre ingredients. I inched around the handful of onlookers who had paused to watch. There's more than one way to desecrate Boston, I reflected as I faced down Park Street. At that instant the skies broke open. Wild cries of dismay came from the street posers. The woman with the parrot stumbled forward putting her knee through Bowditch. The screams behind me, the parrot's included, gathered to a new intensity as I fled down the steep thoroughfare to where Park Street Station lay, at the flat of the hill.

Once back at Cleveland Circle, in my aerie overlooking the Chestnut Hill reservoir, I made a meal of cold beets, broccoli florettes, and sugar snaps, heaped together on a plate and strewn with plain yogurt, toasted quinoa, and a dash of lemon pepper. For something to wash it down with I made carrot juice in the osterizer. It wasn't that Luella's had started me off on another vegetarian binge—I tried that when I got home from Nam, and, after two years, showed up with anemia (which is like having slush in your veins instead of blood). I didn't have time to fuss and this meal took little time to prepare and less to devour. I ate it absent-mindedly while I plotted my agenda for the afternoon. Afterward, I showered and laid out the clothes I'd need for the preview reception. It was then one thirty and, still in boxer shorts (another of my fetishes), I attended to item one on my agenda, dialing Pinckney Street. This time Cleon got me on the first ring. When he heard my voice he said, "I had my hand on the phone to call you when it rang."

"The last one to use that line on me," I said, "was Ronald Reagan when I called to give him some tips on his budget proposals."

"You need some new writers," Cleon said. "Margaret Thatcher sprang that same routine on me last week."

"I'm not surprised." I said. "She got it from me."

"Look, Austin," Cleon said, "First chance we get we've got to sit down together. There've been some developments."

"Are we bringing Eliot in on this?"

"No. That's one of the things I want to talk to you about. What's your schedule for the rest of the day?"

"Eliot's expecting me to call him at two, to compare notes."

"Tell him nothing."

"I'm going to ask him to meet us, at five thirty, at the Athenaeum, for the Ruzicka reception. Does that suit you?"

"How are we going to talk to him in that crowd?"

"That's all been taken care of."

"Fine, then. Perfect, in fact."

"Huddle's last respects go off okay?"

"Okay. Except that Isaac wants his jacket back. Says it was his lucky jacket."

"He was luckier without it. What did you tell him?"

"That, and that the police still had it."

"Did that cool him off."

"In a hurry."

"Does it bother Isaac that the Smedley Barlow papers turned up missing?"

"Like a carbuncle. He's a wreck wondering if Rufus Murdock's going to scoop the *Atlantic*."

"Then he's not so set anymore on suppressing them?"

"That's one of the things we've got to talk about."

"Name the where. Name the when."

"Pinckney Street. As soon as you can get over here."

"Are the barricades in place. Or do I wear my bulletproof weskit?"

"Your Burberry's enough. The way it sheds rain it'll probably shed bullets, too."

"See you an hour from now."

"Be looking for you."

We broke the connection simultaneously. Teamwork.

I dialed Eliot.

"You're punctual," he said.

"Good news should never have to wait," I said. "What would you say if I told you Blackbeard the Pirate has the Smedley Barlow papers and wants to turn them over to you this afternoon, at the Athenaeum, at the Ruzicka reception?"

"I'd say Blackbeard was hanged on Boston Common in the eighteenth century and that you've been idling away a wet afternoon dipping your whiskers too freely into the schnapps."

"Not schnapps. Raw carrot juice."

"And you're still coherent. I don't believe it."

"This is for real. Our adventurous friend is a plausible, twentieth century reincarnation of the old freebooter. Weird though it may seem, he hero-worships Clayton Poole and says that to hand over the papers to Clayton's creator, would be, for him, a foretaste of Nirvana."

"That's not so weird."

"I'm sure you're right. After all, Clayton is one of the immortals. I'll tell him it's set. See you at five thirty." With that I rang off, listened for the tone signal, then, before Eliot could call back, if that's what he meant to do, dialed Ladonna at the Athenaeum.

"Your voice is like honey out of the comb," I told her.

"Thanks for the booster shot," she said. "I wasn't feeling particularly dulcet at the moment."

"You mean you like Rudolph Ruzicka no better than Alma-Tadema?"

"You know better. Rudolph's a darling. It's what Parthenia told me. I'm worried. Ought you to be taking chances?"

"I'm on my guard."

"Still, if Eliot's involved in any way . . ."

"He's not a premium grade suspect. It's probably just

that he's playing detective on his own . . . sitting on information he should've shared with us."

"You think, if we face him as a solid phalanx, he'll cave in and tell all?"

"That's about as far as I've taken it. If I thought there was more to it I wouldn't want you there."

"Am I supposed to be flattered? I'm not. I've never fancied myself a shorn lamb to be shielded from the wintry blasts."

"So much for Lawrence Sterne's comforting thought."

"Even his lamb must have been fattened for the stew pot. That's not the kind of security a woman wants or needs."

"A vegetarian dwelling on lamb's stew! Fie on you!"

"If everyone was a vegetarian I'd find it easier to believe Sterne's shorn lamb had a future."

"He wouldn't. We'd all starve to death and then the wolves would devour him."

"Austin, you're my woolly lamb and I don't want to see you either shorn or sent to the shambles. Have you seen Cleon yet?"

"Talked to him. Would be with him now if I wasn't talking to you."

"Ask him about Lydia Spendlow. Parthenia ought to have told you but didn't. Put it out of her thoughts purposely, I suspect."

"Don't you want to tell me now?"

"It'll keep till you see Cleon."

"Anything else?"

"You could say you loved me."

"Consider it said. Anything else?"

"My, aren't we romantic today?"

"Every day. I have to beat the women off with sticks."

"Since I know that what you're really thinking of is how to tighten the thumb screws on Eliot Bradstreet, I'll overlook that."

"Since I know you're really thinking about how to keep the Stilton from crumbling, I'll overlook being overlooked. When you see me again, though, you've got to make up for it."

"I'll punish you with my lips."

"I'll go willingly to my fate."

"Go see Cleon. He's waiting for you."

"Would that, like the star-filled sky, I could devour you with ten thousand eyes."

"That's nice."

"That's Plato. Sort of."

"You're a nut. You know that, don't you?"

"Sort of."

"Goodby, my firmament."

"You're right. No compliment was ever firmer meant."

"Ouch!" Ladonna said, and hung up.

I'd escaped the noon drive-time traffic and got out of Brighton, in the Sun Runner, and on to Soldier's Field Road and Storrow Drive with almost as much freedom as if I was taking a practice run on the Utah Salt Flats. Twenty minutes after I set out, despite the rain, which, for the time being, had shifted over to drizzle, I was drumming the knocker at 121B Pinckney Street.

19

*C*leon debriefed me over coffee. Though I'd sooner have had Pero, I adapt when I must. If you can't get a dinner to suit your taste then get a taste to suit your dinner. Ladonna would say my mother fed me that line between spoonfuls of Swiss chard. She didn't. I worked it out for myself. Cleon, I found, also worked out things for himself. My debriefing didn't last beyond my third sip of coffee. Most of what I had to tell him he knew already. Only Parthenia's role came as a surprise to him, that and, of course, Jack Cool's. He knew Smedley Barlow was Bathsheba Spendlow and that Bathsheba had been shoved into the pit at Park Street. He knew of the ill-will between Lydia Spendlow and Bathsheba. He even knew Simon had been resolving Eliot's plots for him. No doubt he could've dug all these facts out for himself but he'd found an easier way of coming by his information.

"Julia Parkman Wendell—do you know the name?" he asked me.

"Wife of Sears Wendell, librarian at Harvard for a bushel of years," I said. "Smart as a buggy whip."

"Also, the Athenaeum's only woman librarian—nineteen twenty-eight to nineteen forty-six. Mean anything?"

"The Smedley Barlow years. Hold up, though. What good does that do us? Julia'd be pushing ninety if she was still above ground. Probably couldn't tell us what she ate for breakfast."

"She's eighty-nine and smart as a curricle whip. She knows Spendlow was Barlow and has known it for more than fifty years."

"And never told anyone?"

"Found out by a fluke. Bathsheba asked her if she had any information on James Barlow, an Englishman allegedly swallowed by a whale. 'You mean James Bartley,' Julia told her. 'A seaman aboard the *Star of the East*, who survived being swallowed by a sperm whale in eighteen ninety-one.' 'A kindred soul,' Bathsheba told Julia. 'Troubles engulfed me but I got the better of them.' A little while later, when the Smedley Barlow byline appeared, Julia picked up on it."

"No fluke. That was a whole whale."

"Ouch!" Cleon said, confirming my suspicion that the range of responses my puns elicit is ridiculously narrow.

"Did Julia confront Bathsheba on her moonlighting?" I asked next.

"She'd've seen that as intrusive. She'll talk about it now only because I told her the Athenaeum's become a drop-off point for the Smedley Barlow papers and in jeopardy as a consequence."

"What else did Julia tell you?"

"That Lydia Spendlow once urged her to cancel Bathsheba's Athenaeum privileges, though she wouldn't state her grounds. Julia thinks Lydia guessed Bathsheba was behind Smedley Barlow, though they never discussed it. That would have been a breach of decorum."

Cleon knew nothing about the strategy used to lure Bathsheba to Park Street Station. I'd just got done sketching it out for him when the phone rang. He went into his study to answer it. "Have some more coffee," he called back as he disappeared through the doorway. I didn't need a further infusion of caffeine. My mind was triphammer active as it was. I used the interval to go over the ground we'd covered and remembered I still didn't know how Lydia Spendlow died. That was the first thing I hit Cleon with when he reappeared.

"You don't remember?" he said. "I'm surprised. Locally it almost put the final takedown in Viet Nam out of the headlines."

"Not out of my headlines," I said. "I was over there helping to see us through it."

"I'm sorry. I should have remembered."

"Don't apologize. I've been trying to forget it myself."

"You remember, Eliot was married for awhile?"

"Till his wife left him—for the fellow who portrayed Clayton Poole on the PBS series, wasn't it?"

Cleon shook his head and went on. "Eliot had a younger brother, Burrill, pretty much under Lydia's thumb. When Lydia showed up with Alzheimer's, Burrill stood it just so long then smashed in her skull with a G.H. Mumm's bottle. At Bridgewater, where he was sent for psychiatric evaluation, he hanged himself."

"How did Eliot come through all this?"

"He had a rough time of it. That spelled the finish of his marriage."

"Was he attached to Lydia?"

"Not in the sense you mean. Lydia liked to dominate.

Eliot's marriage to a girl twenty years his junior really set her off. Her father's betrayal all over again, I suppose. He may even have done it to spite her. Theirs was that kind of a relationship."

"Didn't his success as a writer convince her he didn't need her?"

"It puzzled her till she found out he got his plot resolutions from Simon. Then she told him he'd merely shifted his dependency to Simon from her."

"She may have been right about that. To have Simon quit on him must've been a bitter pill."

"Enough to set him on a murderous rampage? Is that what you're hinting at? You know better. There's Huddle, for instance. He was with us when it happened."

"All I'm suggesting is that he's more into this business than he's telling. Let's hypothesize. The one thing he gets credit for doing well, writing detective stories, he can't do anymore because Simon won't help him. There's provocation there. Let's put it in these terms. He had the motivation. Did he have the opportunity? If he did, did he use it? What evidence is there to show that he did?"

"For an analogical thinker you're organizing things in a surprisingly analytical fashion."

"Formulating questions is the easy part. The hard part is coming up with the answers. Let's start with motivation. His mind works this way: Simon thinks he's put me out of business because he's stopped fixing up my plots for me. Maybe I did let him put the wrappings on. So what? The hard part's contriving the complications, not resolving them. I'll show him. I'll contrive the plot to end all plots. And resolve it, too. And when the trap springs, he'll be the one caught in it."

"Okay, there's your hypothetical motivation. Where's the evidence to uphold it?"

"There's this. The note Parthenia got, telling her the papers were in the Athenaeum, had scattered through it idiosyncrasies peculiar to Spendlow's typing. They're easy enough to reproduce once you're familiar with them. Eliot had long acquaintance with them. The pages of closure Simon did for him would have been enough."

"Do we know anything about the machine the letter was typed on?"

"It's one at the Athenaeum, kept for the use of the proprietors. They both had access to it."

"So anyone could have typed that letter?"

"Anyone who uses the Athenaeum."

"Okay, for sake of argument let's say Eliot wrote that letter. That still leaves us with a big problem. What evidence is there that he planted the Smedley Barlow papers in the Athenaeum or even knew about their existence?"

"He knew the shagreen file case is brown. If you'd never seen it the normal thing would be to think it's green since shagreen usually is green, though it needn't be."

"That could have been a slip of the tongue on his part, something not unnatural for someone who habitually confuses colors. I'd hate to hang him on that evidence."

"Another thing. Did you tell Eliot that Quelch returned the file to aisle twenty-three?"

"No. In fact I'd forgotten that."

"Eliot knew it."

"There's still the big hurdle to be gotten over. Eliot was with us when Huddle was killed."

"I admit that stumps me. He was with us every minute,

except when he went to the gent's room."

"How long was he gone that time?"

"A good while. Ten minutes even. In fact I was wondering if I should go see if he'd fallen in when he came out again."

"The first floor men's room has two means of egress. The second one opens into the borning room."

"That changes things, then, doesn't it?"

"I'm afraid it does."

"Let's say we have a scenario now that reads something like this. Eliot pokes his head out the doorway opening on the borning room and sees Quelch's red and yellow tartan disappearing up the stairs. He switches off the circuit breaker that supplies power to the upper floors, slips upstairs himself to the dining room, pockets the gold quill, and continues on to the third floor where he finds Huddle, wearing Quelch's jacket, groping in near darkness. Taking him for Quelch, he kills him, positions the body, comes downstairs again, passes through the men's room and rejoins us in the muniment room. Now all he has to do is sit back and listen to us grubbing for facts that are already old news to him. Wasn't it odd, after all, that Eliot, the intelligence that conceived the exploits of Clayton Poole, had no insights to contribute at all that night? He left the sleuthing to us."

"I guess that's so. It doesn't seem to have impressed me at the time. We might conjecture further that Eliot had the confidence of one of the victims. Hatherly most likely since he hero worshipped Clayton Poole and probably made no distinction between the intelligence of Clayton and that of Eliot. With him, to consult Eliot was to consult Clayton."

"That's creditable."

"One other thing. The white van was real and those bullets were real. Was that Eliot's doing, too?"

"There's nothing to say it wasn't. He was one of the few people who knew we were abroad at that hour. He left the Club when we did and took a cab back to Lime Street. Once there it would've taken him a couple of minutes to fetch his thirty-eight, walk over to Chestnut Street, where the van was parked, move it over to Pinckney and await our arrival."

"How could he have broken into the van and started it without keys?"

"Clayton Poole's always appropriating cars. If teenage punks can do it often enough to make Boston the stolen car capital of the U.S.A., Eliot must long since have found someone who could show him how it's done."

"We still have no idea how Eliot could've got hold of the file. How much was he in Simon's confidence?"

"Simon says Eliot knew Bathsheba was Smedley. He never told him, though, about her plans to publish the *Key* nor about the circumstances that led to her death."

"Maybe he didn't have to tell him."

"What's that mean?"

"That phonecall I had a few minutes ago. That was Simon. He'd just gone through his mail. One letter was unsigned and typed in his own erratic style. It instructed him to go to Park Street Station tomorrow, during the noon rush hour, and to open locker twenty-three. In it, the letter said, he'd find the Smedley Barlow papers."

"The whole thing's weird. They don't even have security lockers in the subway anymore. They took them out a few years ago after a bomb scare. Did it tell him to go stand beside the pit, too?"

"Simon's convinced Eliot's behind that letter. He thinks

Eliot wants to shove him under a train and claim then that he took his own life because he'd killed Huddle and the others and was guilt ridden."

"Wouldn't Letitia show the police the letter Simon got instructing him to go to Park Street?"

"So what? I looks as though Simon typed it himself. They'd figure it was part of his derangement to have sent himself the letter."

"You mean you've been going step by step through all this business with me, hypothesizing up a storm, and all the time you've been sitting on this? You knew Simon would never accuse Eliot unless he was sure of it."

"I thought we owed it to Eliot to go over the ground carefully, to remove as many doubts as possible."

"Now the question is, how do we handle Eliot? This letter to Simon was anything but a smart move. What's happened, I think, is what's always happened when he wrote his books. He's dished up all the complications and doesn't know how to disengage them. I doubt if he appreciates it yet but his whole awful inability to resolve his plots converges on this one moment. He's got to the state where he's passed from wanting to thwart crime through the agency of Clayton Poole to wanting to commit the perfect crime thwarting, through me, Clayton Poole himself. On top of that, if he could let the blame for everything fall on Simon he'd have outplotted the man upon whom he previously had depended for such measure of fame as came to him. The final victory would be his."

A sudden burst of sound made us both jump. The phone seemed ready to spring out of its cradle. I'm sure it rang no louder than it ever did. Our tenseness supplied the difference. Spendlow's disclosure told us that, two hours hence, at the Athenaeum, the verbal jousting would come to an end when Eliot realized his strategems had failed. What would happen then?

"You take it," Cleon said. "Tell whoever it is I'll call back later."

I covered the mouthpiece when I heard the voice at the other end. "It's Quelch," I told Cleon.

"Find out what he wants," he said.

"It's Layman," I told Quelch. "I'm housesitting for Cleon who's off tracking the elusive clue to its lair. Are you fed up yet with being a voluntary hostage?"

"I could be if it wasn't raining so damn hard outside."

"Hang in there a little longer and your troubles will be over."

"I know. Eliot called. He says another day will tell the story."

"Got Clayton working on the case, I suppose."

"I said the same thing to him. He didn't like it. I think all writers are a little crazy. Listen to this. He said the time's come to write Clayton out of the script. Sounded as though he meant it, too, as though an actual Clayton Poole existed whom he could waste with a stroke of his pen. His joke, I imagine."

"A real sidesplitter," I said. "I could die laughing."

20

We got to the Athenaeum at five. With the coming of nightfall the wind was picking up, some gusts quickening to gale force. Rain, carried against the building's frowning facade by the wind, seemed to seep into the darkened stone. Ladonna was waiting by the door to let us in before the authorized hour. Dressed in a pale gold gown of slubbed silk she looked more like a princess welcoming us into an enchanted palace than a staff member of a library staid enough to have a scruple room. When she came up close to me I expected a kiss. Instead she merely squeezed my arm for encouragement. A kiss would have encouraged me more. Cleon's presence wasn't a factor. He knew how things stood between us. Her restraint was occasioned rather by anxiety. She led us into the periodical room, the doors to which had already been closed since it was not one of the places where visitors would be allowed to wander. In our walk through the rain, I'd told Cleon about the melancholy fate of the Discus Thrower. I felt like a humbug, therefore, when, upon stepping into the room, he confronted us, discus in hand, standing intact in his customary place. Alexander Graham

Bell's placard, as usual, leaned against his muscular calf. Cleon addressed Ladonna.

"Does Austin hallucinate habitually? Or merely when he drinks tea at the Athenaeum?"

"The spells come and go."

Cleon walked up to the Discus Thrower and pinged his knee with a gaunt knuckle. "His reflexes aren't that great," he said. "Constricted knee jerk. Otherwise he looks solid enough for someone allegedly a heap of rubble last night."

"Okay," I said, "have your joke. This guy doesn't have a speck of dust on him. Danny O'Discus needed a shampoo so badly I was on the point of asking Vidal Sassoon if he made house calls."

Cleon pretended to confer with Ladonna. Then both laughed.

"The last time our friend here took a dive," Cleon said, "the manufacturer duplicated the replacement order by mistake—either that or he was having a one-cent sale. The Athenaeum accepted delivery of both, figuring, well, you never know . . . "

"I've a feeling," I said, "that if Jack Cool blew up the Athenaeum tonight, a replacement would be standing here in the morning. Come what may, Boston goes on as usual."

"Isn't that why you're here?" Ladonna asked. "To make sure it does?"

"As to the matter at hand," I said. "Do we play this by ear, or what?"

"Parthenia and I have gone over everything," Ladonna said. "It's not only a question of not attracting the notice of the proprietors and their guests. There are staff members to think about, as well. Mostly everyone will be here tonight, including John Craig-Jeffries, the deputy director. He's dyslexic and it's an agony for him to memorize the news notes for these exhibits. He does it though and handles the media beautifully. They never suspect that he has a problem. He'll be so preoccupied we could stand on our heads and he won't notice."

"What about Parthenia and yourself?" Cleon asked. "Wouldn't somebody notice if the pair of you drifted away in the middle of the reception?"

"Parthenia's no problem. She's non-salaried and can come and go as she pleases. She told Apthorp earlier that she had a migraine and wouldn't stay for the reception. He thinks she's gone home. Everyone does. She's here, though, locked in her office, grounded to her radiator."

"You didn't have to lock yourself in your office?"

"No . . . "

"If you change your mind about that, make sure I'm locked in with you."

"If you don't keep quiet I'll lock you in with Parthenia."

"How could I chase her around the desk with all that copper wire strewn in my path?"

"You couldn't. She's reading Trollope. That would inhibit you."

"Trollops never have inhibited me before."

Ladonna shook her head and resumed.

"I have to be present at the reception till at least six-fifteen. Apthorp will activate the electronic warning system just after he comes down from the fourth floor, at five-thirty. Parthenia will deactivate it at twenty to six. The pair of you, along with Eliot, can slip upstairs, singly, as is convenient, any time between then and six. Eliot should be the last to go up. I wouldn't want him there first, alone with Parthenia."

"She looks like she could pin him to the mat if it came to a contest."

"I'll tell her you said that."

"Then she'll pin me to the mat."

"She'll pin your ears back."

"I'd like it better if you left the recognition scene to us and devoted yourself to your official duties—snitching brooches and pendants, lifting wallets, or whatever it is one does on these occasions to swell the coffers of the Athenaeum."

"I'm glad you have such a high opinion of us. I suppose you'll be disappointed when you find that the fifth floor isn't Fagin's garret?"

"You're determined, then, to break away from the orgy to join us?"

"I listened to you before and, as a consequence, never caught sight of Jack Cool. This time I'm not being talked out of anything. Besides, I did my honors thesis on eighteenth century recognition scenes. I adore recognition scenes."

"In that event," Cleon said, "you might want to recognize Apthorp Morison who, in the last two minutes, trying to get your attention through the French doors, has gone through a pantomime routine that makes Marcel Marceau look like a provincial player."

Ladonna jumped up. "I can imagine what he thinks of me," she said. "The lobby must be filled with damp people waiting to come in. I have responsibilities." As she spoke, to Morison's evident relief she moved toward the door. As interlopers we followed contritely at her heels.

Morison knew us both and we knew his fastidiousness. He must have been in a tizzy wondering how he could close off the periodical room without asking us pointblank to depart. His hands already fumbling to secure the lock of the door he gave us a twitch of a smile as we sidled past. "We'll browse till the rest of your guests come in," Cleon told him, meaning that we wouldn't flaunt our cosiness before the dripping throng standing at the inner door, waiting to be told they could enter.

I passed the next five minutes rereading the Bathsheba Spendlow plaque, checking it for typos, and inspecting the huge jardinieres of mimosa looking for leaf mite. On at least three occasions Morison skittered past me, each time giving me a nervous look to proclaim the wretched lot of a librarian who is involved in launching a retrospective. Though he insisted that this business of the Athenaeum reaching out to the larger community with an unending succession of exhibitions was truly democratic, I suspect there were days when he thought that the person who brainstormed the idea deserved to be sunk in the deepest Atlantic canyon, chained to a full scale, cast iron, New Wave representation of Chaos.

Three minutes before the staff was due to admit the tidy throng, which contemptuous of a drenching rain and rising gale had sallied through dusk time traffic to be at the inauguration of yet another Athenaeum exhibition, Cleon gave me the nod and we climbed the stairs to the second floor where, in the exhibition gallery, the Ruzicka woodcuts were laid out for inspection. In the adjacent reading room, which we entered first, at long, nondescript tables—mere boards on trestles, mostly concealed under linen table cloths—barkeeps stood vigil over Le Piar D'Or red table wine and a comparable claret. In an adjacent alcove, on a formidable table of which, since it was buried under a snowbank of linen, little was visible aside from its mahogany claw feet, six sturdy Stilton cheeses reposed on six no less formidable silver salvers, a forest foredoomed to be leveled by glittering blades wielded by a band of art lovers whose appetites equaled if not surpassed their passion for exhibits of every kind. Some, indeed, ignored the gallery to stampede directly toward the cheeses. It was as though they meant to assuage, in one glorious pig-out, the torment they felt at no longer being able to have tea and a cracker at the Athenaeum on a four-cent splurge as had been true in Bathsheba Spendlow's heyday.

A murmur, wafting up the stairs from the ground floor, told us the exhibition viewers had flowed in and, after making a ceremonial circuit of the downstairs reading room to admire the bowls of fresh crysanthemums and the busts and portraits of proprietors and benefactors of yesteryear, would soon be climbing the stairs to the exhibition gallery and refreshment tables. Eliot, we calculated, would, in his eagerness to lay hands on the Smedley Barlow papers, dispense with the rituals of pere-grination. Nor were we mistaken. He didn't even bother with the stairs but came up in the elevator. He hurried to-ward us immediately.

"This is as far as it goes," he said, pointing back to the elevator. "A placard over the push buttons says the floors above are secured for the night. Had you foreseen that?"

Cleon caught his arm and led him into the gallery on the pretext of getting his opinion of "Libertatis Incunabula," Ruzicka's engraving of Faneuil Hall. There, with no one within earshot, save myself, he gave him a quick rundown on our plans to disperse and reassemble on the fifth floor.

"Why must I go last?" Eliot said.

Cleon feigned astonishment. "You must have stage managed scores of such scenes in your books. The grand entrance, of course! This wide-eyed admirer of yours deserves the full treatment."

"Well, yes," Eliot said, mollification beginning to take hold. "There's that, I suppose."

A rising crescendo of voices and bobbing figures advancing into the room announced the arrival of the robust multitude of wine and cheese tasters who, with never varying enthusiasm, came to view every Athenaeum exhibition whether it be Early American Hispanists, the Polaroid portraits of Marie Cosindas, or a retrospective of Athenaeum authors. All were culture, all to be responded to with unrestrained ebullience.

Since the prospect of exulting over Ruzicka's genius did not prevent most of the visitors from accepting a plastic cup of wine at the wine trestles before going into the exhibition gallery, we were noticeably non-conforming in that company, moving about empty handed, and soon drifted back into the reading room where a hardcore minority had gathered to chatter, and would go on chattering till the reception ended, without ever thinking to enter the gallery to examine the engravings that provided the occasion for their visit.

Whoever hit upon the idea of serving Stilton at the Athenaeum's receptions ought to be entered on the rolls that identify the library's major benefactors. Stilton goes far. It crumbles at touch so that two-thirds of whatever is spread on a Bremner wafer drops back onto the tray as the partaker tries to convey it away. Thus, at the end of two hours, most of the cheese still is where it was when the reception began. The Athenaeum is humane enough, of course, to eventually produce a wheel of Brie or a bun of Gouda, and these are fallen upon and devoured rapidly by those patrons who come intending to make the reception do for dinner, of which there are not a few.

I knew some of the people now assembled. Cleon knew many more. Our plan was to stay in the vicinity of the cheese since it was in the vicinity of the door that led to the stairway that led to the upper floors. While we couldn't openly ignore other people, we intended to converse as obscurely as we could about Ruzicka's engravings to make it unattractive for others to break in on our conversation. We had only to keep this up for five or six minutes before Cleon could slip out of view. My problem then would be to keep myself unattached so that I could soon trail after. Having conceded to Cleon, on the toss of a coin, to the mystification of a couple of onlookers, the opening pitch, our exchange took this form:

"Do you think 'Dulce Domum' belongs to an exhibition announced as 'Ruzicka's Boston'? After all, Gore Place is in Waltham."

"For Boston read Metropolitan Boston. Christopher Gore got himself pretty deeply into Boston's early history. Why not show his country seat? It's still one of the finest houses within a ten-mile radius of the State House."

"Visually Rudy's results are gratifying. Carrying the New England red brick into the interstices of the elm gives his conception a beguiling cohesiveness."

Cleon was talking off the top of his head and enjoying it hugely. I only hoped no bona fide artist or architect was in range of his voice, otherwise we could expect to be lectured to for the next hour.

What would have come next? Ruzicka's engravings of the Harvard houses along the Charles? Perhaps. We'll never know. With only three minutes remaining, Ladonna showed up at my elbow, being dragged up to us more or less by Emily Higginson Stedman. It could have been worse. Emily confronted people, unburdened herself of some statement of fact or principle, then departed. Her manner suited our needs exactly. Since we had few moments to give her I wouldn't have disputed her if she said that the White House was made of popsicle sticks. Emerson was her topic.

"Mr. Layman," she said, "since Mary Bradbury never spoke a word in her own defense when she was accused of witchcraft, you will find yourself tempted, when writing about Emerson, to draw a parallel between her behavior and his, when Harvard turned against him because of the Divinity School Address. Don't succumb. Her silence cannot be ascribed to principles. She was old and non-verbal." Good deed done, Emily patted me on the back of the hand, then turned away bent on carrying enlightenment to some other quarter. How fortunate, I thought, that life has treated Emily kindly. Thwarted she could have been another Smedley Barlow. I doubted that Boston was ready for that.

I confronted Ladonna. "Have you noticed the state the Stilton's in?"

"Yes. It's time to relent and bring out the Brie."

"My mother used to say that what the porcupine is to the fauna, Stilton is to the fondu—unassailable."

"You should get up a book of your mother's sayings.

221

Then I could know everything you know, without facing a lifetime of indoctrination."

I glanced around. Cleon was gone. I looked at my watch. Ten to six.

"He got away while Emily had you transfixed," Ladonna said.

I caught a view of Frank Trowbridge edging toward me. He was a sticker.

"Here's where I fade," I told Ladonna. "Tell Frank I've gone to call the Stilton Emergency Service to come make repairs. Then get Emily to tell him what's wrong with the Hallowell School. While she's skewering him, you can flit."

I streaked for the door like a man with a desperate need to get to the john. As soon as it shut behind me I raced up the marble stairs two at a time to get out of view as speedily as I could. I had to do this on tiptoe and it wasn't easy. Someone was coming upstairs from the first floor. I crouched on the third floor landing and listened. I heard Apthorp Morison's voice. He was speaking to another man following along behind him.

"We can use the stairs between these two floors," he was saying. "The rest of the building's out of bounds. With some of the five million we got for the Stuart portraits we upgraded our electronic surveillance system. It's so sensitive now, if you came in here with Listerine on your breath it would trigger it off."

"Peace of mind is a bargain at any price," his companion volunteered.

Glad that I hadn't gargled even with Scope lest Apthorp should loose his attack dogs on me, I froze in position till I heard the two men enter the second floor reading room and the heavy door clamp shut behind them. Then, at desperation clip, I ran the rest of the way up to the fifth floor. Parthenia had done her work well. Had I been steeped in Listerine I still couldn't have triggered any alarms.

Reaching the last and final landing, I felt a sense of elation. I paused a second until my undoctored breath came normally. I didn't care to give anyone the impression I was hyperventilating out of anxiety, when I wasn't. Or was I? Just legitimate excitement. The thrill of the chase. My hand sought the ceramic knob. "One step for Austin," I told myself as I turned it, "one giant step for mankind." I opened the door and stepped through—into the arms of Jack Cool! Correction. This was not the Jack Cool I had seen last in the sub-basement, clad in easy regimentals, but a man dressed now in a Brooks Brothers suit custom tailored to his specifications. Yet, unmistakably, here was my droll adversary.

21

*I*f I took alarm at finding myself face to face again with Jack Cool, the fault rested with me, not with Jack. In exchange for my astonishment Jack offered only cordiality.

"I hope this is warranted," I said, as I returned his handshake.

"Mr. Layman, sir," he said, "at last we're up from the gloomy depths to meet under the arches of heaven where everything good is warranted."

Releasing my hand, his own swept upward to indicate the glorious, high vaulted, pargeted ceiling—Boston's homage to the Escorial—which gives visitors who ascend to the Athenaeum's fifth floor for the first time the impression that they are entering the purlieus of paradise. Though none of the five brass chandeliers was lit (for a private meeting, no matter how consequential, Parthenia's Yankee sense of thrift would never have authorized such a conflagration of watts), the glow from six reading lamps, reflected from the surface of the three cherrywood tables, filtered over the majestic grids in such a way as to make them seem apertures through which one might gaze out upon a distant universe. The light shone down, as well, on the rich crimsons and creams of three Persian carpets which extended along the broad, central hall from which, on either side, the successive book alcoves yielded, each an arched sanctuary announced by the bust of some divinity of letters or statescraft who, in past times, while awaiting immortality, passed profitable hours in this Boston environment. These were not the only witnesses to my unheralded encounter with the ubiquitous Cool. Standing in the dim alcove that abutted the fifth floor terrace, in front of John Quincy Adams's bust, Parthenia and Cleon watched to see how I'd play out my encounter with the man whose presence here at this hour we had fabricated to lure Eliot to our inquisition.

"I wouldn't have thought it possible, Jack," I said, brazening it out, "that you could have exhausted so speedily the contents of the scruples room."

"Boston's scruples rooms," he said, "are elsewhere's open shelves."

"What sets you prowling at this level? Illuminated manuscripts? Pirate treasure maps?"

"Can you think that unkindly of me? Tonight's the night we're moving out our store of gimcrackeries from your hospitable sub-basement. A stormy night suits nicely our purpose. The police are never abroad in the rain if they can help it. On an earlier occasion, I carried away for a leisurely perusal, the library's first edition of *The Barclays of Boston*. I thought it wise to return it tonight. No occasion may offer for me to come here again."

"Was it worth the trouble?"

"The trouble to return? Yes. There's no earlier novel

about your Boston grandees. The trouble to read? Since the author was a lady, I'll pass on that."

"You know we're not alone?"

"That Miss Wentworth is here? And Mr. Entigott?" Without looking around he gestured in their direction. "I do. I do. Introductions have been made. I've even had it from them that I was, in a manner, expected. So I'll stay on a bit so as not to disappoint your coming guest. My buckos below are well able to look out for themselves."

"It's the shagreen file our guest wants to see. You can't have that with you?"

"That would be asking too much of blind luck. It's no great matter though. I'd be a poor Irishman if I could find no plausible excuse for the omission."

Cleon came forward. "Jack was on his way elsewhere," he said. "He got here before I did and Parthenia detained him."

"There's still the matter of the file," said Parthenia. "I've heard his assurances. I wanted you to hear them."

"As I understand it," Cool said, "you're up to a bit of devilment—putting one over on the fellow whose detective gets the better of everyone. A rare stunt, if you carry it off."

"You've read his novels?"

"In paperback. They gave me a taste for Boston—a city where murder is done in such gentlemanly ways. Surely, though, Mr. Bradstreet writes of a wickeder city than ever the Reverend Henry Morgan knew?"

"An author's ego is inexhaustible, Jack," I said, ignoring his taunts. "We're looking to you to lay on the blarney with liberality."

"I can do that well enough. I'll lather him up for you."

"I don't doubt it. I believe you could charm a bird off a tree. It would serve our purposes, however, if you could rile as well as beguile."

"There are turns and twists in the Poole stories that have made me wonder at times about the mind that conceived them. Is your Mr. Bradstreet a wholesome man?"

We were spared the necessity of answering that question when the door opened again and Eliot himself stepped in. By the time it had clamped shut he was at Cleon's side.

"Jabez Brattle got my ear," he said. "He's harder to shake loose than a cocklebur." He stopped, realizing someone he didn't know was present, the man he had come to meet. I introduced them and stood aside, curious to see if Jack Cool's mellifluous surge could overrun Eliot's laconic bulwarks.

"For many a long year, now," Jack began, his tone one of open blandishment, "it's been my fondest wish to pay my respects in person to the man who created so fine a figure as Clayton Poole."

"Mr. Cool," Eliot said, "it dismays me to think of the things you might have wished for in that interval that would have benefited you more."

Had it been addressed to me, this Bostonian dismissal of Celtic sufficiency would have made me wilt. Jack parried it with gusto.

"My admiration for you," he said, "is not so remarkable as your solicitude for me. I know you through your books. You know me not at all. I must feel complimented by your notice, unless, of course, you mean to disparage your own work by suggesting it doesn't deserve my serious attention?"

To have his repudiation of Jack's hyperbole thrust back at him as a statement of yet greater extravagance was not what Eliot had expected. He shifted his ground uneasily.

"I understand you've brought with you some tangible evidence of your good will?"

"The Smedley Barlow papers?"

"Why, yes."

"You know their nature, I suppose?"

"I'm aware of it, yes."

"You must realize then, in that context the words 'good will' go down hard?"

"To credit you with good will in desiring to return them constitutes no judgement on the merits of the papers themselves."

"That's so," Jack said. "It struck me, however, that this is a felicitous occasion. To give those papers a part in it would try my spirits sorely."

"You didn't bring them with you?"

"The wisdom of that is apparent to you, is it? Well, be at ease. They're safe enough. In out of the rain, so to speak, which is more than I can say for my poor helpers down below there." He gestured toward the Old Granary.

With that an irritable angularity seemed to settle over Eliot's posture and gestures.

"I wasn't led to expect this," he said. "To my own profit I might have stayed in out of the rain as well." He was past being charmed by Jack's blather. His eyes bulged, a trait I never liked in Boston terriers and liked no better in him. I half wondered if he'd go after Jack Cool's coattails. It was clear he'd found the provocation.

"Deeds," he said, "not words, connote sincerity."

"I've heard," Jack answered, hardening his line, "that

some Englishman said 'Boston has everything necessary for the most agreeable society, except the spirit of sociability.' Are you bent on making his case for him?"

"How much of that sociability did you find in the Smedley Barlow papers, Mr. Cool?"

"Eliot," I said, "I'm sure the shagreen file communicated to Mr. Cool nothing more than a record of common human failings."

"If that's what you think," he snapped back, "then somebody's sold you the whole Boston myth, lock, stock, and barrel."

"What's your warrant for thinking otherwise?"

"I've seen them! Read them from cover to cover!"

"And that's why you left them at the Athenaeum, then wrote to me to tell me where to find them?" Parthenia exclaimed. "So others could see what you saw?"

"Was that the real reason I was asked here tonight . . . so you could hurl that charge in my face?"

"There's the letter," I said. "Simon didn't write it yet the typing eccentricities are his. You're familiar with them. . . . you've dealt with them often enough in your . . . collaborations."

"He told you about that, did he? Did he say he did all the work? That Clayton Poole was his?"

"Eliot! Few of us can go through life without leaning on others at times. We only wish you'd been more frank with us."

"With your Mr. Cool present, this is hardly the time to air my failings."

"At the moment," Cleon said, "Jack isn't one of your auditors. He's gone out on the terrace."

Cleon was right. Cool was nowhere to be seen.

"He shouldn't be out there," Parthenia said. "The terrace has been closed off. The railings are being reset in lead. The cement's dried out. They wobble."

"His work crew's below," I said. "He's checking on their progress."

Jack popped in again, damp but radiant. "The cases all are on the move," he said. "Little coffins parading in the rain as though there'd been a wholesale exhumation of your hallowed dead like the time twelve Higginsons were removed to Brookline. I hope there are no passersby on such a wild night. They'll think the last trump has sounded."

"I thought the Granary gates were padlocked at four?" I said.

"For special comings and goings, Liam has a duplicate key."

"Evidently," Eliot said, indifferent to the transit of arms under way below, "Mr. Cool tends more conscientiously to his own business than he does to the business of others."

"There now," said Jack. "The darling man is worried still about those trashy papers. He'll shorten his life grieving over trifles. 'The history of Boston,' Beecher said, 'is written in the best things that have befallen our land.' There's an idea to conjure with. Yet your Smut-ly Barlow papers contradict it. They should long since have been fed to the flames."

As Jack stepped closer to us, he skipped nimbly. "A thing's unraveled here," he said, looking down, "unless, of course, you're setting snares for rodents or the unwary."

"It's my grounding wire," Parthenia said. She extended

her right foot disclosing the loop of copper wire encompassing her ankle. "Static electricity's at its worst when there's a storm," she said. "The air must be heavily charged with particles."

Jack's eyes followed the length of wire which, he now saw, connected to a pipe along the wall. It was not in him to challenge a lady's logic. "A grounding wire!" he said. "Every day brings its own enlightenment."

The time had come to put Eliot—nervous now and therefore vulnerable—under fuller provocation. I provided the occasion. "You see, Jack," I said, "what women's liberation has done for Parthenia—made her a tenant of the leash law."

Parthenia bristled on cue. "I fetch sticks at nobody's bidding except my own," she declared.

"That's where you deceive yourself," I said. "Eliot's letter sent you bounding after Quelch at full gallop."

"That wasn't done to oblige Eliot Bradstreet," Parthenia said with a ferociousness worthy of an aroused mastiff. "I was appalled at the extremes Bathsheba Spendlow had been driven to to gain redress in a male dominated society. I wanted her story to be told. Eliot's machinations must have had quite another purpose."

"Machinations!" Eliot muttered.

"So much for the merits of your cause, Parthenia," I went on. "You blundered ahead to avenge someone you didn't know with results you might well have expected if you hadn't been so blinded by your own self-righteousness."

I was hitting hard. It had to be that way to get Eliot to wade in. Parthenia, perfectly interpreting my intentions, fed me the lines I needed.

"I'll take no responsibility for those deaths which, you allege, resulted from the reemergence of the Smedley Barlow papers. If you had any sense of fair play you'd shift the blame to where it belongs. After all, Eliot wrote the letter telling me where he'd hidden the papers. The whole thing took off from there."

That push brought Eliot in. "What right do you have to say that I wrote that letter?"

"Only a few minutes ago," I said, "you admitted you'd seen the papers. What else are we to assume?"

"Yes, I saw them. Quelch showed them to me!"

"Why would he do that?"

"Hatherly came to me for advice. He told me Isaac had them. I told Isaac I could help him dodge a few libel suits if he'd let me see what he had. For my own plots I'd dug a lot into past Boston history. I knew what was there."

A look of smugness settled over Eliot's features. He thought he'd knocked the props out from under the case we'd been building against him. And it seemed as though he had. What he said must have been true. A phonecall to Quelch could establish that. Only why hadn't Isaac told us?

"Why did Hatherly look to you for advice?"

"Eliot Bradstreet—the omniscient detective story writer! To him I was an answer machine."

"Too bad you're short on answers today."

"What else would you like to know? Who did write that letter? Parthenia had the knowledge to have typed it. How do we know she didn't write it and plant the papers as well?"

Parthenia snorted in rage. "My word says I didn't. For those who know me, that's enough!"

Behind us, there was a sigh from the door as it swung inward, and the sound of footsteps changing pitch as they passed from marble to wood. Ladonna came into the room and, at her heels, Liam Cool. Like Jack, Liam was not in common work clothes. In fact he was wearing, unless I missed my guess, one of J. Press's four-hundred dollars suits.

"Liam overtook me on the stairs," Ladonna explained. "He says his brother's here and he has to speak to him."

"Jack Cool, here, Miss Stanton," Jack acknowledged with a prompt bow. "I've had you pointed out to me. It's always a pleasure to meet a lovely lady."

Ladonna's lips formed the words of greeting. They came only in a whisper. A feeling of dread had taken hold of her. I caught her hand and pulled her to me, kissing her cheek. She huddled against me.

Jack approached Liam. "What is it?" he asked.

"Trouble below," Liam said. "They're on to us."

Jack darted, in six steps, across the alcove to the terrace door. Like a puck he skimmed over the wet tiles toward the fragile rails which looked down on the burying ground a hundred feet below. With Ladonna holding my hand in a firm clasp, I followed close on his tracks. The others came, too. When Jack put his hand to it, the rail swayed outward.

"Don't" Parthenia pleaded. "The rail's very unstable."

We could hear the commotion below. That didn't suffice. We had to see. I peered down into the Old Granary. A cry of lamentation broke from Jack's throat.

"Ah! My boys are undone. There's an army of policemen down there and they've pulled the gate shut."

I saw he was right. The pine cases, some broken open

where they had fallen, were strewn along the paths, and Jack's porters, a dozen or more, were either already cuffed or being flushed out of their pathetic hiding places behind the thin slate slabs, protesting to no avail. What astounded me most, though, was the presence of the man who, snapping out orders in a loud, clear voice, was indisputably in command of every phase of the operation—Dunscotus O'Flaherty. If he's as diligent during the day as he is at night, I concluded, the Commonwealth is getting full value for its dollar.

From where we were perched, looking down at the rout, nothing, we saw, was left to be done by us, for the side of the law, or by Jack and Liam, for their vanquished porters. With drizzle collecting on our clothes, we crowded again into the reading room, Liam crooning his dismay, Jack forthrightly deploring the over-confidence that found him absent from his post when his leadership was needed.

"Who was the informer?" Liam exclaimed now, measuring us with a vengeful eye.

"None of this present company," Jack said. "They knew nothing of our plans."

Still with doubts to quell, Liam surveyed us all again till his eyes fastened on Eliot.

"Why here he is!" he said. "The fellow who drove off in my white van!"

"I don't think so, Liam," Jack said.

"You don't do you? Then you're wrong. When I heard the motor start, I snapped awake. I caught a look of him from my bed by the window."

Eliot scoffed. "Your brain's been addled by the setback your plans have received tonight."

"I wondered then where I'd seen him before," Liam

went on. "I know now. Here, at the Athenaeum, in the sub-basement, six or eight weeks ago, traipsing around with that shagreen file under his arm. I saw him there, tucking it on the shelf, though he never saw me. I could never make head nor tail of it then, the likes of him slipping about like a lovesick ploughboy on a moonless night. Now here he is—the very fellow—no mistaking him."

"If my guess is right, then," Jack said, with no great concern, "that gentleman is gathering adventures to put into his next book. A pretty business it's turned out to be, though no business of mine. We must leave that to his friends to thrash out with him."

"So," Eliot said, "they've got you in league against me, too? As if anyone would believe this nonsense." He sought to put assurance in his voice. It wasn't there. Liam's accusations had caught him off his guard. I said nothing, preferring, for the moment, to watch him squirm.

Jack resumed speaking. "Liam, our course is plain and simple. The police will be watching for us at the basement exits and guarding the lower stairs. If we can get down to the second floor and depart with the first nighters we'll miss them altogether, to their sorrow, no doubt, but not to our own."

"So, said Liam, "that's why you sent me home to tog myself out like Lord Bugadee."

"Nothing prudence procures is ever bought too dearly," Jack replied. With that he motioned to Liam to press the button that would bring the elevator. "I don't recommend, Liam," he said, "that you stop to parry lances with Mr. Morison, or to sample the claret and Stilton."

"I couldn't swallow a bite or a sip," Liam said. "I'm sick at heart."

Satisfied, Jack turned to confront us. "My pleasure, good people," he exclaimed. "May your plans this night, whatever they may be, fare better than have my own. Mindful of our difficulties, I'm sure you'll understand when I say it will serve us best if one of you accompanies us—Mr. Entigott, if it suits him. He looks sensible enough not to spark a fracas. Isn't that so, Mr. Entigott?"

"Is this what's known as the illusion of choice?" Cleon asked.

"Don't think of yourself as a hostage," Jack said. "Once we step out the door you're free to return to your friends."

"It's a tribute to your persiflage that I don't feel coerced," Cleon told him.

I positioned myself in front of Jack. "Cleon," I said, "don't go if you don't want to."

"Austin," he said, "from his point of view, Jack isn't being unreasonable."

I knew he had asked himself what was best for Parthenia and Ladonna and had decided that leaving them behind with me and a compromised Eliot was less of a risk than antagonizing the Cools. It was not a high compliment to me. Eliot looked crumpled and used up.

Jack edged toward the elevator as soon as it heaved to a stop. Seconds later the doors parted and Cleon, flanked by both brothers, stepped aboard. Jack brushed aside the placard which warned against seeking the upper floors while the protective system was operative, and pressed the button for the second floor. As the doors slid shut, he tugged at his forelock.

22

*T*hough over those few minutes I had simulated interest in Jack Cool's motions and comments, in truth they had held only a fraction of my attention. My head throbbed as I adjusted to the implications of what Liam Cool almost casually had told us. Certainty had taken the place of suspicion. Liam had identified for us the most wanted man in Boston—not his brother as, with familial pride, he might have assumed, but the Cart-tail Club murderer. Next to Eliot's exposure the discovery that the Athenaeum Library had become a storage depot for IRA arms would be back page news.

Maybe it was pride or maybe, merely, his embarrassing inability to follow through to their logical conclusions the intricacies of his own plots, but whatever it was, it seemed almost as if Eliot never had heard what Liam had told us. Curiously, paramount in his thoughts was a matter that now had shrunk to insignificance.

"That man has the papers," he said. "He means to get a king's ransom for them."

"He'll keep them till he's safe and not a moment longer," I said. "I don't think he even likes having them. To him they're filth."

"He knows we didn't betray him," Parthenia said.

"I don't know what all this arms business is about," Eliot said, "and at this point I don't want to know. I can see though that you had some kind of a deal going with him. Why shouldn't he think you went back on your word? He's seen the Smedley Barlow papers. What illusions about us can he have left?"

"Mankind's more apt to be well-intentioned than otherwise," I said. "Isn't that what the literature of detection's all about—standing up for human decency?"

"I never believed it. That's why Simon's always had to resolve my plots for me."

"How could we have tipped anyone off about Cool's plans when we weren't in on them?"

"He had to move his munitions out some time. Every day that went by increased the danger of their being discovered here. All that was needed was to post round-the-clock observers till signs of activity made it apparent the shipment was ready to move."

"You think we informed on him?"

"This entire business reeks of deception. You, with your little Liam Cool announcing he saw me planting the file one day, driving away the next in his white van. You needed a scapegoat and chose me."

As Bradstreet spoke his body began to vibrate. He was overwrought. His agitation increased till it seemed his paroxysms would shake him asunder. Before I could intervene, Ladonna left my side, moving toward him, wanting to help. As she came within reach, he gripped her suddenly by the shoulder and spun her around till she faced Parthenia and myself. Then, instantly, his hand slid down from her shoulder to grip her hand. His other hand,

I saw now, clasped a small Colt automatic snatched from the left inside pocket of his jacket. Ladonna's instincts told her to wrest herself free. Mine told me to bring him down in a flying tackle. A cry from Parthenia checked us both.

"Don't! If you challenge him, he'll use that gun."

"Smart lady," Eliot said. "Let either of you try anything and Parthenia's worries about static electricity will be over for good because I'll shoot her right off her ridiculous tightrope."

"If that's your threat," I said, "then you've got nothing to gain holding Ladonna hostage. Let her go."

"I never thought you'd make it as Clayton Poole, Layman. Now I'm certain you wouldn't. So long as I have Ladonna subdued, you won't make a move. So long as I have Parthenia under the gun, Ladonna won't make a move."

"What will you do if I make a move?" Parthenia asked. "Shoot me anyway?"

"If you challenge me, I'll shoot Ladonna. I'm in an enviable position. I'm dealing with three people willing to lay down their lives for their friends. Yet none of you is willing to risk the life of either of the others by making an ill-considered move."

"Isn't this a lot of bother to go to," I said, "merely to stimulate my imagination?"

"What's your imagination got to do with this?" he countered.

"Isn't that what all this is about? You stumbled upon the Smedley Barlow papers, probably at the Athenaeum where they could have been all along, and decided to stir up some excitement, and maybe, in the process, provide yourself with some new plot material—something you desperately need now that Spendlow has quit on you—by getting the papers noticed and talked about. You weren't sure you'd done that, even when your fellow Cart-tailers started dying off in spectacular ways. Then Cleon came along with his idea of signature murders. Here, you saw, was something with fictional possibilities, even if it was far-fetched. You threw me into the equation, then, figuring that if I portrayed Clayton Poole for you, your creative faculties might, for once in your life, be stimulated enough to carry you through a plot to the end."

I piled phrase on phrase, not knowing what was coming next yet hoping I was making some kind of sense. I had to convince Bradstreet nothing was known against him that could put him in jeopardy of any kind. He studied me now, wondering how far he could credit what I was saying. Then he recalled the van.

"You admit," he said, "it was at your prompting that Liam Cool said he saw me drive off in his white van the night Huddle was murdered?"

"No," I said. "That was you. You shot at Cleon and myself."

"I needed corpses for my next book. Is that it?"

"We had a corpse. Huddle's."

"Which, incidentally, I couldn't have provided."

"We have no problem there. We know where you were when Huddle was murdered."

"To have shot you would hardly have served my turn."

"You never meant to shoot us. I know that. After we found Huddle, though, you were afraid I wouldn't want to go on posturing as Clayton Poole. You shot at me. If I quit after that I'd look as though I was chicken."

"Your faith in my good intentions is touching."

"Put your armament away. If you produced it to stimulate me further, it wasn't needed. Even without that this business totally engrosses me."

"I'm sure you don't intend to hurt me," Ladonna said, twisting until she could confront him, "yet I can't help being frightened. I've never been this near to a gun before. It terrifies me. Any gun would!"

Eliot shifted his stance. From what I knew about body language I had a feeling he was about to shift more than that. I'll never know for sure. Parthenia wasn't one for letting things work themselves out slow and easy. "The girl looks terrified," she said. "Can't you see that?" She moved a step in Eliot's direction. That decided him.

"Stop!" he commanded. He pressed the muzzle of the gun against Ladonna's left temple. "Another step and I'll kill her."

Parthenia halted, tense and quizzical. She hadn't looked for this rebuff. Yet Eliot resolved to proceed as he had begun.

"You're fools," he said, "the lot of you. My public's no better. Wouldn't you like to be a great detective like Clayton Poole? That inane question's been dinning in my ears for three decades. Do you want to know what the real answer to that is? No, I would not! My ambition is not to be the epitome of detectives but to be a paragon of crime—a peerless criminal, never caught, never suspected. And what better cover than to appear before the world as creator of a God the Father figure who safeguards civilization from the tyranny of wrongdoers?"

"We all have our fantasies, Eliot," I said, still determined to beguile him into submission, and wondering, wildly, if I'd stumbled on the truth. "All that's needed to put them to rout is a moment of clear reflection. Your conditioning's all against it. The apple doesn't fall far from the tree."

"Funny you should say that," he said. "Remember what you've heard about the Smedley Barlow papers. Some of those trees rotted out a long time ago. Mine, for instance. I don't have as far to roll as you may think. You never knew Lydia."

"Your mother . . . ?"

"She was right out of Greek tragedy—the Electra thing. Old Simon deliberately sought to put distance between them. He had her to psychiatrists. She married Eliot, my father, only because one doctor told her that, with a new attachment, the old one might wane. It didn't. Her bitterness grew. My father drowned himself in Jamaica Pond. After that her obsessions settled on me. I deliberately cultivated Simon because I knew it incensed her. I liked to antagonize her. Sometimes, when I stayed overnight at Simon's place, I snooped. When I found out about the *Key* I told her about it. She went further than I foresaw. She . . . had Burrill push Bathsheba under that train and take the papers. She planned it all."

A hectic glow suffused Eliot's face as he came to the end of his disclosures. I had a feeling that that didn't augur well for us. Sooner or later he was going to have to reclaim the exclusivity of his secrets. Our best hope, I saw, was to keep him believing we thought he was displaying his skills as a storyteller.

"Eliot," I said. "Terrible things have happened. That's true. No blame falls on you."

Some invisible force seemed to turn back my words

before they could reach him. "Hatherly!" he said. "The damn fool actually did bake himself to death. I had nothing to do with that. I liked Tom. He confided in me. What I had in mind for him was fugu liver. He was always crazy for new foods. Just a pinhead's worth and he would've been paralyzed and dead in minutes. It would've been a much better way for him to go."

"You thought about it," I said, "as a writer plotting. That's all. Thinking isn't doing."

He paid me no heed. "They all had to go," he went on, "Quelch, too. He botched it."

Parthenia turned to me and shrugged. "What's next?" she said, making no attempt to muffle her words. I could see why. Eliot seemed to be conversing with himself. If it wasn't for the reality of the gun pointed now at Parthenia, it would have seemed as though we could have walked away without his taking any notice. His supposed state of abstraction misled us.

"Move quickly," he said suddenly. "All three of you, out on the terrace. Now."

"In that rain?" Parthenia exclaimed.

"In *that* rain," Eliot mocked.

"I think Eliot means to lock us out there and let us get a good soaking," I said, making certain I spoke loud enough to include him. Moving past Parthenia, ostensibly to hold the door for her so she could trail her wire through, I whispered. "Can you fake a death scene with all the trimmings, on cue?"

"Count on it," she said, and fetching along the ubiquitous wire, stepped out onto the terrace. "Good," she called out, "the wind's shifting around and there are breaks in the clouds."

The slate tiles that formed the surface of the terrace seemed slipperier now than they'd been on our first visit. Or maybe it was our proximity to the precarious railing that made me think so, or the realization when I met, at eye level, the upper limits of the steeple of the neighboring Park Street Church, that the Athenaeum's lofty fifth floor paralleled the eighth stories of the adjacent buildings. It was, I reflected, a long drop to the Old Granary below. I looked about me, hoping Bradstreet had made no arrangements for us to walk the plank. I hoped for too much. At the doorway he paused, released Ladonna's arm at last, and ordered her to go ahead of him onto the terrace. She came directly to me and gripped my hand as much to reassure me as to find reassurance.

"If I could marry you this minute," she said, "I would."

"I hope your life insurance is paid up," I said, "and that you've made me the beneficiary."

"What?"

"That's the usual precaution when people are contemplating deathbed marriages."

Ladonna looked out into the night. The mist gathering on her cheeks might have been tears. She squeezed my hand. Then she smiled. "You devil," she said. "Anything to take my mind off the fix we're in."

Her words became a buzz in the background. I was watching Eliot. His eyes still were riveted on us. Never for an instant unmindful of his gun—still pointed at Parthenia—with his free hand he fetched a small tube from his pocket, loosened the cap, and squeezed some of what the tube contained onto the latch bolt of the doorlock. Then, immediately, as though it had seared his fingers, he flung the tube over the railing and emerged onto the terrace, shutting the door firmly behind him.

"Kimura," he explained, "a Japanese glue used by American embalmers to seal shut the lips of corpses. An instrument of symbolic fitness on this present occasion, wouldn't you say? It secures a bond instantly. Had I gotten even a speck on thumb and forefinger I wouldn't be able now to separate them with a chisel. It works equally well on metal and wood."

"So the door is sealed shut?" I said.

"No force known to science can open it again without dismantling it. None of us can reenter the Athenaeum from the terrace. You can forget the alternative of breaking the laminated safety glass to get back inside. It won't yield to fracturing blows." He stopped, hugely pleased with himself.

"What comes next?" I asked. "Do we all sit around under one of these potted weeping figs and pretend we're shipwrecked on a desert isle in typhoon season?"

"Credit me with more imagination than that."

"If we're trapped here," Parthenia pointed out, "then so are you."

"Not quite. Facing the door, to the right, you'll see there's a cement cornice, a survival from the era before the fifth floor was added, that extends along the side of the building, all the way to the fire escape, just where the building arches toward Tremont Street. It's minimal—barely wide enough to secure a foothold on—yet with the help of the railing that's set in behind it, it can serve as an escape route for someone who can maintain his balance and isn't intimidated by the prospect of falling eight stories into a flotilla of tombstones. It's by that route that I'll make my exit."

247

"What's to prevent us from exiting by the same route?"

"Anyone who attempts to vacate the terrace after me will be picked off the cornice with this," Bradstreet said, gesturing with the Colt. "I'm an excellent shot and, from the fire escape, I'll have all three of you in full view."

"If you mean to station yourself there on a permanent basis," Parthenia said, "why leave the terrace at all?"

"Oh, didn't I tell you?" said Bradstreet. "That would be the wrong place to be when the bomb goes off. The large, potted *ficus benjamina*—Austin's proposed desert island rendezvous point—presently is supporting in its branches a highly volatile packet of gelignite which I had put there this afternoon. It was rigged for me by a demolition expert whom I consult every now and again on Clayton Poole matters. To accommodate me, he even put aside a fireworks display he was working on for MUSH—Mothers United for a Safe Halloween. It has a timing mechanism set to detonate at exactly eight o'clock. At eight-oh-one the Athenaeum will look like Brighton's Grand Hotel looked after the Provisional IRA paid a call on Mrs. Thatcher—an avalanche of cascading masonry, floor collapsing into floor. And think of it! Fortuitously that same IRA has been caught tonight, red-handed, in the act of moving a cache of arms out of the Athenaeum. Everyone will realize that this assault, resulting in the tragic deaths of all three of you, as well as of certain others—Cleon Entigott, for example—lingering on the floors below, was the work of that band of IRA terrorists headed up by the ineffable Jack Cool. I, in fact, will attest to Cool's presence on the terrace less than an hour before the blowup."

"Of course," Parthenia said, "you will be untouched by the explosion, having flitted away, like Peter Pan?"

"Yes," Eliot said. "I'll be outside the zone of destruction. As a measure of prudence, though, I've left ajar, adjacent to the fire escape, a window which opens on a row of steel filing cabinets which will, at the necessary hour, serve as an effective buffer, shielding me, though we've calculated for a downward rather than lateral thrust, from flying debris, should any debris chance to travel that far. My departure will come too late to benefit you. Whoever is on the cornice when the fig tree outgrows its pot can expect to disintegrate about the same second the cornice itself does."

"Look, Eliot," I said, "you've worked out a foolproof plot. Now why don't you go home and write it up and give Clayton another triumph and forget all this nonsense about keeping us out here on a cold, damp October night. I can take it. After all, I lasted through a couple of monsoon seasons in Viet Nam. I'm not so sure about Parthenia and Ladonna."

In line with my expectations, my praise of his ingenuity set him preening and, with the usual blinding effect that vanity has, a little off his guard. I used that split fraction of time to whisper to Parthenia, "Go into your act."

That's all that was needed. Suddenly, her hands clawing at her chest Parthenia emitted a low, choking gurgle. At the same time, stumbling rather than staggering, she pitched two or three steps closer to Eliot.

"Get back! Get back!" he yelled, darting closer to us to keep his distance from her.

Parthenia's body jerked in convulsions. Low moans rose from her throat and her mouth twisted horribly. She dropped to her knees on the wet slates, with a thump that sounded like a sack of potatoes being flung to the floor.

Then, plunging forward, she lay across the path Eliot had identified as his escape route.

"She's epileptic!" Ladonna cried out. "We've got to help her. She could choke. . . . "

"Too risky," I said. "The way she's writhing about she may knock out the railing any minute and take us with her."

This observation seemed to galvanize Parthenia into new activity.

"Better stay clear," I told Ladonna. "My mother always said there are two times when you stay out of other people's way—when they're praying and when they're thrashing."

"Your mother . . . " Ladonna began, and then stopped. She knew I invoked mother when I wanted to get her goat. It got through to her. What she saw happening was a hoax. She squeezed my hand to signal her awareness. I wondered what she'd say when she found out some day that I never knew my mother. She'd died when I was two.

Parthenia's legs flailed. Her body seemed to bounce against the slates till finally she flipped over to rest on her heavy buttocks. Her tweed skirt was streaked with water. Light filtering from the reading room caught the glow of globs of spittle dribbling from her mouth. Her eyes, glaring widely, suddenly became fixed. Her knees, drawn up as though to ease some agony, shot forward and her legs locked rigidly. Ignoring Eliot, I did the obvious thing and crouched down beside her, supporting her head with my left forearm. I spoke her name. I repeated it. She remained motionless. I felt for her pulse, then shrank back in revulsion. "She's gone," I said.

Eliot uttered a low, wailing sob. He sprang to get past

Parthenia, to get away from the sight and presence of a dead body and onto the cornice that was to be his pathway to freedom. As he leaped, I seized the copper wire attached to Parthenia's ankle and pulled it tight across his path, catching him smartly just below the knees. With every ounce of strength in my being I jerked it taut over the distance it stretched from where it was trapped in the irrevocably sealed door to where Parthenia lay. Eliot had forgotten about Parthenia's "ridiculous tightrope." He shouldn't have. He sprawled through the air, stretching forth his hands instinctively to save himself, to catch hold of something. The Colt skittered across the slates and flew off the edge of the terrace to disappear silently into the darkness below. Desperately grasping, Eliot's hands came into contact with the weakened terrace railing. As he propelled against it, it swayed outward. Then, like boots being hauled out of thick ooze, the rail supports, with a violent slurp, tore loose from the cement and, propelled by Eliot's momentum, spun over the side of the terrace, carrying him with them. For a split moment they held as the uprooting process continued. Then, in a quick succession of wrenching sounds, they unmeshed themselves from the cement like a succulent zipper, shaking Eliot loose. With a hideous wail of terror, he pitched downward through the night directly above the spot where, I knew, stood the tomb of John Bellingham, governor of the Massachusetts Bay Colony in those days when Hester Prynne and Arthur Dimmesdale swooned into another's arms and, for one exquisite moment, forgot the bleakness of the Puritan world.

Parthenia was already on her feet, plucking mechanically at her defiled clothes and backing with Ladonna and myself toward the sealed door to the reading room when we heard the squelch of Eliot's body strike and shatter the lid of the tomb that had waited three centuries to record a further judgement against another sinner. Later, the press would recall the words engraved on Bellingham's tomb— "Virtue's fast Friend within this Tomb doth lye"—words obliterated when Eliot's body pulverized the lid and sprawled grotesquely in death amid Bellingham's musty bones.

There was one thing to think of now. While Parthenia and Ladonna hugged one another in terror and uncertainty, I parted the dense branches of the weeping fig and, lifting out the ticking mechanism Eliot had had concealed there, looped my pants belt around it and my necktie as well, knotted also in a loose loop, and heaved the resultant package with all my might at a mammoth tree of heaven which, thirty feet away from us, spread its great pagoda of branches over the Old Granary. I prayed that one of the loops, either of belt or tie, would be caught in its heavenly embrace. In a state of near panic, I heard my missile bounce from branch to branch, then, suddenly, the sound cut off and a menacing silence followed. Either the packet had lodged in the cleft of a branch or some twig had snagged it. The silence persisted. The packet apparently had completed its journey intact. The all but impossible had happened. I turned to Ladonna and Parthenia.

"I've put a little distance between us and it," I said. "I haven't bought us any additional time. We've got about four minutes to get across the cornice and inside, behind that bank of files."

"I'll lead off," Parthenia said. "I've crossed rope bridges in the Peruvian Andes at greater hazard. Do as I do."

"For a lark," I said, "this time do it blindfolded."

Parthenia wasn't interested in banter. "Shed your shoes, Ladonna," she instructed. "Those heels are a menace."

Parthenia's own brogans were another story. She could have scaled the Great Wall of China in them, hauling a backpack. Giving the railing that paralleled the cornice a vigorous shake to ascertain if it was securely in place, she decided it was and swung over it nimbly. The moment she was certain of her foothold she began to move along the cornice at a no-nonsense pace.

"If you want to play Tarzan," Ladonna said, "there goes your Jane. I'm not that agile. If I look down at all I think I'll experience total paralysis."

I picked her up in my arms. "Get a tight grip around my neck," I said, "like you're daddy's little girl, and I'll lift you over the stile."

Her arms came warmly about me and I felt her lips brush my cheek.

"Once your feet make contact with the cornice keep holding on to me with your left arm till your right hand grips the rail. Then let go of me and start moving along. I'll be right behind you."

We soon were sidling across the cornice as rapidly as we dared. I tried to think of it as a sporting venture, though I wanted to cringe every time I thought of the packet swinging from the branches of the ailanthus.

"Mark deWolfe Howe's office was right behind the terrace," Parthenia reported gustily. "Looking across the burying ground at people passing on Tremont Street, he used to say, 'I relish my view of the world beyond the grave.' "

"Parthenia," I said, "I'm sorry we had to leave your grounding wire behind. If we come through this, I promise you, I'll replace it in platinum."

"No urgency," she answered. "Whatever static electricity I had in me has been scared out."

A fragment of mortar, loosened by Parthenia's tread, bounced along the lip beneath our feet. Ladonna froze. Holding the rail with my left hand, I gave her a damp hug.

"If you want to play Juliet," I said, "I'm sure I can find a better location for the balcony scene." The tension left her and she resumed the crabwise, sideways scuttle that was taking us step by step closer to the fire escape. Hey, I thought to myself, wrong play, this is *Hamlet*.

We had less than a dozen feet to go when a rising hissing noise, which seemed to gather volume second by second, carried to us above the rustle of the leaves in the wind. Even without turning to look we knew it came from the branches of the ailanthus. Enough light showed from the windows of the Athenaeum for me to see the hands on my Omega. It was eight o'clock.

"Hold tight and keep moving," I called out. Suddenly there was a whoosh and a fierce, white glare brightened the night and made the shadows of the tree limbs dance against the walls of the Athenaeum. I waited for the impact of the blast, moving, staying close enough to Ladonna so that, if it came to that, I could grab her in my arms and share with her whatever fate awaited us. Even in this desperate moment we gained another few feet in our progress. Then, all at once, Parthenia called out, "Look! Look! You'll never believe this!"

We looked and saw that Eliot's infernal packet was spewing out raging balls of fire, soaring off into the night sky above the burying ground, above the Athenaeum, above the steeple of the Park Street Church itself—dazzling balls of light that burst into glorious cascades of radiant, multi-colored sparks, hosannahs of delight which seemed to carry with them the brightness of noon for brief seconds before darkness overwhelmed them.

"Powers of heaven!" I said. "Roman candles!"

Joyously, with no assurance that we had sufficient reason to be joyous we came to the end of the cornice and leaped onto the fire escape. There Parthenia had stayed, looking on in astonishment at the pyrotechnical wonder that flamed through the sky above us, like a finale to Arthur Fielder's Esplanade rendition of the "1812 Overture." One faulty ball of fire dove at us, colliding with a window pane. It didn't seem to matter. We had no idea of what was to follow. We could have been in mortal danger. That didn't seem to matter either. This, after what we'd steeled ourselves to face, seemed a fantastic relief. For a minute or two more, fiery orbs continued to eject from the packet, then followed a great surge of startling lights which flew out in every direction, a gigantic crysanthemum blooming in the sky and, finally, a solemn boom, like Old Ironsides discharging its annual broadside, over Boston Harbor, on Independence Day. With that something emerged from the packet, catapulted into the sky soaring straight upwards. Then a scarlet parachute blossomed against the night, steadied itself and, after a tentative flutter, began to drift earthward. From it, garishly lit by the waning bloom of light, we saw some indiscernible object dangling. Buffeted by the tired gasps of the dwindling gale, the parachute now alternately bounded upward or sunk uncertainly toward the burying ground below. Above us, the storm passing, the clouds still thinning, for a sudden moment the moon broke through, its rays coating with silver the stiff array of stone slabs marshalled in rows across the graveyard, and playing over the brilliant parachute as it hovered, dipped, and rose. At length, on a sudden sweep of wind, it came close enough for us to identify its burden. It was an effigy of a witch, conical hat rivaled by a chin as sharply pointed. It rode a tiny broomstick—an incarnation of the very horrors that had terrorized Boston three centuries ago. Nor was that the whole of the direful shudders it evoked as, at once, mindless yet purposeful, it edged closer to us. Its maker had endowed it with a computerized soundtrack. Over the soughing of the subdued wind there came from it now a hideous, prolonged cackle and then the words, spoken in a shrill, raucous voice, and repeated again and again, the refrain interspersed with fiendish cries—"Whither dost thou wander? Whither dost thou wander?"

"My God!" Ladonna gasped. "Mother Goose!"

"Whither dost thou wander? Whither dost thou wander?" came the voice again, the words growing fainter as the parachute drifted downward.

"There's a second verse to that Mother Goose rhyme," Parthenia said. "Whoever rigged that contraption could never have guessed how horribly fitting it would be."

"If I ever knew it, I've forgotten it," I said.

"I haven't forgotten it," Ladonna said. She recited it softly:

> " . . . I met an old man
> Who wouldn't say his prayers;
> I took him by the left leg,
> And threw him down the stairs."

I recalled Eliot's words, "One retires only from fantasy to reality." Was the distance that separated them so great?

23

*I*n 1938, a play rehearsal at the Cart-tail Club began six hours late owing to the unannounced arrival of the great September hurricane. There was no other precedent for letting passing events interfere with the production and presentation of Cart-tail Club plays. Indeed, in 1978, although this time the weathermen were on hand with their predictions well in advance of the storm, the entire cast showed up for rehearsal of the Shrove Tuesday play on the day of the great blizzard. As a result, they were left snowbound at Dyer Place for three days with nothing to eat but a bushel of Macouns and six Cajun shepherds pies which had been prepared ahead for Mardi Gras night and stored in the freezer. An account of their plight (all seven, not having Cajun digestive tracts, came down with acute gastro-enteritis), was incorporated into the Club's annals so that future generations would remember how "the Cajun Seven" had, against catastrophic odds, upheld the tradition that Club plays were not to be interfered with by mere whims of nature or mere strokes of doom.

Long-standing members, therefore, were not surprised

when, the week following the tragedy at the Athenaeum, the final dress rehearsal of *Nile Bodies* was held on its originally scheduled date. Only one departure from tradition resulted from the unusual circumstances that had led up to that event. Cleon Entigott was authorized to bring to the Club, on rehearsal night, not one but four guests—Parthenia Wentworth, Ladonna Stanton, Dunscotus O'Flaherty, and myself. Parthenia did not come. Her alleged hostility was not a factor. At noon that day, she had left for Lapland to captain a group of activists protesting the slaughter of seals in Nova Zembla. She sent sincere regrets. As for the rest of us, curiosity routed any notions of propriety that might have deterred us. We were further bolstered by the realization that propriety, as defined by others, did not determine how the Cart-tail Club comported itself. That Boston's Mrs. Arthur Newell had worn black for fifty years after her husband went down on the *Titanic* was no doubt touching, yet periods of mourning, whether protracted or brief, did not suit the temper of the Club. The thing to do was to pick up with life and go on.

As author-director-producer of *Nile Bodies*, Cleon had continuing obligations, even on dress rehearsal night. Accordingly, at his suggestion, we arrived an hour ahead of the general inrush of members so that, equipped with drinks provided us by Thaddeus Nebble, we could sit in the muniment room and pass in review the events of the preceding week.

In the library Ladonna paused to confront a curious item, at rest on a corner pedestal.

"It's a scold's mask," I explained. "A few hundred years back these were in hot demand. They were fitted over a woman's face if she nagged too much—the equivalent of wiring her jaws shut."

"Men actually did that?"

"And how! Brattle says any man who'd take the initiative to put them back into production today could make himself a bundle."

"Parthenia was right! This place is a bastion of reactionism."

"See now. You couldn't have said that if you were wearing a scold's mask. You've vindicated Brattle's stance."

"I knew there must be some purpose to life."

"Of course, as a concession to your considerable feminine charms, I could have yours enameled in the color of your choice and set with rhinestones. Would that suit you?"

"Beauty should be seen and not heard. Is that it?"

"You're mixing aphorisms. If that sums up your viewpoint, however, it's all right with me."

"And to think I came here tonight without my geologist's hammer."

I nodded to the lady in the mask. "Hang on, sister," I said. "One of these days Ladonna will liberate you."

"Or obliterate *you!*" Ladonna said.

In the muniment room we found Cleon and Dunscotus O'Flaherty already waiting for us.

After he saw that we were comfortably seated, Cleon exclaimed, "I wanted us to have this time together here because I have something to report. Before taking his leave of me Jack Cool told me that, if he managed to give his pursuers the slip, I'd have prompt tidings from him. This morning's mail brought me a letter from him written at St.

Andrews-by-the-Sea, from whence, he said, he was about to embark on a long voyage."

"Did he say anything about the Smedley Barlow papers?" Dunce asked.

"Dunce!" Cleon said. "What are you trying to do to us? There was nothing in the newspapers about Smedley Barlow. How did you ring in on it?"

"One listens. I'm listening now. You were about to tell us about the deal you struck with Jack—his freedom for your papers."

"No deal. It was his Brooks Brothers suit that earned him my cooperation. I figured that anyone who could fine tune his operation right down to such a detail as that probably would outsmart me anyway if I tried to thwart him."

"Aren't you forgetting that his operation came a cropper?"

"There's that, of course. And thanks to your intervention. I don't know how you managed to come upon the scene when you did. Somehow, though, I don't think it had anything to do with faulty planning on Jack's part."

"Nor did it. Jack's a master strategist. We planted a mole in his organization. There was no real way he could have known that."

"Your discretion in not naming Standish openly reflects, I suppose, your hope that you can make further use of him?"

"Standish? Who are we talking about? Do I know him?"

"It's your loss if you don't. He told Jack Cool about the Smedley Barlow papers. Then he told you what Jack did to make them serve his turn."

"I stand mute," Dunce said.

"Don't worry. I . . . we . . . intend to do the same. We have no wish to put him in danger."

"I'm glad you've worked that out," Ladonna said. "Now, if you'd only work the fate of the papers into the equation."

"Jack," Cleon said, "thought an apposite repository for them would be a serene and pleasant nook where documents concerning Boston and its first families are habitually sequestered and forgotten."

"There was a time," Ladonna replied, "when I would have taken that to mean the Athenaeum. Now I wonder if such a place exists anywhere in Boston."

"It does and Jack found it. Don't ask me how, but he did."

"Don't tell me," I interrupted, "let me guess. We're in it—the Cart-tail Club's muniment room, a catacomb for Boston documents, a place where, like the Dead Sea Scrolls, they can be hidden away, untouched, for centuries. Did I hit it?"

"On the button."

"If Jack's on the high seas when will he ever get the chance to effect the transfer?"

"He did that before he left Boston. Austin, since you're the only one here who's ever seen the shagreen file, suppose you point it out to us."

Scarcely crediting what I'd heard, I let my eyes travel along the shelves. "It's there," I said, after a minute. "Behind the glass doors with the Franklin memorabilia." I kept my seat, flabbergasted that Jack had successfully penetrated yet another holy of holies, and uncomfortable knowing the ill-begotten papers were again within arm's reach.

261

"Austin doesn't seem anxious to verify his find," Cleon said. "Would someone else like to do it?"

Ladonna shrank back in about the same way she would have if someone had tried to hand her a legless lizzard.

"I prefer to admire them from afar," Dunce said.

"Jack Cool thought there might be some squeamishness about reclaiming the papers," Cleon said. "He took care of that by sealing the file and fixing a label to it stating that it's to remain unopened for a hundred years, dating the time from the present. The precaution is adequate. No one here will think of looking at them a day sooner."

"I wish that ended it," I said.

"There are wounds to be healed, of course," Cleon said. "Still, I think it does end it, more or less."

"I don't know about that. I've gone over the facts a dozen times and they don't add up to what they should. Less so each time, it seems."

"You've talked to Simon, I suppose. What does he say?"

"That's the strange thing. When I told him about Burrill's involvement, he was stunned. He hadn't anticipated that. I reminded him that Eliot was overwrought when he told us those things, that they could have become terribly twisted in his mind. He didn't think so. It upset him badly. He cared about very little else, it seemed."

Cleon turned apologetically to Dunce. "More details that were excised from the text before it was released to the press."

"I don't feel deprived," Dunce said. "I sense I'm better off remaining in ignorance."

"Simon's attitude changes nothing," I went on. "I'm less complacent about one or two other things. Take Eliot's Colt revolver for instance. The police have it. They found it under some of the cement debris that fell from the terrace when the railing gave way. They got one good fingerprint from it which they were able to identify as Eliot's. The thing is—it wasn't loaded."

"To have it there . . . to threaten us with it as he did, can't have been mere bravado on his part," Ladonna said. "I don't see . . . "

"Remember," Cleon said, intervening, "he didn't have much lead time. Harassed as he was, he forgot to load it. And, after all, he did have a superior weapon on hand, or thought he had—his infernal mechanism."

"And what about this liquid adhesive he used to seal up the door?" Dunce said. "That was an effective part of his strategy."

"That's the other thing that troubles me," I said. "It wasn't. Go ahead, Ladonna. Tell them."

"When somebody thought to try the door in the morning it opened quite as readily as it always had. We thought that maybe the storm, the high humidity, kept his cement from holding as he said it would."

"That answer's too easy," I said. "When Ladonna told me that, I checked it out. The only tube the police found in the Old Granary contained a handcream used by Scandinavians who fish the Arctic. You can buy it in any chain store that deals in toilet articles."

"So we've got a gun that doesn't shoot, a glue that doesn't stick, a bomb that doesn't blow up," Cleon said. "The picture that's coming together isn't quite the one we bought."

"No, it isn't," I said. "I thought I'd accounted for the bomb being what it was. Now I'm not so sure of that either."

"What was your theory?" Dunce said. "I'd like to hear it."

"I think we all would," Cleon said.

"It's this. Eliot said his demolitions man was someone whom he'd consulted in the past when, for his books, he needed information on infernal devices. You or I, if we wanted that kind of information, would go to someone in construction work or someone who had experience in such matters while in the military. In pursuit of credibility, Eliot seems to have established connections with people who operate outside the law. Since that's so what would be more likely than that his contact here in Boston should have been a demolition expert with the IRA? Even though, invoking his assistance on short notice, Eliot would have had to settle for some item that could be provided him out of stock, as it were, he would have had to tell his supplier how he meant to utilize it. In this instance, of course, that would have put the expert on the spot. Assuming that he was aware of the taxing demands that had been made on the ingenuity of his colleagues in recent days, the last thing he would have wanted to do was to blow up the Athenaeum while it had a crucial shipment of IRA arms stored in its sub-basement. Yet, without putting the whole gun-running operation in peril, he couldn't tell Eliot why he was unable to accommodate him. Accordingly, he said nothing but gave Eliot, not the conventional bomb he asked for, but, instead, a harmless package of fireworks he'd assembled for some other occasion, probably, taking into account the addition of the witch—for some upcoming Halloween celebration. While he knew, naturally, that Eliot would be outraged when he found he'd been deceived, meantime he would have kept him from going elsewhere for his explosives and thus assured the safety of the IRA's cache of arms at the Athenaeum. Bear in mind, too, human nature can take some strange twists. Quite possibly our bomb-maker might have been appalled at Eliot's intentions. A man who, in pursuance of political aims, could, with impunity, blow up random Christmas shoppers to dramatize his cause, might, conceivably, be morally outraged at the thought of someone blowing up a world renowned library for mere personal revenge."

"Your explanation covers the essentials," Cleon said. "Certainly it can't be too far from the truth."

"It shouldn't be. Nonetheless my gut feeling is that it is. If we buy this, then we might as well assume that Eliot's provisioners all were bibliophiles who saw to it that he had a gun loaded with blanks and an adhesive glue that wasn't glue at all, as well as a bomb that wouldn't detonate. Somewhere along the line the train went off the track and I think I may have been the one to pull the switch."

"Austin," Dunce said, "Standish Hegarty has talked with the man who supplied Eliot with his skyrocket. Since you've already figured out Standish's role in this business and things need some clearing up, there's no point in my remaining coy any longer. You mightn't like everything I'm going to tell you but these are the facts. To begin with, you're right, Eliot's supplier was an IRA demolitions man. Eliot never intended to blow up the Athenaeum. That packet of fireworks you saw bursting skyward was precisely what he asked for. It was a Halloween assemblage, put together, actually, for Mothers United for a Safe Halloween. The only alteration made to accommodate Eliot was the Mother Goose sound track which, at his direction, was substituted for the usual menacing threats and cackles."

"Eliot mentioned MUSH," I said. "I thought it was a sick joke."

"Austin," Ladonna said. "You told Eliot you believed in his innocence. You told him he'd convinced you he could resolve a plot on his own. No one could have done more. If only he'd listened." The color flew into her cheeks as she spoke. She was looking, I knew, for a way to extenuate me. I wished it was that simple.

"For a guy who thought he had all his ducks in a row," I said, "I must look pretty stupid right now."

"Eliot isn't in the clear," Cleon said. "We know he killed Huddle."

"That's not so," I said. "How much of what he confessed to doing is true is anybody's guess. Never at any time, though, did he admit killing Huddle. We worked that out for ourselves, making a lot of assumptions to give validity to a foredrawn conclusion. Don't forget. Eliot fainted when he saw Huddle's corpse. That was genuine enough."

"The wrong corpse."

"Our assumption. We could've been wrong."

"Liam Cool saw him in the sub-basement and saw him take off in the van."

"It could've been someone else."

"It's possible. Simon and Eliot, for example, had enough of a family resemblance to be mistaken for one another in poor light. Then, too, Liam was not in his most settled state of mind when he identified Eliot. He was scapegoat hunting."

"With all these negative points surfacing," Dunce said, "you probably have no use for a piece of information that clears up so trivial a point as where Jack Cool hid the rounds of ammunition for the weapons he stored at the Athenaeum."

"You know?" I said.

"In the wine cellar here, at the Cart-tail Club."

"The muniment room? The wine cellar? He seems to have had the run of the place. How did he manage it?"

"Mr. Gookin helped him."

"This needs some explaining," Cleon said, flabbergasted for once.

"Enoch venerated Mollie Osgood—Mrs. Erskine Childers. She was a Bostonian, you'll remember. Enoch's father, Josiah, managed Doctor Osgood's Brookline estate for more than fifty years. Enoch convinced himself he owed it to the Osgoods to help the IRA when he could. I think Standish's straightened him out on that subject now. Earlier, though, Standish kept his counsel because he didn't want to imperil our operation."

"You knew about this right along?"

"Yes. The night your alarm sounded, the reason I was so persistent about gaining admittance had to do with that. I was afraid something had gone wrong relating to the ammunition. I didn't want to see the Club blown sky high."

"Is that stuff still down there?" Cleon asked.

"Oh, no. Jack had it taken out the day following the murder. He thought you people played too roughhouse to be trusted with it."

"It was in coffins, too?"

"In crates supposed to contain wine shipped from Raymond Colesworthy's Saranac vineyards. Jack's a stickler for keeping up appearances."

At that point our conversation was interrupted by the sound of someone running in the hall. Loud cries split the air—"Entigott! Layman!" We stood up in time to face Quelch as he burst into the room. Dunce stepped back so that Ladonna could stand next to me. Her hand in mine, she looked at me quizzically. I gave her a reassuring hug. This was getting to be a habit.

"What more can happen?" Quelch said when he saw us. "Trowbridge came in on the subway from Harvard Square a few minutes ago. He says there's near chaos at Park Street Station. An hour ago Spendlow threw himself into the pit right into the path of an incoming train!"

"Simon?" I said. "How can they be sure already that that's who it was?"

"Letitia called the police and said that's what he meant to do. She called as soon as he left the house."

Stupified we moved back down the hall to the library where, over the past half hour, a throng of members and their guests had gathered. Maybe Cart-tailers didn't find death a congenial topic. No matter. Tonight there was no escaping it. I said little, listening mostly. My palms were sweating. I was surprised how warm and dry Ladonna's hand was when it slipped into mine. Her eyes sought me till mine met hers directly.

"It seems as inevitable as something out of Sophocles," she said. "It couldn't have happened any other way than it did."

I felt someone plucking at my left sleeve and turned to face Lorna Greenstockings who'd angled her way through the mass of bodies to get to me. "Mr. Layman," she said, "there's this." She handed me a small envelope. "I never thought to give it to you when you came in. I heard what

Mr. Trowbridge said about Mr. Spendlow and then I remembered. Mr. Spendlow was here this afternoon and left this for you. He said you'd understand." Pinkness suffused Lorna's cheeks. It could have been the glow of health. It was, for once, I think, the glow of excitement.

Inside the envelope was a key to security locker twenty-three, the Greyhound Bus Terminal, the only place in Boston which still had security lockers. I looked around for Cleon, then remembered he'd gone back upstairs to his playmakers, taking Dunce with him. I caught hold of Ladonna's arm and pulled her along with me to the borning room where we put on our coats.

"We've something to do before dinner," I said. "It won't take us long and the cold air will do us both good."

We walked up Boylston and turned the corner into Park Square. I told Ladonna what our mission was.

"What do you expect to find when you open the locker?" Ladonna asked.

"The final page of a play by Sophocles," I said.

We walked on in silence.

I found locker twenty-three without any trouble. Inside was a second envelope, same size as the first. Still no fifty thousand dollars. That didn't matter. I didn't think there would be. When I opened the envelope I found a single sheet of paper, folded once. The lines of type spread across the page offered, in evidence of their origin, Spendlow's distinctive mannerisms. Ladonna looked away while I read it.

"Does it say what you thought it would say?" she asked when I turned toward her.

"It tells me what I needed to know," I said. "Here, read it to me to see if I've missed anything."

She took the page and read it in low, firm tones: "My mother's papers were sent back to me by Burrill the day before he killed Lydia. He didn't explain how he came to have them. Thanks to your efforts I've at least learned that much. Eliot, of course, told me what Hatherly and Quelch told him about the papers once I put them in circulation again. With my mother's vindication at stake, I couldn't let them botch it. As for Eliot, he never could get the ending right. Once again it falls to me. This is as close to writing a confessional piece as I intend to get. Spendlow." An earthworm was sketched under the signature.

Ladonna and I retraced our steps to the Cart-tail Club. If we said anything at all to one another, I don't remember it. When we came in, the members and their guests already were climbing the stairs to dinner. We hung our coats again in the borning room and I sat, for a moment, on the deacon's bench while Ladonna went to the ladies room to undo the mischief the wind had done to her hair. I was alone when Raymond Colesworthy came through. He stopped and shook hands.

"The turmoil's behind us now," he said.

"Mostly so, I guess," I answered, "though there's one thing that still aggravates me. I'm not positive who shoved Bathsheba in front of the train at Park Street Station— Burrill, Eliot, or Simon. Are you able to tell us now?"

Colesworthy shook his head solemnly. "Lamentably," he said, "when viewed from your coign of vantage, there's no statute of limitations governing sacerdotal confidentiality. Since I'm not willing to calumniate the innocent by saying nothing, however, I find myself obliged to tell you this much. It was none of those you've mentioned."

He clasped my hand again in his for a moment, in the spirit of a blessing, then turned away sadly.

Ladonna and I ate baked stuffed haddock, and saw *Nile Bodies*, which was probably very good, and went through the motions of normalcy because that's how you get normalcy back when you've lost it. After the third curtain call, which confirmed that the majority of those present felt they'd sat through a fine evening's entertainment, Cleon joined us.

"Trowbridge tells me you've been accepted for membership," he said. "That is, if you can stand us."

"Oh, I can stand you all right," I said. "The question is, can I stand myself?"

I passed him Spendlow's note. He read it, reinserted it in its envelope, and passed it back to me. "Don't lose it," he said. "That's what lets you off the hook."

"How do you figure that?" I countered.

"Don't you see? Simon gave up plotting Eliot's stories so that he could concentrate on bringing to a satisfactory resolution the mystery that had hung over his own life for so many years. Ironically, when Eliot's nerves failed him and he blurted out the facts about Bathsheba's death, Simon still wasn't satisfied that he'd achieved his goal. His sense of symmetry was outraged. Eliot's bungling had brought everything to a distorted climax. Simon, of course, wasn't looking for public recognition for his deeds. He was unconcerned that others ascribed to Eliot the cunning and ruthlessness he'd exercised in pursuit of his goal. What bothered him was the general assumption that with Eliot's death everything was resolved. That was uncivilized. The revelation he'd sought had come at high cost. Accordingly retribution had to be forthcoming in equal measure. For Simon that meant nothing less than his own immolation."

"And I'm dispensed of all blame?"

"Your method was a bit involuted. Nonetheless, you did bring the Smedley Barlow murderer to justice. Simon knew whom to credit. Hence his note is addressed to you. And remember, whatever the immediate circumstances, you aren't to blame for Eliot's death. His own wilfulness tripped him up."

"How much of all this is going to come out now?" I said.

"I shudder to think. Certainly, though, Eliot's name will have to be cleared."

"Somehow," I said, "I have the feeling the seal on the Smedley Barlow papers will be broken sooner than a hundred years from now."

"It's at times like this," Cleon said, "that one feels thankful for the Club—a place to make a stand, no matter how much the world alters."

We stayed for the Welsh rabbit and Bass ale because, for a newly elected member, that was the civil thing to do. Dunce stayed too. Cleon and Isaac were proposing him for membership and wanted to introduce him around.

At eleven o'clock Ladonna and I set out for the parking garage at the east end of Park Square where I'd stashed the Sun Runner. Boylston Street at Tremont is the windiest spot in Boston and, along Piano Row, the wind already was soaring into a Sarasate concerto.

"Look!" Ladonna exclaimed when we came abreast of the Boston Music Company, "a pigeon's trapped inside the window. There—perched on the Larry Adler harmonica."

Poor fellow, I thought, and his best friend on her way to Lapland, stalking bigger game. I made a mental note to phone the SPCA come morning. I owed Parthenia that much. As we got under way again I called out to him, over the cry of the wind—"Hang in there, buster. And lay off those cactus needles. They're murder!"

ABOUT THE AUTHOR

JOHN MCALEER is a vice president of the Mystery Writers of America. He is the author of the Edgar Award-winning biography of Rex Stout, and critically acclaimed studies of Emerson, Thoreau and Dreiser, as well as the definitive novel on the Korean war, *Unit Pride*. Professor of English at Boston College, Mr. McAleer lives in Lexington, Massachusetts where he is at work on a second Austin Layman mystery.

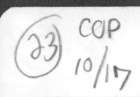

(23) COP
10/17

" stiff + tedious "   9/88